Broslin Bride
(Gone and Done it)

Includes bonus novella: Guardian Agent

DANA MARTON

CONTENTS

ACKNOWLEDGMENTS

With many thanks to Sarah Jordan, Diane Flindt, Kim Killion, my wonderful editors Linda and Toni, and to all my amazing Facebook friends: Ginger Robertson, Anita Reilley, Judy Morse, Morse Dawn, Barbara Veal, June McFall Saltiel, Renea Panzer, Chrissey Matherson, Christopher McMinn just to mention a few.

Chapter One

Luanne Mayfair might have killed her boss a little. Fine, a lot. Pretty much all the way. God, that sounded bad. But he *was* a sleazebag. Honest. The maids at the Mushroom Mile Motel that Earl Cosgrove managed often prayed for lightning to strike the lecherous bastard. Alas, God had seen fit to send Luanne instead.

Now you've gone and done it, she thought the morning after as she stood on the sidewalk in front of the fifties ranch home she rented in her hometown of Broslin, PA. She squinted against the early summer sun. Her red 1989 Mustang sitting by the curb had come from the used-car lot with its share of nicks and dents. But the damage to the front was new.

Gone and done it.

She'd done a horrible, terrible, despicable thing. Guilt and regret made her knees wobble. Whatever the punishment was, she deserved it.

Except, she couldn't go to prison. She had her four-year-old twin sisters to take care of. She was Mia and Daisy's sole guardian.

Luanne drew air in big, gulping breaths to wrestle down the shock and nausea. *Get moving. One foot in front of the other.* She couldn't stand there and stare all morning. She had to find a way to get away with murder.

* * *

Twelve hours earlier, Mushroom Mile Motel, Broslin, Pennsylvania

Luanne Mayfair stopped her cleaning cart in front of room #44 and glanced at her list. *One occupant, not checking out today.* Only a quick

1

cleanup then; she wouldn't have to change the sheets. On the other hand, no tips. Most guests only tipped on their last day.

She knocked on the door, hoping the room was empty so she wouldn't have to come back later. She was almost done, ready to get off work. *Finish the last two rooms. Catch Earl. Pick up check.* Then she was free. "Housekeeping."

After some rustling inside, the door opened, a blurry-eyed man filling the gap. He looked her over, then stepped back to open the door wider. His wrinkled wife-beater shirt was stained under the arms, his blond mullet dangling to the middle of his back, his wide face covered in stubble. "Come on in, darlin'."

Luanne flashed an apologetic look. "I'll come back later."

"I'm stayin' in all day. Catchin' up on sleep. My rig's gettin' fixed. Now's as good a time as any." His smile showed cigarette-stained teeth.

He'd better not smoke in here.

Scents clung to wallpaper, heavy drapery, carpet, and the comforter that wasn't changed from guest to guest. More work for her. More trouble too. If she took too long in a room, she'd be blamed for being too slow, be accused of stretching her hours for extra pay, would likely be docked some time as discipline.

And if the smell of smoke lingered, the next guest would complain and wouldn't leave a tip.

Not all the guests were truckers, although the Mushroom Mile Motel had its fair share. The small town of Broslin—the mushroom capital of the US—shipped fungi to the four corners of the country. The truckers mostly slept in their rigs if they were in town overnight. Except if their rigs had problems, or if the air conditioner quit on them in the middle of summer, or if they hooked up with someone and wanted room to entertain.

"Who's fixing the rig?" Luanne watched the guy's eyes and measured him up. Being in a room alone with a male guest could turn into trouble in a hurry, but she had to at least give him fresh towels.

"Company sent a guy." He blinked slowly. Yawned. Looked half-asleep still.

In and out in a minute. She grabbed a set of towels from the cart, added a small soap, her spray bottle of universal cleaner, and hurried in by him, holding her breath against the smell of sweat and beer.

She stepped into the bathroom and set out the fresh supplies, even though he hadn't used anything yet. Didn't look—or smell—like he'd taken a shower when he'd gotten in.

Towels done. Countertop neat. She grabbed the extra washcloth and wiped off a few errant water drops.

"Would you like me to clean?" she asked on her way out, glancing into the room.

Judging by the dent in the middle of the comforter, the guy had been sleeping on top of the covers. Nothing else seemed out of place.

"I'm good." He leaned forward, crowding her in the doorway. His grin widened, his small, watery green eyes focused on her body.

She moved around him, swinging abruptly to the left when she felt his meaty hand on her butt. *Oh, for heaven's sake.*

"What if I'm hungry?" His voice dripped with innuendo as he tried to cop another feel.

She laughed off the attempt, shifting away. "We're not that kind of a motel."

She wouldn't let the smile slide off her face. Tips were more important than smacking grabby men over the head with her spray bottle. Although, someday, when she was ready to quit—she didn't plan to scrub toilets for the rest of her life—one of the jerks was going to get it.

Or probably not. With her luck, she'd probably be booked for assault. As satisfying as fighting back against a slimy guest would have been, even just once, the grief she'd get wouldn't be worth it. The twins needed her, had nobody but her. So Luanne kept a tight rein over her violent fantasies.

She kept right on smiling as she said, "Broslin Diner on Main Street is having a free dessert special."

A disappointed, semiannoyed look crossed the man's face. No doubt he'd expected a different kind of answer. *Tough tooties.*

He grunted, giving up for the moment. "What's the nearest place I can get some smokes?"

"Gas station on Main Street. It's just a few blocks from here," she said. "All our rooms are nonsmoking, but we have a nice spot out on the back patio of the main building to sit." He'd better not smoke in the room. Not cigarettes, and nothing else either.

The motel had a certain...*history.* Until recently, the locals had been calling it the Magic Mushroom Motel. Before the current owners, the place had been pothead heaven. The previous night clerk had been a dealer. But all that was in the past now, and the motel did good business with tourists who came for the Mushroom Festival, the Chadds Ford Days, the Hot Air Balloon Festival, or Longwood Gardens.

Convenient and inexpensive for the guests, steady employment for Luanne. She just had to keep the occasional jerk from getting under her skin.

"Will that be all?" Her cheeks were beginning to hurt, but she kept her smile in place. She was going to have a good day. *A great day.* She had a date tonight, for the first time in ages. She had to keep focused on that. *Friday night, baby.*

"Maybe you can bring me the paper later." The trucker stared at her breasts, an oily grin spreading on his face, his mouth opened to say something she knew she was going to hate, so she turned on her heels and walked away.

"No problem," she called over her shoulder. She could bring the paper and leave it outside the door for him.

She skipped room #45—unoccupied, according to her list— stopped in front of room #46. Two occupants, checking out. She knocked on the door. "Housekeeping."

No response.

She opened the door with her master key, called "Housekeeping" again before she stepped in. She didn't want to catch anyone in the middle of anything. She'd seen enough on this job to sometimes wish she could wash her eyeballs with bleach.

No guests. The room stood empty.

She hurried to the dresser first and could have cried when she looked at the tip, a dollar and change. For cleaning after two people for nearly a week.

Luanne did her best to work herself into a grateful spirit as she changed the sheets. She had her health. She had the twins. She had a place to live. She had food to eat. She had a job. She was so much better off than a great many people in the country. She was grateful, truly grateful for everything.

But another truth was that deep down she was bone tired. She was exhausted from dancing on the sharp edge of barely making it. No security net. Nothing to catch her if she fell. Making rent was a monthly challenge. If she lost the rental, social services would take Mia and Daisy away.

She had no close family left save her twin sisters. She swore she was going to raise them if she had to eat broken glass and walk through fire. So she worked hard and worked fast, and never complained about the guests. She desperately needed the job; that was the truth of it.

When she finished with the room, she moved on to the bathroom. All the toiletries were gone, even the toilet paper and the box of tissue. She grabbed the garbage and went out to her cart. No more tissue boxes. She pulled the door of the room closed and hurried down the hallway back to the supply room, pushing her cart. She was in the main building, so she didn't have to go outside.

Four separate buildings made up the motel, nothing fancy, but all clean and trim. The smallest building housed the main office, its roof crafted by Amish carpenters to resemble a mushroom cap. The giant round cap was visible from the highway, free advertisement. Good location too, on the Mushroom Mile—over a dozen mushroom producers lined up on Route 1, one after the other, along with specialty stores that sold fresh local mushrooms and other produce.

Earl Cosgrove, the manager, stood behind the check-in counter, avoiding her eyes, mumbling something under his breath as if calculating something important, completely absorbed in the task. *Do not disturb*, his body language transmitted.

He didn't normally spend a lot of time out in the open on paydays. She'd expected to have to track him down in some distant corner of the place to receive her money.

She parked her cart by the wall and waited. Then she waited some more. Then she finally said, in a voice as undemanding as possible, "Any chance I could pick up my check? If it's ready."

Better grab him now, before he hid.

"Are you done?" He looked at her at last, pushing his glasses up his nose, his face without humor, his beady brown eyes narrowing with displeasure.

"Almost. I just ran back to grab some supplies."

He scowled. "You should have a fully stocked cart. Walking back and forth is a waste of time."

He stepped away from the computer and shuffled down the short hallway that led to his office in the back, mumbling something about ungrateful employees who cared only about money.

She followed his uneven gait into his rat's nest of an office, stuffed to the ceiling with paperwork and supplies, and stayed standing while Earl dropped onto the ripped leather chair behind his desk that had seen better days. His hemorrhoid pillow lifted him up a few inches, making him look like an aging rooster on his perch.

"If it can't wait..." Thinning hair in a comb-over, cheap black tie in a disorderly knot, he scowled at the schedule and counted up her hours. From the top of the hour, even though the maids were required to show up fifteen minutes early to stock their carts. The end of their workday too was usually rounded back to the nearest hour.

Luanne shifted on her feet. "I appreciate it."

She figured she, and the other girls, could take home at least a hundred extra bucks per month if they were paid for all their time, money they all desperately needed, but Earl wouldn't hear about that, so she tried for what she might actually receive. "I worked those five hours for Jackie."

Jackie moonlighted as a cashier at Arnie's gas station and she got stuck there Tuesday when the second-shift girl didn't come in.

Earl looked up. Frowned. Patted his hair into place. "I don't remember."

"You can ask her."

He made some noncommittal noises. Then he wrote a check for her regular hours with a half-mumbled promise to check into the extra time later.

The Pennsylvania minimum wage for tipped employees like waiters, hotel maids, and bartenders was $2.83 per hour. The law also required that tips and wages added up to the real minimum wage, $7.25 in PA. Since the maids at the Mushroom Mile Motel made roughly $3.50 in tips, Earl had to pay them $3.75, about which he griped, moaned, and groaned regularly.

He owed Luanne $18.75 for the five hours. A small windfall. Which he wasn't going to pay today, or ever, if he could help it.

She stood there, disappointment washing over her.

The twins were turning four tomorrow. The real bakery in town had always been out of her reach, but she could have sprung for a grocery store cake. The girls had been begging for weeks for the ladybug cake from the grocery store's bakery. For the first time, she planned on them having something fancy, something better than the boxed cake mix she made every year, the cake flat and square and frosted in the pan. This year, she'd planned on real candles, not the old tea lights she'd been reusing. With an extra $18.75 in her pocket, she could afford all that *and* ice cream.

All of which she'd stupidly promised already.

She put on her nicest smile. "Are you sure I couldn't have the extra hours now? I wouldn't ask." She swallowed. "I'm sorry if I sound pushy. It's just that I kind of promised something for the kids."

Earl shot her a black look of disapproval. "Now's the time to save on them. No sense wasting your money. They won't even remember these years."

He had five kids with three ex-wives, decades of dubious experience he doled out freely to his employees, usually to convince them that they didn't need to get paid.

He pushed to his feet and shuffled around the table. Stopped too close to Luanne, his coffee breath hitting her face. "If you're looking to pick up some extra, I still need someone to clean the house." He put a hand on her arm and rubbed the inside of her elbow with his thumb.

Cold dread crawled up her spine as she held still.

Some of the more desperate maids had fallen for Earl's trap over the years. Work at Earl's house included hours on their knees, scrubbing floors, tub, toilet—all of which Luanne could handle—then more time on their knees in front of Earl—which she couldn't.

She stepped back. "I wish I could. But I already clean at the library. Two jobs are all I can handle for now. I have to take care of the twins too." She hoped she sounded appreciative of the offer and full of regret that she couldn't take advantage of Earl's "generosity."

He watched her with a calculating look. "I might have to cut hours here for some of the staff. You could pick up those hours at my place."

She flashed one last smile, then fled the office, bumping into Jackie in the hallway.

The other maid took one look at her face and raised an eyebrow.

Luanne shook her head: *You don't want to know.*

"Weatherman's calling for a storm later this week," Jackie, a hardworking black woman in her forties with a heart of gold, announced cheerfully.

Luanne grinned. The maids had a running joke about their hopes for lightning to strike the general manager. "Cars drive off the road every day," she countered with her own favorite revenge fantasy. Earl lived nearby and walked to work and back since sitting—in an office chair or in his car—was hard on his hemorrhoids. He'd rather walk, even in bad weather. Plenty of chances for an inattentive driver to skip the curb.

Jackie grinned back at her. "That's the spirit." Then they went their separate ways.

Veronica, Earl's third ex-wife, was back in her place by the front desk. She must have been on a break earlier. She was a Jersey girl, with Jersey girl hair from the eighties. The big hair went with her electric blue eye shadow.

Earl came out of his office and passed by Veronica, looked her over, winked. "Hey, I think I need to put my mouth where my money is."

His standard joke for his ex. He was referring to the breast implants he'd paid for when they'd been married.

Veronica narrowed her eyes and puckered her lips in a confused-blonde look. "Are you talking about that expensive hemorrhoid surgery of yours? Honey, you ain't that bendy."

Luanne choked, holding back laughter.

Earl focused his displeasure on her, his eyes narrowed to threatening slits. "Are you still wasting time here? I'm not paying you to hang out in the hallways. People are waiting for their rooms to be cleaned. I'm the one who has to listen to them complain."

"You're right. I'm really sorry," she said as Earl marched outside in a huff.

"Guests will gripe, no matter what. Everything's not your fault," Veronica said. "You know, you don't have to apologize to Earl for everything."

Veronica could get away with saying whatever she wanted since she was the mother of two of Earl's boys. But Luanne knew that the rest of the staff better toe the line. "I should be getting back to work."

Veronica rolled her eyes after her ex-husband. "Can't tell you how many nights I spent lying awake, thinking about holding a pillow over his head." She sighed. "I still can't believe he cheated on me with Stacy Lucado. Couldn't resist all the sweet innocence, he said."

Veronica snorted. "She had more truckers in and out of her than this motel."

She shook her head, waving the words away with fingers tipped with the fanciest gel nails Luanne had ever seen, white and red flowers on pink. "Oh, forget I said that. Let's just pretend I've been gracious and ladylike. He is paying child support. He's terrible with women. But he's pretty good with his kids."

Earl Cosgrove, a complex human being. One of the mysteries of the universe, Luanne thought. She grabbed a newspaper from the counter. "Room #44," she said, and Veronica added the charge on the computer.

Luanne dropped off the paper in front of the trucker's door, then she finished room #46 and moved on to #47, her last one for the day. Thoroughly trashed, that one, pizza boxes on the bed, garbage everywhere, the furniture moved around, mud ground into the carpet, shampoo bottles floating in the toilet.

She had a fishnet she'd picked up at a garage sale for twenty-five cents for things like that. Live and learn was the name of the game in the hospitality industry.

She decided to leave the toilet-fishing expedition for last and headed over to the dresser, keeping fingers crossed. With a nice tip, she could still salvage some of the birthday celebration. She could at least spring for a boxed mix for the cake. Otherwise, she was going to have to frost her half box of graham crackers.

She cleared off the dresser. But under all the garbage, she found absolutely nothing.

Okay. No big deal. She closed her eyes for a second and swallowed the lump in her throat. People had more serious problems than not being able to buy a cake.

Friday. Date. Good things ahead.

She finished the room, doing the best damn job she could, then put the biggest smile on her face and went to pick up the kids from Jen.

Jen O'Brian had been her best friend in high school. They went their own ways for a while when Jen shipped off to college and Luanne stayed home to work and help her mom pay the bills. Even when Jen came home, she got married and had a baby, too busy to hang out. But Luanne and she became friends again once Luanne took guardianship of the twins after her mother's death, and Jen began watching the girls.

Jen was on the phone when she opened the door. *Doctor*, she mouthed, then said into the phone, "Okay, yes. We can try that."

Luanne gathered up the girls and left her friend to take care of business, simply whispering a "See you later," as she headed out the door with the kids. Jen was desperate for another child, currently in the throes of her sixth round of fertility treatments.

"Bobby cut Daisy's hair with the play scissor," Mia tattled on their way home.

Luanne whipped back to look. Okay. No chestnut curls were missing. Thank God for plastic scissors.

"I pushed him down," Mia said proudly, her brown eyes glinting. "We're family, and we protect each other."

Luanne winced. "When I said that, I meant that I'll protect you two chipmunks, because I'm the big sister."

"I'm the big sister too," Mia argued.

"No fair. One minute," Daisy mumbled. "I'm not a baby."

"No, you're not." Luanne smiled at them in the rearview mirror. "You're both big girls. You'll be four tomorrow. You'll be going to preschool soon." Her throat tightened. She wasn't ready for the girls to head out into the world.

She drew a deep breath and took the opportunity to add a teachable moment into their day as they got out of the car in front of the tiny two-bedroom ranch home she rented. "You shouldn't push anyone, Mia. Okay? If you do that at school, you'll get in trouble with the teacher."

"I don't want to go to school."

Daisy looked doubtful too, but she didn't say anything. For the most part, she let Mia do the talking. Luanne worried about how that would work at school if the two got separated, put in different groups. Something she'd have to ask about when they went in to register. A problem for another day.

For the next couple of hours, she focused on nothing but Mia and Daisy. She wanted them to feel loved and wanted, not a problem she'd inherited that she had to shuffle around in between her chores and work. She played with them, read to them, fed them, bathed them, got them into their pj's. Only when they were settled in front of the TV for their favorite cartoon did she go to get ready for her date.

She began by showering the spray-cleaner smell out of her hair. Next, she dragged on her best jeans, topped it off with a cute silk top that she'd found at Goodwill, fitted to her curves but with a decent neckline, not too slutty, not too nunsy, just right for a first date.

She had no money for drinks, but Tayron, the bartender, had promised her a drink on the house the other day when she'd given him a ride. She could nurse that one drink all night, no problem. She wasn't a big drinker. She'd picked Finnegan's because it was public, and because if they went to a restaurant and her date wanted to split the bill, she wouldn't be able to pay for her half.

She put on fresh makeup, tried for smoky eyes, ended up looking like a raccoon on drugs, wiped it off, tried again. Her eyes were a lighter shade of brown than the twins', not exactly pretty, but maybe interesting.

You always emphasized your best feature to draw attention from the worst. If you emphasized everything, you came off overdone and slutty, which she wasn't. And she didn't like her lips anyway; she had a stupid crease in the middle of her bottom lip.

Okay, clothes, check; makeup, check. She sprayed perfume in the air, then walked through the cloud of scent so it'd cling equally to her shirt, skin, and hair. She never sprayed perfume directly on her clothes. No sense in staining a perfectly good top.

After she finished, she drove the girls back to Jen's for a prebirthday sleepover.

"Ready for the party tomorrow?" Jen asked Luanne after hugging and kissing the girls silly. She loved them as if they were her own.

"Almost." Luanne bent to take the girls' shoes off.

"How about for tonight?" Jen grinned, offering her a cola. "You look sexy."

"I wish." Luanne tugged at a stray lock of hair as she accepted the drink.

Without a curling iron to give her blond locks body, her hair was seriously limp and way too fine for any kind of volume, unlike Jen's thick reddish-brown waves that could have starred in a shampoo commercial. Where Luanne was too thin from running around and being on her feet almost constantly, Jen actually had curves, especially since Bobby had been born—the kind of curves men noticed.

Luanne looked at her own chest. "Do you think this top is too low-cut?" she asked, hit by a sudden wave of insecurity. "What if Brett thinks I'm a total hussy?"

"Yeah, because that's what guys think when they get a glimpse of boobs." Jen rolled her eyes.

Then she glanced at the girls giggling on the couch, her gaze distant, an odd look coming over her face as she turned back to Luanne. She blinked, then a smile replaced her strange expression. "Oh, to be single and going on hot dates."

"You don't want to be single and going out on hot dates."

Jen was a family gal through and through. She wanted a second child badly to give Bobby a little brother or sister, so her son could have what the twins did.

"Fine. I want to be home with a bushel of kids." She smiled a little wider. "I do. But you deserve a hot date."

"I'll settle for *nice*." Her first date in a year, Luanne thought. *Nice* would have been an excellent start.

"How about hot sex with a nice guy?" Jen suggested ever so helpfully.

"Not on a first date."

"You've known Brett for a while now."

"Over the Internet."

"He's a dog walker. You met him in a goldendoodle online fan group. I don't think anyone who's into poodle–golden retriever mixes so much can be a creep."

Luanne nodded. In their online communications, Brett had never been anything but a gentleman, kind, funny, romantic. She was more than looking forward to meeting him. She had butterflies in her stomach. "I better get going."

"Kisses!" Mia launched into a frenzied hug immediately.

Luanne hugged her, then Daisy in turn. "You behave for Jen, okay? Go to bed without giving her trouble."

They promised, with angelic faces that seemed impossible to doubt. If only she didn't know better. She gave them the mother look. "I mean it."

"Relax. They'll be fine." Jen walked her to the door, then dropped her voice. "I'll want every dirty detail tomorrow. Take notes so you don't forget anything."

"What, no video?"

"Video will work. Hey, I'm a married woman, living vicariously through you."

"Billy is a great guy."

"Except when he has one too many beers and gets into a fight with one of his dumb Irish relatives."

"Again?"

Jen rolled her eyes. "I'm sick of his Irish temper and his fifty Irish cousins. Well, at least he knows he's done wrong, so he's sweet as pie, trying to make it up to me. I'm so gonna milk that for all it's worth."

Okay, so that was a little messed up, but being in a relationship still seemed like an incredibly nice thing, not having to make all the decisions alone all the time, have someone to curl up against at night. Billy wasn't perfect, but for the most part, he was one of the good guys. Luanne had high hopes for Brett in that regard.

"So what was the phone call with the doctor? Everything okay?"

Jen shrugged. "Switching me to a new drug. No big deal. I swear, some of the hormone injections make me wacky."

"I'm keeping fingers, toes, eyes, and legs crossed for you."

"Yeah, that'll make you attractive for your date," Jen deadpanned, then shook her head with a grin.

Luanne walked to her Mustang with a last wave. She was smiling too as she slipped behind the wheel. *Okay. Here we go. Hot date.*

Finnegan's was just a few blocks away, within walking distance. But she wasn't sure how late she'd stay out and as safe as the town was, she didn't like walking through Broslin in the middle of the night. She was all the twins had. If anything happened to her, they'd be all alone in the world.

She shot down the road and was at the neighborhood bar in three minutes. Honestly, so fast she didn't even bother switching the ABC song to adult music.

Finnegan's kept with the Irish theme, green booths, *Sláinte* signs all over the place. As soon as she walked in, she could smell the bacon they sprinkled on their famous baked potato soup. Guinness flowed freely at the tap at the gleaming mahogany bar, the clientele several steps above the dive bars along Route 1. The owners' son, Harper Finnegan, was a local cop who helped out when he wasn't working at the station. His presence kept the shady element away.

Music filled the cavernous room, a local band covering everything from old Beach Boys hits to mournful Irish ballads. The bar was a safe place for a single woman on a Friday night, or any other night of the week.

Luanne scanned the hundred or so people around the tables and on the dance floor. No sign of Brett. She'd never met him in person before, but she'd seen dozens of pictures of him on his Facebook page. She didn't think she'd have any trouble recognizing him.

Tayron, tall, kind-eyed, spotted her as soon as she walked up to the bar.

"Hey, girl." He flashed a wide smile. "What are you drinking tonight? My treat."

She thought about a beer, then decided to go wild. "Something colorful and fancy." She raised her chin. "Something with an umbrella."

She could have one drink, spend a couple of hours here with Brett, then be perfectly fine to drive home later. "How's school?"

Tayron studied engineering at West Chester University by day, bartended in the evenings. He also fit a second job into his schedule, at the local lumberyard—which gave him the muscles that got him the big tips, which helped to pay tuition, everything coming together in a circle of life, according to him.

"Finals are a bitch." But he grinned, always upbeat.

In less than a minute, he had a cocktail glass in front of her, an orange-red drink with an umbrella *and* a plastic thingy that looked like a burst of fireworks. "Meet Finnegan's very own Irish Comet."

She sipped and moaned from the sweet, tangy flavor. She cast him a look that she hoped conveyed her full gratitude. Sipped again. "Makes me feel like I'm on a cruise ship." The fanciest place she could imagine that would serve drinks like this.

Tayron grinned at her. "So who's the guy?"

She sipped again. "Who says I'm here on a date?"

"Your sexy shirt."

Too sexy? Okay, no. She was not going to start obsessing over that now.

"Someone I met on Facebook a while back." While the twins were at story hour at the library Tuesday nights, she usually hung out online. "He's single. Dog lover."

Which was pretty important to her. She and the girls sometimes volunteered at the local shelter. They used to have Macy, the best dog that ever lived, had lost her last year, and were waiting until money wasn't so tight to get a new puppy.

Tayron leaned forward so he wouldn't have to shout over the music. "From around here?"

"Philly. He has three goldendoodles. He's a dog walker." Apparently, you could make a living from something like that if you lived in a big city. Seemed like a dream job to Luanne. Like being a resort-spa secret shopper. "He has two sisters. Loves kids."

He'd told her he was usually the default babysitter for his two nieces, ages two and three. "He gets me." She smiled. "Not the type to look down on a small-town motel maid who is raising two little girls." One of his sisters was a single-mom waitress.

"Sounds like a good guy." Tayron moved off to serve another customer.

Luanne stirred her drink and allowed herself a dreamy smile. Brett was great. Easy to talk to, at least online. She glanced at her watch. He was also five minutes late. Not a big deal, considering he was driving out from the city. Friday night traffic could be crazy.

She stayed at the bar, facing the door, and slowly sipped her drink as she kept an eye out for a tall blond guy with a dimple in his chin. She was looking forward to a great night. Not that she could stay out too late. Big day tomorrow. She had a lot planned for the twins' birthday.

They were going to go to the playground in the morning. Then home to a party with friends, super simple, just games and sandwiches. Then the park had a free children's play that afternoon, *The Wizard of Oz*. Broslin had its own amateur theater company that put on several plays each year.

The presents were already bought but not yet wrapped, all from garage sales. Amazing how people gave away twenty-dollar toys for a dollar when their kids got tired of them. Their loss, her gain.

Luanne considered the ladybug cake. Well, no help for that. She took another sip and thought several uncharitable thoughts about the guests who'd stiffed her on the tip.

While she was at it, she allowed herself a brief daydream where she smacked the trucker upside the head when he'd grabbed her ass. She felt the weight of the spray bottle as she swung it, heard the satisfying clunk, saw the dazed expression in the man's eyes, then the shame as he came to his senses. He issued a hasty apology, then a ten-dollar tip to make up for his assholery.

There, that made her feel much better.

She glanced at her watch. Brett was definitely late. Didn't matter really. She had nothing else to do. She didn't have to work until Monday. She shuddered at the thought of another encounter with Earl.

He'd be walking home around now. He didn't like to get up early, usually ambled into work around noon, but then he tended to stay pretty late. He lived two blocks from here. For a moment, she thought about going out back—he usually cut through the alley behind the bar—to demand her five hours of overtime money.

But since she knew it would be pointless, she stayed in her seat and slipped into another little daydream. This one involved her red Mustang in the back alley, speeding toward Earl, making him dive for the garbage containers. She lingered over the thought of him emerging coughing and cursing, covered in rotten banana peels.

She rather liked that image.

But she liked her job better, so she stayed where she was and entertained herself by watching the crowd. A couple of inebriated college kids performed some pretty interesting dancing. By the time she glanced at her watch again, Brett was forty-five minutes late.

"You look bored," a pleasant voice came from behind her before she could admit to herself that she was seriously disappointed.

She turned to look into nondescript brown eyes, in a nondescript but pleasant face, matching brown hair. The guy was in his midthirties, a couple of inches shorter than her.

A shy smile made his face interesting. "Can I buy you another drink?"

Before she could decline, he flashed her a puppy-dog look and added, "I was stood up. Giving up and going home seems too pathetic. If I at least have a drink with a pretty woman, it'd do wonders for my self-esteem."

She found herself smiling back at him.

"Okay," she said, and finished her drink. "I'm Luanne."

"I'm Gregory." His eyes moved in a good-natured roll. "I know. Even the name is geeky, right? You're probably thinking I'm the kind of guy who deserves to be stood up."

"Nobody deserves to be stood up," she told him. And when he ordered another round for her, she thanked him.

Chapter Two

Luanne struggled in a dream where someone was using a chain saw to slice up her head like a watermelon, the noise as overpowering as the pain.

She woke with an unbearable headache, forced her eyes open to a slit, and glared at the phone ringing on the nightstand. Ever so slowly, the events of the night before came back to her. The bar. Brett not showing. The other guy. She closed her eyes again. She couldn't remember the name. Then it came to her on a thunderclap of pain: Gregory.

She groaned. Good God, how much had she had to drink? She hoped she'd had the good sense to walk home instead of driving.

The phone kept ringing, each chirp drilling into her brain. She picked it up just to quiet it.

"Luanne!" Jackie yelled on the other end.

Luanne pulled the phone a little farther from her ear. "What is it?" Was she late for work? She blinked. No. She had the weekend off. *The twins' birthday.* She glanced at the clock. She had to pick them up from Jen in an hour. In spite of the pounding in her head and the rolling in her stomach, she forced herself to sit.

"I thought you might not have heard yet," Jackie rushed to say. "Earl's dead."

"What?" Luanne's hand froze in the middle of rubbing her forehead.

"The police found his body in the alley behind Finnegan's. A car ran him over. He was covered in garbage."

The alley. Earl. Car. Piles of garbage. Fuzzy images swirled in Luanne's mind, making her dizzy. Her stomach rolled.

"Luanne?" Jackie asked, but then kept talking even when she didn't receive a response. "The police are here at the motel. They want to talk to all the employees. Can you come in?"

Luanne cleared her throat. A long moment passed before she

could line her thoughts up straight. She could probably ask Jen to keep the twins for another hour or so. "Sure."

She hung up, fell back into the bed with a groan, but after a pain-filled moment got up again, all the way to her feet this time. She cleaned herself up, then she called Jen.

"Oh my God. What do you know? I just heard," Jen tore into her before Luanne could say a single word.

Why was everybody shouting today? "I need to go to the motel. The police want to talk to the employees. Could you please keep the twins a little longer?"

"Of course. They're no trouble. Call me the second you find out anything. I can't believe this is happening. Let me know what the police say."

Luanne promised, her mind struggling to catch up to full speed as she made coffee, only half hearing as Jen said, "You sound terrible. What time did you get in?"

Luanne tried to think back. "Not sure."

"Date went that well?"

"Brett never showed." But she couldn't think about Brett. Last night was a fuzzy mess in her head. Her thoughts circled around Earl.

She hung up with Jen and caffeinated, hanging on to the hope that some java would untangle her brain. Her mind was a disjointed, foggy mess, the mother of all hangovers using her head for a punching bag.

Her dollar-store coffee was as dark and thick as tar, and just as tasty, but it did the trick. She felt half-human by the time she walked to her front door, ready to leave, dark premonitions circling in her semicoherent brain.

Think.

But she couldn't remember anything past meeting Gregory.

Prior to that, she could remember being mad at the trucker, Brett, Earl. She could clearly recall thinking about Earl in the alley, her hands gripping the steering wheel.

She walked through the door, squinting against the morning sun, biting her bottom lip against the pain.

Earl. Dead. She had a very bad feeling about this.

She tried not to panic. She might have fantasized about fighting back, but so had the other maids—a harmless way to blow off steam. She would never have acted that fantasy out, could never cross over to actual violence. Could she?

"No." She said the word out loud to settle her brain.

Earl was an equal-opportunity jackass. He harassed every woman he came across, stiffed every employee he'd ever had. There had to be at least two dozen people in town pissed enough to want to kill him.

But how many of them had a dented grill?

OhGodohGodohGod.

She came to a staggering stop in the middle of her lawn to stare at her Mustang parked by the curb, the same color red as the fire hydrant ten feet or so in front of it. Both the car's bumper and the grill were crushed in the middle. Clearly, at one point last night, she'd run into something.

She wished and hoped she'd just bumped the fire hydrant, but that didn't show any damage. She couldn't bear thinking of the alternative.

She almost threw up, prevented only by the fact that her stomach was empty. *Shit.* Had she... She swallowed hard, her head spinning.

Gone and done it, run him over. The 1989 Mustang had come from the used-car lot with its share of nicks and dents, but the damage to the front was definitely new. *Gone and done it.*

Cold panic cut through her, an ice blade. She'd done a horrible, terrible, despicable thing. Guilt and regret made her knees wobble. Whatever the punishment was, she deserved it.

Except, she couldn't go to prison. She had her four-year-old twin sisters to take care of. She was Mia and Daisy's sole guardian.

Luanne drew air in big, gulping breaths to wrestle down the shock and nausea. *Get moving. One foot in front of the other.* She couldn't stand there and stare all morning. She had to find a way to get away with murder.

Her head pounded, her mind in a stunned haze. Her fight-or-flight response was firmly locked into the flight setting. She stopped by the car. Squinted. Was that blood on the bumper? Her stomach rolled again.

If she was put away, the twins would go to foster care. They were cute and young. They'd be adopted out faster than she could say "termination of guardianship." She'd never see them again.

The thought brought a new flash of pain coursing through her body.

She felt guilty as hell, horrible about what happened to Earl. She wished more than anything that she could take it back. She deserved to go to prison, she really did. But she wasn't going to give up the twins. Not ever.

Nobody could find out what she'd done.

As panic gripped her hard in its cold clutches, her gaze fastened onto the fire hydrant. *Nobody could ever find out.*

She squared her shoulders, then looked up and down the quiet dead-end street. Not a soul in sight. She slid behind the wheel, revved the engine, and, pedal to the metal, drove straight forward.

The crash rattled her brain, threatening to split her head in half, the explosion of water instantaneous. She leaned back in her seat, not having to bother with airbags, the car too old to have any.

Oh God. Fighting back tears, she closed her eyes and waited for any incriminating blood residue to be washed away by a thousand gallons of water.

After a minute or two of sheer misery, she filled her lungs, put the car in reverse and backed away. She had to get to the motel. The police were waiting.

On her way over, she called the fire department to report the hydrant accident, cringing as she lied through her teeth.

What's next? Her brain felt like gelatin. This here was why she didn't normally drink.

Think.

Who'd be at the motel? Probably Captain Bing. Murder was big news in Broslin. She didn't care who came, as long as it wasn't Chase Merritt.

She'd gone to high school with Chase.

She'd been in love with Chase.

She'd lost her virginity to Chase.

That last bit hadn't gone well. Afterward, she'd shared her disappointment with Jen, blaming Chase for the lack of earthshaking pleasure she'd read about in romance novels. Unfortunately, Jen told her other friends, and the rumor spread that Chase was less than adequate between the sheets. He hadn't been amused.

Luanne wasn't one of his favorite people. Mostly, through the years that had passed since, he'd avoided her.

She didn't need to think about that now. But as she shoved the past aside and turned her focus to the trouble she was in, a heart-stopping thought popped into her head.

Had there been witnesses?

Her muscles froze. *Oh God.*

No. Wait. If there'd been a witness, Luanne decided, she would have been woken by the police knocking on her door, instead of Jackie's phone call.

Okay. So, very likely, nobody had seen her in the alley. A lucky break.

She had no alibi, but so what. Earl had been murdered in the middle of the night, and she was home alone. Plenty of people were home alone in the middle of the night. That shouldn't be overly suspicious.

The damage to her car…hopefully, she'd taken care of that. She made a mental note to donate money to the fire department, even if she had to scrape it together a penny at a time.

What else? She was too nervous, her brain pounding too hard to be able to think clearly.

The mushroom cap on the motel, which she always thought cute and quirky, now loomed like a prison tower as she pulled up.

She scanned the single police cruiser up front and went to park in the back. Then she hurried inside, hoping and praying that she'd be able to keep her composure.

The rest of the employees were already gathered around a single detective in the middle of the reception area. Several inches taller than the tallest of the women, he wore dark dress pants—his badge clipped to his belt—with a light blue shirt that did nothing to disguise his massive shoulders. He stood in the typical police power stance, feet slightly apart. She didn't think he was trying to be intimidating, but the solid mass of his body had that effect anyway.

That she'd once slept with him now seemed utterly surreal.

He turned as Luanne came in, his gaze settling on her face.

"Luanne Mayfair," Chase said dispassionately as he looked her over.

* * *

Luanne looked in rougher shape than he did, and that was saying something, since Chase was on his second shift. His crazy night had included a street fight, checking out the crawl space under a house after reports of suspicious sounds that turned out to be raccoons, and

21

saving a pet turtle from a tree. He'd also handled half a dozen traffic violations with their share of cursing and crying and threatening with powerful friends. And that was just his first shift. The second started off heavy-duty right away, with a murder.

And then Luanne Mayfair had walked in.

Chase reached to his hair to brush away any cobwebs he might have acquired in the crawl space, but caught himself and dropped his hand to his side. He was *not* prettying up for Luanne.

He was a grown man. A detective. He was not going to feel like an awkward, rejected schoolboy when he talked to her. That decided, he strode over for a private word. He'd already interviewed the other maids and the two front-desk clerks.

"Luanne."

She looked even worse up-close, mouth tight, her whiskey-color eyes spaced out one second, then nervously darting the next.

"Detective Merritt."

He'd braced himself against her voice, but the low, velvety pitch got to him anyway. "Let's stick with Chase. Everything okay with the twins?"

"Fine." She bit out the single word, then cleared her throat, clasping her hands in front of her, her fingers red from scrubbing.

Of all the employees, she seemed the most upset. The others were shocked and dismayed that something like this could happen in Broslin. But not one had shed a single tear over the manager. Yet Luanne looked on the verge of breaking down in tears.

Maybe she'd been closer to Earl than her coworkers.

Chase let his gaze pan over her again. Long, blond hair barely combed, no makeup, a wrinkled silk shirt topped blue jeans that accentuated her slim legs. Long legs. She'd run track in high school. "You don't look fine." The assessment came from the analytical-cop part of his brain. The stupid-guy part still thought she was the prettiest woman he'd ever seen. Her whiskey-color eyes, bleary or not, drew him in.

She cleared her throat again, and he could see as she gathered herself little by little, with effort. She held his gaze. "Exhausting date last night."

The jealousy that cut through him was beyond stupid, so he refused to acknowledge it.

She has an alibi, he thought instead. *Good.* He didn't want to have to interrogate Luanne. She had plenty on her plate with raising her sisters.

He pulled out his notebook and pen. "I'm going to need to talk to your date. Need the timeline for your night. Step one in the investigation is to just rule out as many people as we can. Name?"

She cleared her throat. Looked away. "Gregory."

He wrote it down. Waited. "Last name?"

She bit her lower lip. "I can't remember."

Not like Luanne. Then again, it'd been a pretty long time. Maybe she'd changed since he'd known her. "You have his phone number?"

She shook her head.

A one-night stand? He hated the idea, frankly, but it wasn't his place to judge, so he went on with his questioning.

"Anybody see you with him?"

"We had drinks at Finnegan's."

"Who was at the bar?"

"Tayron."

He nodded. "I'll check with him." He watched her for a second or two, trying to see her impartially, instead of as the first girl he'd fallen in love with, even if all that silky hair and those supremely kissable lips made the task difficult. "What time did you get home?"

"I'm not sure."

"Alone?"

She hesitated. "Yes."

Okay, by an exhausting date, maybe she'd meant dancing. He liked that idea much better. "Any idea who might want Earl dead?"

"Every woman he ever met?" Even as the last word left her lips, she slapped her hands over her mouth, her eyes turning large and horrified. "I'm so sorry." She looked genuinely stricken. "What's wrong with me? What a terrible thing to say." She really did look like she might cry.

"Relax. It's pretty much what everybody else told me." How did he not know that Earl was such a colossal jerk, taking advantage of his employees? "Anyone hate him in particular? Enough to do him harm?"

"I don't know." She clutched her hands. "He was the boss. He wasn't well liked, but..." She gave a resigned shrug.

Right. Earl was a jackass, but he was the jackass who signed the paychecks.

"When did you see him last?"

"Near the end of my shift." She wrung her hands. "Here at the motel."

She seemed to struggle with the interview. She was probably dead tired after being out most of the night. Chase saw her from time to time but hadn't been this close to her in a while. He hadn't realized how skinny she was. When had she lost weight? According to the other maids, she put in a full shift here, worked Saturdays at the library, plus took care of two toddlers.

From what he'd picked up from general town gossip over the years, after her parents' divorce, her father had gone up to Alaska. He'd always been a hard-core alcoholic. Whether he was still alive or not was doubtful. Luanne had gone off to business college once her mother moved in with a new man. The guy—not into crying babies—took off after the twins were born, never to be heard from again. A year later, Luanne's mother died of breast cancer. Luanne took guardianship of her sisters, quit school, and came home to work.

Regardless of the fact that she'd single-handedly ruined Chase's manly reputation back in their younger years, he had nothing but respect for her. She was a hell of a woman.

Even if she currently had trouble meeting his gaze.

Maybe she felt embarrassed at having to tell him that last night she'd hooked up with a stranger whose last name she couldn't remember.

She cleared her throat. "Anything else?"

"Earl ever try anything with you?" He hated the idea and the images popping into his head.

She pressed a hand over her stomach.

His muscles tightened. "Like what?"

"Some…touching. Trying to talk me into…more under the guise of becoming his housekeeper." She repeated what the other maids had already told him.

"Sounds like a gem." He swallowed his anger. "Has he ever pushed anyone too far?"

She looked at her feet. "I wouldn't be surprised. But not that I know for sure."

Chase nodded. He put away his notebook. He didn't see much point in questioning her further right now. He had plenty to do this morning—subpoena Earl's financial records to see if he'd been in some kind of money trouble, track down next of kin, interview his neighbors, go to the morgue in West Chester and see if he could hurry along the autopsy.

He had only one thing left to do here. He stood and turned toward the group of employees chattering around the front desk, six maids and two front-desk clerks. "If you wouldn't mind, ladies, I'm going to have to take a quick look at your vehicles."

The women headed outside immediately.

Chase glanced back at Luanne.

She'd gone two shades paler.

Chapter Three

Okay. She was doing fine. At least, she thought she was—difficult to tell in her current mental state. She just had to get through the car check, then she could go home. Luanne desperately wanted her head to stop pounding, so she could think.

She hung back and let Chase inspect all the other vehicles. When he finished and told the staff they were free to go, she led him to the back, to her poor, abused Mustang, which she'd parked nose to the fence so the damage would be mostly hidden.

He walked right up to the busted front end, with that relaxed gait of his, never rushed, always calm and collected. He scanned the bumper silently, then looked from the car to her. "What happened?"

His voice was soft, kind, and low, and for some reason it made her throat burn.

She swallowed hard. *Can't go to prison. Can't abandon Mia and Daisy.* "When I got the call this morning from Jackie, I was upset. I ran into the fire hydrant in front of the house. Stupid mistake."

"Did you call it in?"

She nodded.

He'd been one of the hottest boys in her senior class in high school, in a natural, non-flashy way, no hair gel, no gallons of aftershave. He really didn't need embellishment—straight nose, strong jaw line, ocean-deep blue eyes that wouldn't dream of rushing over a person. He took his time then, and he took his time now. Of course, he'd grown into an attractive man, with his easy smile and calm presence that she appreciated.

He walked around the car, back to the front, examined the damage from the other side, bending low. "Have you called your insurance company yet?"

"I haven't really had the chance to think."

He nodded as he straightened. "Too much going on this morning." He was looking at her with regret in his deep blue eyes.

"I'm going to have to have the car towed for lab testing."

She blanched, nerves shooting through her. *Breathe.* Everything was going a lot faster than she'd thought. How could they be at lab testing already?

Stay calm. Don't panic. Don't look scared.

She tried to smile. Her head hurt, her brain fuzzy. *Think.* Okay, lab testing. How thorough can that be in Broslin? The PD didn't exactly have a high-tech CSI team. With luck, the fire hydrant had washed off anything incriminating.

"I'll give you a ride home," Chase offered.

She didn't want a ride from him. She didn't want any of this. She wanted to go back to yesterday, not go to the bar, spend Friday night home with Mia and Daisy.

"The twins are with Jen," she told him.

"No problem." He called in the tow, then tucked his phone away. "Arnie will be here in a minute. We don't have to wait if you're in a hurry. We can leave."

He escorted her around the building to his cruiser, opened the front passenger-side door for her. At least he didn't make her sit in the back. That had to be a good sign.

He went around to slide behind the wheel, and the space was suddenly all filled with his tall, wide-shouldered body that bordered on husky. He was all calmness, as he'd always been. Steadiest person she'd ever met. He was the quiet type, fair, always ready to hear people out. Rumor was even the criminals liked him.

For a moment, her gaze snagged on the short stubble that shadowed his masculine jaw, and her hangover-disabled brain wondered what that stubble would feel like scraping against her sensitive skin. She blinked. Shook her head. What was wrong with her?

He didn't start the car. Instead, he turned to her.

His gaze carried nothing but kindness as it held hers, the blue deepening as he watched her. "If you need a ride anywhere while the PD has your car, I'd like you to call me. I'd like you to think of me as a friend."

"You don't even like me," she blurted, stunned at the unexpected offer.

He drew back. Waited a beat. "Why would you think that?"

She could feel heat creep up her face. *Oh God.* Did they really have to talk about the past? Deep breath. *Fine.* "I started that rumor. I'm sorry. I was a stupid teenager."

She didn't want him to hate her. He was investigating the case. But even beyond that, the apology felt right—the only thing that felt right in her crazy, confusing morning—and she realized she should have said those words years ago.

His lips twisted. "I'd like to think I've moved on since high school. I don't hold a grudge like that, Luanne."

Huh. "You barely said two words to me ever since."

He shrugged. "You always avoided me, so I gave you space."

She stared. Had she avoided him?

She had.

"Water under the bridge," he said with a sure, slow smile after a moment, then turned the key ignition and backed up the cruiser. "Anyway, what I was saying... We were friends before. If you need help, I hope you'll let me know."

Because he knew that she was lying?

Cold panic spread through her chest. She didn't let it show on her face. She couldn't let on. Chase could not find out what she'd done. *Ever.* She thought of the twins and forced a smile as she fastened her seat belt. "Yeah. Thanks. Sure." *Look calm. Don't look criminal.* "How soon do you think I can get my car back?"

"Tomorrow the earliest. Possibly not until Monday."

Her heart sank. What was she going to do all weekend without a car? She was *not* going to ask Chase for rides, no way.

He drove her to Jen's, lost in thought, stayed in the cruiser, on the phone, while she went in.

"What happened? Why are you getting a police escort?" Jen asked as soon as she opened the door.

"Crashed the Mustang into the fire hydrant this morning." Luanne stepped inside.

The kids were in the living room, piled on the carpet, watching cartoons. They were happy and safe, and she was going to keep them that way. *Smile.*

"Hey ya, chipmunks. Had a fun night?"

"Not ready yet. Five more minutes. Pleease!" Mia begged, and Daisy's quieter, more polite, "Please," echoed her.

"Jeez. It's nice to feel missed." Luanne shook her head at the girls, wanting to scoop them up, hold them tight, and never let go, but it was better not to act over-the-top strange.

"What's with Chase?" Jen whispered, rubbernecking to see him from the front window.

"He offered to give me a ride home. Just being helpful."

Jen's perfectly plucked left eyebrow lifted slightly, the thoughtful look in her eyes saying she wasn't entirely buying that. "You haven't talked to him in what, since high school?"

Luanne began gathering the twins' bags. "I guess."

"And he just offers you a ride?"

"I crashed my car." She didn't want to go into the whole thing about the car getting towed by the police for lab testing. She didn't want Jen to ask if she'd had anything to do with Earl's murder. Because to keep the twins, Luanne would have to lie.

The weight of that hit her, the sudden realization that she *would* have to lie, for the rest of her life, to people who loved and cared about her. Her knees folded, and she dropped to the couch.

"Are you okay?"

Luanne rubbed her hands over her face, then dropped them. "It's been a crazy morning."

Jen turned into the kitchen and brought her a glass of water and a bag of vanilla cookies, looking lost in thought for a moment.

"Thanks." Luanne's stomach was nowhere ready for food, but she drank the water, then set the glass on the side table. "Is everything okay with you?" Jen seemed preoccupied.

"Got back some lab results. One hormone level fixed, now another goes out of balance. It's a never-ending story." She shook her head ruefully.

Luanne reached over to squeeze her hand. "They'll get it right one of these days."

Everybody had tragedies in their lives. Everybody had heartaches. She couldn't dump her problems on Jen. She had to solve them herself.

She filled her lungs and looked at the kids, all focused on the TV and ignoring the adults. "All right girls, who's ready to come home?"

Two sets of identical begging eyes and pouty lips turned toward her. "Can we finish? Pleeease?" Mia entreated, and her sister chimed in with "Five more minutes. Pleeease?"

They had no sense of time. Everything was five minutes to them at this stage.

"Hey, we're going to ride home in a police car," Luanne said with exaggerated excitement, eyebrows up, her voice high-pitched, trying hard to sell it.

The kids all ran to the front window. Bobby stared wide-eyed and vibrating with excitement, every part of his little body moving. "Can I go too, Mom? Pleeeeease?"

Jen shot Luanne a see-what-you-started look. Then she shrugged. "I suppose we can go out and see if Detective Chase will let you sit in the backseat for a minute."

The kids screamed in excitement like a pack of wild monkeys.

The pounding in Luanne's head intensified, and she squinted, as if somehow that could hold back the noise. "All right. Shoes first," she ordered, hoping that getting the kids busy with something would turn the volume down a little.

She wasn't sure how Chase would react to three toddlers storming him, but he let them climb all over his backseat.

"Can we turn on the siren?" Bobby batted his long eyelashes, hope shining from his face, the expression downright angelic.

"Siren, siren, siren," the girls chanted.

"Not the siren," Chase told them firmly. "That's for official police business."

He was friendly about it, but his tone carried enough authority so the kids didn't protest.

"How's Billy?" he asked Jen, in between helping the kids in and out of the car.

"Back to shift work now that his back is healed," Jen said. "Better pay, but I hate the night shift. Being home alone."

Chase nodded. "It's a pretty good neighborhood. You'll be fine. I'll make sure to drive by when I'm on duty."

Okay, watching Chase with Jen was a revelation. Since he'd been avoiding Luanne—apparently in response to her avoidance of him—she'd begun to think of him as standoffish. But maybe he was right and she was the one who'd put that distance between them all along, staying out of his way, sending out signals that told him to stay away from her. He was plenty friendly with Jen and the kids, chatting easily.

Luanne cleared her throat. "I should get home. You probably need to get back to work."

Chase looked at her, nodded, flashed a parting smile at Jen. "I probably should. Say hi to Billy for me."

"Will do." Jen lifted a protesting Bobby out of the car, then turned back to Luanne. "We'll be by later for the girls' birthday party. Do you need me to pick up anything?"

Right. No Mustang. "Can I call you later? I need to sit down for a second and figure out what I'm doing. I have pretty much everything but dessert."

"Sure." Jen dragged Bobby toward the house with promises of popsicles and setting up the sprinkler in the back. She was at the front door before she turned back. "How are you going to get to work?"

"I already cleaned the library yesterday morning before it opened, so I can be home all day for the birthday festivities today. I can walk to work at the motel. That's no big deal."

They had guests in the rooms. They couldn't close down, not even temporarily until things got sorted out. For the time being, they had to manage without Earl, until the owners hired a new manager.

Jen's forehead furrowed. "Do you think they'll close the motel?"

Cold spread through Luanne's chest. With everything going on, she hadn't thought about that yet. "God, I hope not." Or they'd all be out of a job, which none of them could afford.

The owners, Mildred and Harold Cosgrove, were retired, had moved to Rising Sun, Maryland, a year before to be closer to their grandkids. Without Earl, a distant nephew, here to manage the motel for them, they might just sell, deciding it was one less worry for their old age.

Luanne was still worrying about that on the drive home with Chase, until Mia interrupted with "Did you get the ladybug cake?"

Oh, how small yesterday's problems seemed when compared to today's.

Deep breath. "I didn't. I'm sorry, honey. But we'll make dessert together. That way, you'll get to lick all the leftover frosting." She tried to put a positive spin on it and was grateful when the girls responded to the promise of extra sugar with huge grins in the backseat.

Then they were distracted from further questions about the party by the view when Chase turned down their street.

One of the smaller fire trucks parked in front of their house, plus the fire chief's car, three men working on the hydrant, Chief

Kendall supervising.

He came right over, a handsome man in his fifties, milk-chocolate skin, tall, fit, just beginning to gray at the temples. "Are you all right, Luanne?"

"Better than my car. And the hydrant." Luanne winced, guilt flooding her. "I'm really sorry." She *was*, sorrier than anyone would ever know.

Chase let the girls out from the back of the cruiser. Of course, they immediately began jumping in the water, splashing each other.

Luanne looked toward the men repairing the hydrant. "How bad is it?"

"Nothing these boys can't fix. Chase." The chief nodded at him. "I heard about Earl. Anything?"

Chase shook his head. "It's pretty early in the game."

Mia hopped across the biggest puddle and stopped in front of the chief. Daisy followed, stopping one step behind her.

"We rode in the police car," Mia announced proudly.

The chief played right along, bending to them and narrowing his eyes. "Did you rob a candy store?"

Daisy blinked, glanced at Luanne as if to ask *are we in trouble?* But Mia said with an impish grin, "We did!"

"Where is all the candy?" the chief wanted to know.

Mia giggled. "We ated it!"

And that got Daisy smiling. She was the shy one, even anxious at times. Mia brazened things out, game for anything. She was the one Luanne would have to watch like a hawk when the twins became teenagers. Hopefully, she'd still be here with them at that stage and not sitting in prison for murder.

"I need to get the girls inside before they're totally soaked," she told the men, then scooped up Mia and Daisy and carried them off as they protested. She needed to get behind closed doors, where she could stop pretending that all was well in her world.

Well, could almost stop pretending. She couldn't fall apart even at home. The girls needed her.

"Happy birthday, chipmunks." She set them down inside. God, it was good to be home. "Let's take off our shoes and clean up this place a little, then we'll set up the food for later. Who wants to frost graham crackers for dessert?"

"Me!" Mia and Daisy jumped up and down.

"All right. But first, cleaning." The house was small, but plenty enough for them, the furniture they inherited after their mother's death old but functional. They were used to the lumps in the frumpy brown sofa and the scratches in the pine coffee table. Luanne had grown up with the furniture, the only thing of her childhood that still remained. "Who wants to put away all the shoes?"

The girls moaned dramatically. "Do we have to?"

Right. Luanne felt like a wicked stepmother, making them clean on their birthday. "Or, you can use your birthday passes and play, as long as you don't make a big mess."

That cheered them right up. "Play! Me too!" They bounced around her.

Her head spun from all the movement and energy. She had to steady herself for a second before the dizzy spell passed. *Okay, all right, take it easy. Lot's to do.* She had no time today for frivolities like passing out today.

Since she had no car, the playground visit planned for this morning was canceled, and so was *The Wizard of Oz* later. She'd just have to make the most of the party.

She made herself a cup of coffee that actually helped her headache a little, then, while the girls played in their room with their plastic dolls and horses, she began vacuuming, which made the headache worse. Oh well.

She sucked up dirt from the tan living room carpet first, then lifted the green sofa cushions one by one and sucked up all the fuzz-covered cheese puffs. Which visiting kids *would* find and eat, if past experience was anything to go by.

The couch done, she turned and jumped a foot. Chase was standing behind her, inside the front door, watching her. She turned off the vacuum cleaner, her heart racing.

"Sorry." He took another step in and looked around. "I knocked. You probably didn't hear me."

Having him in her home felt weird beyond weird. She found it impossible to look at anything but him. He definitely had a strong presence, a certain energy that drew the eye. Not that his well-built body didn't do that already.

He'd never been skinny, not even in his youth, but he'd packed on serious muscle since Luanne had last seen him up close and personal. And since she'd seen him naked before, her mind ever so helpfully provided an image of what he would look like now without his clothes, all grown up with the aforementioned muscles.

She choked on her own spit. Squeezed her eyes closed for a second. What was wrong with her? She could *not* think about a naked Chase Merritt. Did she still have alcohol in her system from last night? *Okay. Just get through this.* She opened her eyes and smiled.

"Did you need to ask me anything else?" She held her breath, willing him to say no, to tell her that he was just leaving.

He pulled a business card from his pocket and handed it to her.

The plain white card had the Broslin PD's logo on it, his name below, then the word *detective* and a phone number. "In case you need me."

Meaning *in case you want to confess?* She kept smiling so he wouldn't think she was nervous. She was probably being paranoid. He couldn't have guessed what she'd done. She'd covered it up. She'd fixed the problem with the car. Nobody had to find out. Ever. "Thanks. And thanks for the ride."

He watched her for a long moment, the expression on his face unfathomable. He looked as if he was preparing to say something, but, in the end, he turned and walked away, stepping over a rag doll and a toy tiara in his path.

Her shoulders sagged as she deflated when the door closed behind him.

That relief lasted about a second. As she turned back to work, she caught her reflection in the mirror above the fireplace. She looked...almost normal. She patted down her hair and straightened her shirt, her hands freezing in midmotion.

The dazed shock that had carried her through the morning abated, the pounding in her head stopped long enough for her to have her first clear thought of the day.

She was a murderer.

As that word popped into her mind, her entire body began shaking.

I ran over Earl.

Killed him.

She'd killed, and she'd covered up the evidence. Her knees gave out, and she folded onto the couch. Filled with enough guilt, disappointment, and regret to drown in, she shook her head at her mirror self, then she crumpled completely, burying her face in her hands as she tried to just breathe.

She couldn't do this.

Who was she kidding? She was never going to get away with murder.

The girls' laughter reached her from their bedroom.

She *had* to get away with it.

But she couldn't live with the guilt for the rest of her life. At one point, she'd have to make this right. *She could...* She let her hands drop and straightened her back a little. *Okay.* Once the girls reached eighteen and could manage without her, she was going to turn herself in.

In the meanwhile... She sighed. At least nobody suspected anything.

Chapter Four

Luanne looked guilty as sin. Sexy as hell too, but that wasn't something Chase had to address at this very moment, so he was willing to table it.

The Mustang was in rough shape, he thought as he walked up to it behind the police station where Arnie had dropped off the car. The front was smashed. Of course, she *had* hit a fire hydrant.

He'd been damned relieved to see the chief and the boys out there working on that. He'd hated to think that Luanne might have hit something else entirely.

Not that Earl didn't have it coming, judging by what the employees had said in their interviews. The stories they told spoke of him pushing Maria up against the wall in the supply room, grabbing Jackie in an empty guest room, pressure to "work" at his house. Hundreds of dollars held back in wages. That the women hadn't liked him was an understatement.

But none of the employees had a big dent in their car, except for Luanne.

The thought of Earl putting his hands on her, pressuring her, forcing her... Chase rolled his neck to ease his tightening muscles.

His phone rang just as he set his evidence kit on the ground. He glanced at the display and took the call. "Hey, Mom."

"I ran into Cindy Jenners at the store today."

"No."

"She's such a nice young woman."

"Not interested."

"Your sisters abandoned me."

"They didn't abandon you. They got married."

"They moved to other states. I don't have a single grandchild within driving distance. How can they be so cruel?" She gave a guilt-laden pause. "Mrs. Ottmann said she saw you talking to some blonde with Massachusetts license plates by the feed store yesterday."

Chase closed his eyes and brushed his thumb and forefinger over his eyelids. "I was giving her a speeding ticket, okay?"

"Oh." She sounded mollified. "Cindy Jenners teaches at the elementary school now, did you know that? Such a nice girl. I'm sure she doesn't speed. Promise me to take a Broslin bride. I'm begging you. Please."

Oh sweet Jesus. "I'm at work. I have to go."

"My dishwasher stopped working," she said quickly.

His finger hesitated on the button. "All right. I'll come over tonight and look at it. But I swear, if Cindy Jenners is accidentally there for tea…"

"I can have whoever I want at my own house for tea, thank you very much," his mother snapped, then mumbled something about ungrateful offspring.

"Mother," Chase put some official, police-grade warning into his voice.

"Don't you *mother* me in that tone, Chase Mortimer Merritt," she said and hung up on him.

He groaned. His mother was an intelligent woman with plenty of energy and brains, widowed, children out of the house, retired. Lots of time on her hands, which made Susan Merritt a bachelor son's worst nightmare. Chase loved her anyway. But if he was going to find Cindy at the house tonight instead of a broken dishwasher, he and his mother were going to have words.

He rolled his shoulders. All right. Forget Cindy Jenners and matrimonial traps. He had a job to do here.

He sat on the ground and opened his evidence kit, took out the first swab, ran it along one side of the red bumper, sealed it away, grabbed a second, swabbed the other side. He used four swabs on the grill. Other than some negligible dirt and red paint from the hydrant, he didn't see anything suspicious with the naked eye.

He relaxed a little and eased under the car next. The fire hydrant had washed the outside, but the undercarriage was pretty dirty. He pulled the flashlight off his belt and panned it around. Stopped.

Was that hair? His neck muscles tightened all over again.

He slid back out, grabbed an evidence bag and tweezers, crawled back in, bagged the short, whitish hair, even as he told himself it could be from a cat that had slept under the Mustang. He panned the light around again. Froze.

Was that blood?

He used a wet swab for that. The white cotton came back dark red. His stomach sank as he took several samples.

Let the lab have it. Don't jump to conclusions. But he was swimming in dread and regret as he bagged the piece of evidence.

He went by the book, collected second and third samples, took his time, didn't rush the process. Then he walked back into the station with his bags and his kit.

Only the captain and Leila, the admin assistant slash dispatcher, were in. No, one more. The new officer was coming from the break room with a cup of coffee, Gabriela Maria Flores, ex-inner-city cop, a recent hire, straight from Philly.

She nodded in greeting, tall and lean, crisp uniform, dark hair in a tight bun at her nape. She had a steel core that one, not to be messed with. Chase nodded back at her. "Gabi."

He dropped the bags on Leila's desk. "Would you please pack these up for me?"

Leila worked the front desk first shift, a single mother of three teenage boys, no-nonsense short hair, drill-sergeant attitude, a sensible woman, save for her dubious taste in footwear. Today's affront to modesty was high-heeled pink sneakers covered in black lace.

There could not be enough people willing to wear something like that to make it worthwhile for a manufacturer to make them, Chase thought, and put the shoes down as one of the womanly mysteries.

Leila pulled a large, heavy-duty envelope from a drawer and dropped everything inside, sealed the tab, and handed the package back to him. "Is that Luanne Mayfair's Mustang out back?"

Chase nodded.

"I hope she's not in trouble."

He made some noncommittal sounds, and she let the topic drop. She knew better than to ask questions about an ongoing investigation.

Captain Bing gestured from his office, so Chase walked over to talk to the man.

"Anything?" Bing was in his midforties but had grown five years younger in the last couple of months. Marriage clearly agreed with him.

"Not yet."

"Is that Luanne Mayfair's car out back?"

Chase nodded. "She hit a fire hydrant."

"I'm guessing you already checked that."

"Checks out."

"What's in the evidence bags?"

Chase hesitated, hating to say the words. "Some blood and hair from the car. Could be roadkill," he quickly added.

Bing raised an eyebrow. "We have a hit-and-run, then a car with blood and hair." He shook his head. Reached up to rub the back of his neck. "Let's hope for the roadkill scenario. I like Luanne." He thought for a moment. "She worked with Earl."

"She did."

"You're thinking of her for the homicide?"

"Just covering all the bases."

Bing shook his head again. His lungs filled, then deflated. "Motive?" he asked in a tone that said he really didn't want to be asking that question.

Chase didn't want to answer it. "Same as for all the other employees. Earl was a sleazebag who cheated people out of their wages when he could. He also pressured his staff into sexual favors."

Bing's face hardened. "Why is this the first time I'm hearing about this?"

"Good question. I suppose nobody wants to lose their jobs in this economy."

Bing stayed grim as he thought. Shook his head. Gave a disgusted grunt at last. "All right. Let's walk through this. Opportunity?"

Chase was equally grim as he responded. "Luanne was at Finnegan's last night. Earl was killed in the alley behind the bar."

Bing leaned back in his chair, putting both hands on his desk. "So we've got motive and opportunity. And for means, her Mustang. Dented. With blood and hair on it."

"Fire hydrant and roadkill," Chase put in, wanting badly to believe it.

"Or she could have hit the fire hydrant to destroy evidence. Makes her look even guiltier."

Chase nodded. He'd already considered all of this, hated the picture the details painted when added up together. "Could have been an accidental hit-and-run. Then she panicked and tried to cover it up."

Bing watched him. Flattened his lips. "We've put in for arrest warrants on less evidence."

They had. "It's Luanne. She's got the twins."

And Bing nodded. "Let me know when the lab results come back." His eyes narrowed after a moment. "You think she has a lawyer?"

"I got the impression she doesn't have a lot of money."

Bing nodded again. "Any other suspects? Girlfriend, wife, ex-wife?"

"No current girlfriend. Three ex-wives. The last ex-wife, Veronica, works the front desk at the motel. I already talked to her. Solid alibi, bridal shower with a dozen other women. The second ex lives in Downingtown. The first is down in South Carolina. I'll be checking them out next."

Bing considered that for a second. "All right. I want to know as soon as you have something."

Chase went straight to his desk, grabbed a permanent marker, and wrote his name, contact information, and the case number on the evidence envelope, then set that aside for the time being. He got his notes out, including the interviews with the maids, signed in to his computer, and updated the case file.

He looked for any other angle besides Luanne, all other possibilities. Standard procedure. Once a suspect was identified, it was too easy to focus only on him or her, look at all evidence from that light, and maybe miss something significant. So he set aside the possible evidence from the Mustang and considered the case afresh, as if Luanne wasn't in the picture.

Maybe Earl had been accidentally killed by someone driving through town. A stranger. Hit-and-run. That would have been Chase's favorite option. Except the evidence didn't bear out that hypothesis.

People driving through town drove down Route 1. They didn't get into the neighborhoods to wind their way through back alleys. Yeah, people got lost. But at this stage, that was the less likely scenario. He thought it more likely that the killer was someone local.

Maybe somebody who regularly took the alley as a shortcut. Or maybe one of last night's bar patrons, Chase thought. He needed to go in tonight once the place opened, and ask around. The Finnegans would cooperate without giving him any trouble. Maybe he'd ask Harper to go with him, just to make everything go smoother.

Harper would want to be there if somebody was questioning his parents.

So, hit-and-run. Hit, hide, and run, technically. The driver had gotten out and covered the body in garbage bags. Maybe someone who'd been driving drunk?

He tried not to think how bleary-eyed Luanne had looked when she'd walked into the motel this morning.

He finished his initial report, then uploaded the crime scene photos. A messy, dark back alley. The body from every angle. Nothing in the pictures jumped out at him as a screaming clue.

Accidental hit-and-run with a cover-up.

There *was*, of course another option. That the hit had been planned and Earl specifically targeted. Motive, means, and opportunity, Luanne had all three, but so could any number of others.

He didn't like Luanne's name as the only one on his suspect list. He was determined to expand that list significantly before the day was over.

He rifled through his notes until he found the motel owners' phone number. Mildred and Harold Cosgrove were originally from Unionville. They'd bought the motel twenty years ago as an investment, run it for fifteen years before they retired and moved to Rising Sun, Maryland, to be closer to their daughter and grandchildren. Earl Cosgrove had been hired at that point to take over, and he'd been managing the place for the past four years.

Chase dialed the number and waited until someone picked up, then introduced himself to Mildred Cosgrove on the other end.

Her voice was thick as if she'd been crying. "I've been expecting a call. Veronica told me what happened to Earl." She sniffed. "I just can't believe it." She sniffed again. "Harold and I are driving up tomorrow."

"I'd appreciate if you could give me a call when you get here." He'd meant to talk to them over the phone, but in person would be better.

"Do you know who…?" She couldn't finish the sentence.

"Not yet, ma'am. But we're doing everything we can to catch the perpetrator. I have a couple of questions I'd like to ask when you get here, but in the meanwhile, I'd appreciate it if I could have access to the motel's employee records." Technically, he needed a warrant for that, unless Mildred volunteered it, but he was pretty sure she would.

She sniffed again. "Of course. Harold has everything on the computer. He can probably e-mail the files."

"Thank you." He dictated his work e-mail address. Waited a beat. "You wouldn't know anyone he'd been fighting with, would you? Any enemies?"

Mildred sniffed louder. "I don't think so. He ran the motel, but we weren't that close, I'm sorry to say. I'll ask Harold when he gets home. If he knows something, I'll let you know."

After they hung up, he went through all the information he had up to this point—none of which looked good for Luanne. But things improved once Harold sent Earl Cosgrove's employee record fifteen minutes later.

Among all the basic information, Chase quickly found what he was looking for. Earl had life insurance through his workplace. The beneficiaries were his three ex-wives. Probably so they could take care of the kids if something happened to Earl and the child support checks stopped coming. Okay, so the man wasn't a total jerk in every area of his life. At least he cared about his kids.

He updated his report, doing his best to tune out the two men who staggered into the police station, dragging each other.

"I want you to arrest this idiot bastard," the taller one shouted, face contorted with rage. "He shit on my front porch!"

"Your dog shits all over my yard every day," the other one countered, shoving.

"Calm down, please," Leila said when they reached reception.

The tall one thumped a fist on the counter. "I want to make a police report. I stepped in that shit!"

Chase checked out the floor behind them, the questionable footprints. Made a mental note to walk around them when he left.

"Good, you deserved it. My kids can't play in my yard because of your stupid dog." The short guy swung and missed, knocking the pot of lucky bamboo off the counter. Miracle of miracles, the pot didn't shatter.

Leila snapped to standing, her eyes narrowing, chin down, hands on her hips. "Calm the hell down, I said!"

Her voice cut through the office, quieted the men for a second, but only for a second. The tall one stuck his head forward and got right into Leila's face.

Her eyes narrowed to dangerous levels. The air seemed to vibrate around her.

"It's all fun and games until someone gets her foot up his ass," Gabi murmured at her desk, and rose to keep the idiots from coming to harm.

Chase grinned as he pushed to his feet. "Leila would never treat her footwear like that. I'll take care of it. I'm heading out anyway."

As Gabi sat back down, he grabbed the evidence envelope and walked up to reception. "Do we have two open holding cells?"

The men's heads whipped around.

"Wait a minute," the short one sputtered. "I'm here to make a report."

"I'm here to take you back for disorderly conduct and disturbing the peace," Chase said calmly. "Plus battery." He looked at the blood on short guy's lip and on tall guy's brow.

Leila sat, not entirely able to wipe the smug off her face. "I'll put that call in for Animal Control. We have leash laws in Broslin."

Chase nodded. The PD didn't get involved with animals unless abuse was involved, but these two dumbasses didn't need to know that. "Once you bring the police in the middle of something, we do look at every little detail," he told them, his voice holding nothing but kindness. "You came to the right place. Every detail of this will be fully investigated."

"That's what we do," Leila added in cheerfully.

Chase gestured toward the back. "Let's go back to holding. I can take your complaints about the dog shit there. There are benches in the cells. You'll be more comfortable sitting."

The tall one ducked his head. The short one looked at his feet, hands shoved into his pockets. They suddenly looked sheepish, the wind gone from their sails.

Chase shrugged. "Or you can just have a discussion and come to an agreement like reasonable men. Split the cost of a fence. Tell Ed at the lumberyard I sent you, and he'll give you a discount."

Tall guy slinked one step back, then another.

Short guy turned with a frustrated gesture and marched out of there. Seeing his escape go unchallenged, his buddy quickly followed.

Chase shook his head as he picked up the lucky bamboo and set the pot back on the counter. "I'm driving over to the lab. In case anyone's looking for me. Then I'm heading over to Downingtown to interview Earl's second ex-wife."

"They're lucky they didn't make me mad," Leila said.

Chase had a feeling that would happen when she discovered the questionable footprints. Best not be here at that point. He headed for the door, keeping to the clean surfaces.

Half an hour to the lab in West Chester, fifteen minutes there— he put a rush order in—half an hour to Cathy Cosgrove's house.

He found her, a sporty brunette, unpacking travel bags from the back of her car in the driveway, her face stricken, her two teenage daughters who looked just like her crying, all three wearing Girl Scout uniforms.

Chase introduced himself and noted her blue SUV. No damage.

"We came home as soon as we heard." Cathy sounded exhausted. She invited him in, and he helped her to carry the bags inside. "Do you have any suspects?" she asked, shaking her head over and over again. She waited until the girls went upstairs with their backpacks. "Earl wasn't the best man I've ever known," she lowered her voice, "but he didn't deserve this."

"No, ma'am."

She buried her face in her hands for a second, then dropped them, drawing a deep breath. "Do you have any idea who or why?"

"Not yet. Did he have any enemies?"

She closed her eyes for a moment. "We haven't been very close since the divorce. Since Chloe got her license, she's been driving herself and her sister over to Broslin when they wanted to spend time with him. I don't think I've even seen him yet this year."

Chase glanced at the bags on the floor. "May I ask where you've been?"

"Week-long camping meet for the Girl Scouts over in Jersey."

"You stayed there the whole time? Didn't run home for anything?"

She shook her head.

"I'm sorry, but I have to ask," he prefaced the next question. "Could you tell me where you were last night?"

She swallowed. "At the midnight hike with the girls."

"Can anyone confirm that?"

"About a hundred people. I can give you names and phone numbers."

"A few would be enough. I'm sorry." He didn't want to sound as if he was accusing her of anything. Maybe she no longer loved Earl, but he'd been the father of her daughters, and their grief had to hurt her.

She grabbed an empty envelope from her coffee table, turned it over, scrolled through her phone, and began writing down numbers. "You need to eliminate people so you can find the one who did this. I understand."

"I appreciate it."

He liked working with nice people. Truly most people were honest and accommodating. The troublemakers were the exception to the rule. You got the kind of energy out of an interaction that you put in. His SOP was to solve problems politely, either with humor or gentle coaxing. No sense escalating anything into an outright confrontation, usually not even when he was faced with criminals.

On his way back to Broslin, he called all four of Cathy's scouting friends and confirmed her alibi, then mentally crossed the woman off his suspect list.

Then he called the first ex-wife, who ran a staffing agency in Myrtle Beach, April Cosgrove, now April Barton, remarried. The housekeeper informed him that Mr. and Mrs. Barton were on their second honeymoon in Paris and had been there for the past ten days. Chase had to confirm with airline records, but if that checked out, he'd have to cross April off his suspect list too.

Which would once again have only one name on it: Luanne.

He was tempted to curse.

He called Harper on his way back to Broslin. "I'm heading over to Finnegan's if you want to be there."

"I'm already over here. Anything new?" Harper sounded sleepy. He'd had the night shift too, but had the morning off today.

"Not much yet. I'm still interviewing people." Chase didn't want to make a big deal about the samples he'd collected from the Mustang until he knew for sure that he had something.

"I want in on this case."

"Like the captain told you, conflict of interest." The murder had happened on property owned by Harper's parents.

Harper swore, plenty of bristle in his voice as he said, "I want to

45

be updated on every new clue. And if anyone talks to my folks, I'm going to be here with them."

"Which is why I called you before I headed that way." Harper was a friend. Chase saw no need to antagonize him. If his mother was in the same situation, he'd be acting the same.

He grabbed lunch from a drive-through, then headed over to Finnegan's. He'd rather have Rose's famous potato soup, but asking the person you were questioning for a bowl of soup didn't seem professional. He ate his burger, was long finished by the time he reached the bar.

Only three cars sat in the parking lot: Sean Finnegan's pickup, Harper Finnegan's SUV, and a beat-up old Ford Focus. Chase checked the front of each, then checked out the back alley one more time before going inside.

The place wasn't open, but Sean and Rose Finnegan were there, as well as Tayron the bartender, setting up behind the bar, all looking pretty grim. Harper, tall, reddish-blond hair, Irish down to his toes, leaned against the wall in the corner, glowering. He wore civilian clothes, jeans, and a green T-shirt with the bar's logo on it. He nodded at Chase.

"Chase." Sean, the older Finnegan, gave a friendly greeting. "I've been expecting your call." Either due to good genes or Guinness, he looked twenty years younger than his age. He could have been Harper's slightly older brother. They looked alike in every way.

"I had plenty to do this morning. Figured I could wait until you were here to get ready for opening. I might come back later tonight to talk to some patrons."

Sean nodded. "Any news?"

"Still in the information-gathering phase," Chase told him. "Were you here last night?"

Sean Finnegan offered a half smile. "Took Rose on a date. Fortieth wedding anniversary. Any man who values his hide better make a big deal out of these things."

Sean and Rose Finnegan were made for each other, a small-town love story. She had plenty of fire left in her, even at sixty—slim figure, startling blue eyes, short hair in a fashionable cut—and Finnegan was smart enough to appreciate it. The couple reminded Chase of his own parents, before his father had passed away.

Now his mother was lonely. Of course she was. He made a

mental note to stay a little after he fixed her dishwasher tonight. Maybe they could watch a movie together. And have a chat about the matchmaking that was getting out of hand lately. All right, so he was the age where guys started to get married. It wasn't as if he had one foot in the grave.

"I'm going to need the credit card receipts for last night," he told Sean. "Need to come up with a list of everyone who was here last night." He paused. "I'm not going to lie to you. I probably couldn't get a warrant, since neither the bar nor any of the patrons have been implicated so far, but having a list of who was here would sure make my life easier."

"All right," Sean said without hesitation. "Just be discreet when you go talk to people. We usually have men here whose wives don't know they come to Finnegan's. Don't want to get anyone in trouble. Bad for business."

Chase nodded.

Since Sean and Rose hadn't been here the night before, after a brief conversation, Chase let them go back to work, Rose in the kitchen and Sean in the back office. Chase sat down to interview Tayron. Harper stayed right where he was to listen in.

"Did you hear anything suspicious out back?" Chase asked the bartender.

Tayron lifted a shoulder, dropped it. "Can't hear anything with the music going and the big-screen TV in the back, people talking. Too much buzz."

"Was the place hopping?"

"A couple of hundred people, coming and going. A hundred or so in here at a time." He paused. "I was alone. The waitress who was supposed to work couldn't come in. Things were a little rushed. Normally, I'd have called Harper to give me a hand, but he was on duty. We try to not have just one person serving drinks. Have to watch out for VIPs."

Chase lifted a questioning eyebrow.

"Visibly Intoxicated Persons," Tayron spelled it out. "Normally I tend bar, keep an eye on the people ordering. The waitress serves the tables, keeps an eye on people in the back. If I'm alone, people will come up, buy a round for their friends, and take it back. I don't see the friends at the table, what shape they're in. If one gets drunk, gets into an accident, Finnegan's could be liable."

Chase nodded. He knew that part. "I need you to give me a list of everyone you remember."

"Mostly locals. A carload of college students I've never seen before. Probably on a drive from WCU."

West Chester University, the nearest college. Could be something. A carload of drunk frat boys had potential. "They pay with credit cards?"

Tayron narrowed his eyes for a second, then shook his head. "Cash. Mostly one-dollar bills. I remember thinking maybe they'd set out for a strip club, then somehow ended up here."

"Who else? Off the top of your head."

Tayron began listing names, mostly people Chase knew. He'd lived in Broslin his whole life. When Tayron came to Luanne Mayfair, Chase held up a hand.

"Alone?"

"For a while. She doesn't come in much. You know, since she got the twins. Some guy bought her a drink."

"You know him?"

"First time here. Couple of years older than her. Geeky. Brown hair, brown eyes. Average guy."

"I don't suppose you caught his name."

Tayron pursed his lips. "Gregory," he said after a second. "I think that's what she called him."

Not enough.

"When did Luanne come in?"

The bartender rubbed his chin. "Early. Around nine. And she didn't stay long. Less than an hour."

So she left around 10:00 p.m. The coroner's preliminary report put the time of death between 10:00 p.m. and 11:00 p.m.

Chase's muscles tightened.

Tayron leaned forward suddenly, shock on his face. "You looking at Luanne? She's not like that, man."

"I know." That was the trouble. In his heart of hearts, Chase couldn't see Luanne as a murderous villain, not even under provocation. "Did she leave with the guy?"

"Can't say for sure." Tayron drew his eyebrows together. "I was serving people. One minute they were there, making small talk, the next they were both gone. I didn't think much of it. She's not the one-night-stand type. You know what I mean?"

He did. Back in the day, it'd taken him an eternity to talk her into his bed...um, backseat. And then she couldn't wait to get out, which was a different story entirely. Not that she'd bruised his fragile teen male ego or anything.

He still couldn't think about that night without wincing, so he didn't. He went back to questioning Tayron. "Was she under the influence when she left?"

"She had two cocktails. Light. She's not a boozer. I wouldn't have let her drive if she was seriously drinking." Tayron thought for a second. "Guy didn't look like a player. She said he was a dog walker. That's all I can remember."

Sean Finnegan brought a stack of papers from the back office and handed them to Chase, photocopies of last night's credit card receipts. Of course, most people paid with cash, so it was a given that the list of patrons would be incomplete.

Chase didn't like that word in relation to his investigation.

He spent another twenty minutes with Tayron, thanked him, then walked to the door, turned back for one last question. "Do you remember, by any chance, how the guy who was with Luanne paid?"

Tayron closed his eyes for a second. "Cash. I remember because I had to break a hundred. I was thinking, kind of jokingly, *Hey, Luanne hooked a high roller. Good for her.*"

Chase stepped back toward him. "How many hundred dollar bills did you get last night?"

"Just the one."

"You still have it, by any chance?"

Tayron glanced at Harper, who was already on his feet.

"Let me see," he said as he walked off to the back office. He came back a minute later, holding a bill with a salad tong.

"I was just about to take the money to the bank," Sean said. "You think you'll find fingerprints?"

"Far shot," Chase admitted. Money, in general, went through way too many hands. But he was determined to follow every possible lead. "I'll need the prints of everyone here who touched it so those can be eliminated. I'd appreciate it if you could come down to the station today."

Both Sean and Tayron nodded.

Chase pulled an evidence bag from his pocket, waited as Harper dropped the bill in. "I'll let you know if anything comes up," he said before Harper could ask, then walked out, turning one word around in his head: *Gregory.*

He needed a last name. Technically, the guy wasn't a person of interest in the investigation at this stage, but something about him pricked Chase's instincts.

Luanne had said she'd driven straight home. Alone.

He wished somebody had seen her.

On his way back to the station, he swung by her house. A birthday party was in full swing in her backyard, with about a dozen screaming kids.

For a second, he thought about running over to the store and grabbing the girls that ladybug cake. But he wasn't sure how Luanne would take it. He wasn't family. She didn't even consider him a friend. Her friends were in the backyard at the party.

He didn't normally frequent toddler birthday parties. Odd that all of a sudden he wanted to walk back to see how this one was going. He hoped the girls were having a blast. He hoped Luanne had been able to get everything ready. It couldn't be easy to be the single caretaker of twins.

He didn't want to interrupt, so he went back to the station, gave the hundred dollar bill to Leila to overnight it to the lab since he didn't want to drive back to West Chester again today, then he finished off his shift, going through every scrap of information he had.

Earl's financial data came in finally, but Chase found nothing suspicious there, no big debts, no odd purchases, so he closed down his computer and headed out again. He went to see Earl's neighbors, didn't mind throwing in an extra hour, but they didn't tell him anything that sounded even remotely relevant to the case. On his way home, he swung by Luanne's again. The row of cars was gone from the curb, the backyard empty.

He pulled over and just sat behind the wheel for a minute, looking at the brand-new fire hydrant. Then he got out, against his better judgment.

She opened the door on the first knock. "The girls are sleeping," she said in a hushed tone.

Her low, velvety voice got him, like it did pretty much every time. He could close his eyes and listen to her all day. Although, under the circumstances, she'd probably find that weird. "Tuckered out from the party?"

She nodded, her eyes strained, her face tight. "Any news about my car?"

He watched her closely. "If someone's in trouble and they come in and give themselves up, that counts big-time as far as what happens later."

She paled.

She wore a different shirt from this morning, this one black with some ruffles. Maybe it was the color, but she looked even skinnier.

"Would you mind if I came in for a few more questions about last night?"

Her hand tightened on the door. "Am I in trouble?"

"No. But you knew Earl. You were at the bar. You might have seen something. I'm off duty. It's nothing official. I'm just trying to help here, in case something comes up later. Let's just talk for a minute."

She stepped aside with plenty of reluctance, but she did let him in.

He headed for her kitchen table and sat, thought about the cake she couldn't afford, and wondered about food. He rubbed a hand over his stomach. "I didn't have a chance to eat much today. Would you mind if I ordered a pizza and grabbed a slice while we talked? I swear I'm getting lightheaded."

Her whiskey-color eyes watched him with suspicion as if trying to figure out his angle. But after a moment, she said, "Sure."

So he grabbed his cell phone, asked for a large pie with everything, and had it delivered.

He got straight to his questions while they waited. "So Gregory's a dog walker. Do you know where?"

"What?" Confusion sent her eyebrows sliding up her forehead.

"Gregory. Dog walker. Do you know where?"

The look of confusion disappeared. "That's Brett."

"Brett who?"

"Brett Bellinger. We had a date. He couldn't make it. While I was waiting, Gregory came over to talk to me."

Huh. He couldn't say he approved of all those men around her. He wanted to ask more questions about the Brett guy she was apparently dating, but since he hadn't actually been at the bar, Chase had no excuse to drill her about him.

"Can you think back to when you were leaving Finnegan's? Did you walk out with the guy you met, Gregory?"

She blinked a couple of times. "I think so."

"And then what?"

"Got into my car and drove home." But she didn't sound sure.

"See anyone in the parking lot?"

She shook her head, her long blond hair slipping all over her shoulders.

He wanted to reach out and tuck the golden strands behind her ears. He didn't. "Hear any noises from the back alley?"

She shook her head again.

"Did anyone see you get into your car, other than Gregory?"

"I don't think so."

"And when you got home? Did any of the neighbors see you?"

"They were probably all settled in for the night. I'm sure they don't stand by the window all night to see who comes and goes."

Still, a nosy neighbor might have looked out the window if he or she heard the Mustang, could confirm the time when Luanne had come home. He hoped more than anything that he'd have no need to check, but the Mustang was stuck in his mind, setting off all his cop instincts.

He kept up that line of questioning until the pizza arrived, then he switched to Earl.

"Who knew that he always cut through the alley on his way home?" He bit into a slice and waved a hand toward the box. "Help yourself. I can't eat all this."

"Pretty much everybody." She took a slice after a moment of hesitation. Ate. Relaxed marginally. "Thanks."

"So I get it that he wasn't averse to putting his hands on his employees. How far did he push? I don't mean you. In general. Place like that, people working together, you must have heard stories."

She took her time chewing, maybe to put off the answer. But eventually, she said, "Just groping." She hesitated.

"But?"

"If somebody wanted extra hours, he'd hire them to clean his house."

Chase set his pizza down. "And?"

"Certain things were expected," she said quietly.

His blood began to heat. "Did he ever offer you a cleaning

position?"

She put her pizza down too. "Yesterday."

The way she looked just then, her eyes haunted, brought Chase's protective instincts to the surface. He wouldn't have minded spending a minute or two in a dark alley with Earl. He cared about Luanne, dammit, and he hated the thought of some asshole messing with her.

"Anybody ever reported him to the owners?" He knew nobody had talked to the police, which filled him with frustration. How was he supposed to fix problems he didn't know about?

"Not that I know of," Luanne told him. "He's one of the family."

Right. The maids probably worried that instead of Earl the slimeball getting reprimanded, they'd be fired.

Chase kept asking questions, and kept eating, even though the pizza felt like gravel in his stomach. But he had the feeling if he stopped, Luanne would too, and he wanted her to have a good meal. Only four slices remained by the time they finished eating.

He was out of questions for the moment, so he thanked her for her cooperation, then stood. Gestured to the box. "I hate wasting food, but would you toss that for me? Unless you think the girls might be interested when they wake up. I have some things to do, and I don't want to carry the box around in the cruiser."

She nodded and walked him out, nervous and wary.

He opened the door but hesitated before stepping outside. "If you remember anything else, please call me. From what we know so far, Earl was killed at around the same time that you left the bar. Anything you remember could be significant."

She promised, but she looked as if she couldn't wait to get rid of him.

She looked beaten down. Scared.

He cursed himself for not paying more attention to her these last couple of years. He'd known about her mother's death, the twins. But he'd just assumed she was managing, since he hadn't heard otherwise. "I want to make sure you're all right."

She stuck her chin out. "I'm a tough cookie."

"Under the right circumstances, even tough cookies crumble." He didn't want to see Luanne crumble. He wanted to see her naked. *Shouldn't be thinking that.* He tried to think friendly thoughts. "I really meant it when I told you I want you to consider me as a friend. You can tell me anything. I'll help if I can. I swear."

But she kept that fake, brittle smile on her face and looked at him as if she had no idea what he was talking about.

He wanted to shake her. He wanted to kiss her. Which clued him in that he shouldn't be at her house off duty.

He left her, his thoughts troubled.

For the first time during an investigation, he wasn't looking forward   to   the   lab   results   coming   in.

Chapter Five

Luanne spent Sunday with the girls, racked with guilt. She decided several times to turn herself in, then changed her mind each time. She had no idea how criminals lived like this. Her conscience about killed her.

What had she done?

She felt horrible about Earl's death, and she felt just as bad about covering up her involvement. She had no idea what she'd been thinking the day before. She'd felt as if someone had melted her brain, which was only just beginning to clear today. She'd reacted with panic and her childhood reflex of hiding from trouble.

Her daddy had firmly believed in tanning her hide for even the most minor infractions, like a messy bed or a bad grade, sometimes for illogical things like putting the newspaper on the wrong spot in the kitchen. He'd loved that old belt of his, used to fold it in half for discipline. As a child, she'd learned in a hurry that the best way to avoid a good licking was to hide her mistakes and failings.

She was aware of the ingrained tendency to hide from trouble, had corrected it as an adult, raised the twins with a completely different method of parenting. But sometimes, evidently, she still reverted. She had a sneaky suspicion that her actions the day before might not have helped any, might have made things worse in the long-term.

What to do now?

She knew the right thing was to drive over to the station and confess. But then she would look at Mia and Daisy, think about them being taken away by Social Services, and she simply couldn't do it.

These were the times when she longed for family, even if her parents had been less than perfect. If she'd had aunts and uncles and nieces and nephews, grandparents, then if something happened to her, the girls wouldn't be all alone in the world.

She knew nobody on her father's side. He was an only child. His parents had died early, and he'd pretty much raised himself. Her mother's side, the Desirees, were somebody down in Virginia at one time. But they'd disinherited Luanne's mother when she'd run off, pregnant at seventeen, with a northern boy, a hired farmhand.

In her nostalgic moods, Luanne's mother used to talk about the big farm, all the cows and horses, the log cabin up in the hills built by the first Desirees, where she'd had her trysts with the handsome young farmhand who'd caught her eye.

When Luanne's father was at his most raging drunk, her mother often threatened to leave him and move right on back into that old empty cabin. She never did. He'd left Luanne and her mother first.

None of the Desirees ever so much as called, except a Great-Aunt Hilda who sent a card once a year for Christmas. Luanne's mother never answered, but after her death, Luanne had gotten into the habit of sending a simple card back, a few lines of well wishes, a fragile connection that was the only tether she had to family.

A tenuous tether at best. Even if she had her great-aunt's phone number, she couldn't call up and ask if anyone in the family wouldn't mind raising two little girls—should worse come to worst. In any case, her family would be as much strangers to the twins as whomever Social Services might select.

No matter how little Luanne made, she squirreled away a few dollars each month for life insurance. She'd been meaning to ask Jen to be the girls' guardian if something, like a car accident, happened. But if Luanne went to prison, there'd be no life insurance money. And Jen and Billy had spent everything they had on fertility treatments to give Bobby a little brother or sister.

Without contributing anything, Luanne couldn't just ask them to take on the huge financial responsibility of raising the twins. She had to figure out some kind of solution. She thought and thought, but all she accomplished was making herself sick with worry.

What little sleep she caught was filled with guilt-laden dreams of her mother taunting her. *"It's your fault that your father left." "It's your fault that the twin's father left. You should have been home to help with the girls." "It's your fault I got cancer. I got it from the stress you give me, I swear." "It was your fault I had to marry your drunk of a father in the first place. I was pregnant with you. What else could I do?"*

By the time Monday morning rolled around, Luanne was dizzy from lack of sleep, tired from being up all night again and trying to make herself remember what happened in the back alley behind the bar.

She even considered that she might have been roofied. That kind of thing happened in movies all the time, right? Then again, in real life... Not to anyone she'd ever known. And the thing was, Gregory had never touched her drink.

Since she still had no car and it was pouring rain outside, Jen picked up the girls. Jackie was on her way to pick up Luanne. They were both working today.

Luanne downed the last of the coffee, then detoured by the bathroom to dab on some more concealer. She had circles under her eyes stark enough for a heroin junkie.

She had one eye done before her doorbell rang. "Coming!" She dabbed the other eye quickly.

She hurried out and opened the door, stopped in her tracks at the sight of Chase. He pretty much filled up the doorway, all imposing and very intent this morning. She stood there, frozen for a second before she remembered to step back so he could come in out of the rain.

Act normal. She swallowed. "Am I getting my car back?"

"Luanne." He cleared his throat and held her gaze. He looked troubled, his blue eyes shadowed as they seemed to search her soul. That easygoing, relaxed air that always surrounded him was gone, replaced by something darker and heavier. "Is there anything you'd like to tell me?"

Panic spread through her. Suddenly, she couldn't catch her breath. "I'm late for work. Jackie is coming."

He shook his head. "The lab results are back on the Mustang."

The world came to a sudden halt around her. "And?"

He watched her for another long moment, drew a deep, long breath. "Luanne Mayfair, you are under arrest for the murder of Earl Cosgrove. You have the right to remain silent..."

She gaped as he read her rights, then her peripheral vision narrowed, and she was suddenly lightheaded, and the next thing she knew her legs were folding.

He caught her, moved farther into the house with her, seated her on the couch, and went for a glass of water. Looked around. "Where are the twins?"

Her mind couldn't catch up with what had just happened.

Arrested for murder.

"Jen took them already," she responded on autopilot.

"Good." He brought her the glass.

She took the water but was too frozen with fear to drink. The lab results were in. Her car had definitely been involved in Earl's death. Even while she'd feared that, part of her had hoped that somehow it had been something else. That she'd hit a deer on her way home from Finnegan's.

Why couldn't she remember?

She would swear that, even drunk, she couldn't hurt anybody. She never even spanked the kids. Yet while she'd been sitting at the bar, she'd thought about Earl in that alley. *Oh God.* She set the glass on the side table and leaned forward to bury her head in her hands, but instead, her stomach heaved, and she threw up right there between her feet on the carpet.

She groaned with misery and embarrassment, then felt Chase's hand on her shoulder. He gently tugged her hair back from her face.

"You're going to be fine." He reached down and took her hand. "Come on. Let's clean you up." He pulled her to her feet and walked her to the bathroom, a cramped little place with a pink toilet, sink, and a worn tub littered with yellow rubber duckies. "You okay in there alone?"

She nodded, shaking as she closed the door behind her. Her face looked ashen in the mirror. Thank God the twins were with Jen. Thank God, thank God for that.

She washed her face, the cold water making her feel marginally better. She brushed her teeth, glanced down, and realized that her pant leg was stained. *Oh gross.* She shoved her pants down and kicked them over to the laundry pile.

Then she stood there, unsure of what to do. All alone, all her defenses down. Tears gathered in her eyes.

"You all right in there?" came from the other side of the door.

"I need pants," she said numbly after a moment.

"Hang on." And two minutes later he was back, opening the door to a gap and handing in a pair of jeans.

His blue eyes met hers, held no judgment, just concern. "You should call Jen before we leave. Once you're booked, you'll only get the one phone call. I don't know how long you'll have to wait for the bail hearing."

She blinked hard, trying to hold back the tears that suddenly flooded her eyes. "Thanks."

He nodded and closed the door, and she dressed, then washed her face again. Stared at herself some more in the mirror. She didn't want to go out there and face reality. She wanted to hide, wanted to run, but of course, neither was possible. The small bathroom was windowless. *All boxed in.* And wasn't that just a metaphor for her life right now? Her chest tightened.

She drew a deep breath and gathered herself. She had to call Jen. She had to make arrangements for Mia and Daisy. The thought of her sisters got her moving.

She opened the door and stepped outside, found Chase kneeling by the couch in the living room with a roll of paper towels.

He stood as she walked over to the battered coffee table that had been scarred and scribbled on by the girls. He looked up and flashed her an encouraging smile. "All done. I found your cleaning supplies under the sink."

He'd cleaned up after her.

"I'm so sorry," she told him. She was truly sorry, for a great many things.

"Don't worry about it," he said easily, as if he cleaned up after vomitous women on a daily basis. "Want to sit and take a few more minutes?"

She nodded, sat, then grabbed her phone from the coffee table and dialed.

"Hey," she said when Jen picked up. "I'm not sure when I can come for the girls." Her voice broke. "I've just been arrested."

A stunned silence on the other end, then, "Don't worry about the twins. They'll be fine here. Are you okay? What can I do to help?"

She couldn't think. She couldn't talk. "Just the girls."

She thanked Jen and hung up. Looked at Chase as she stood. "I don't want Mia and Daisy to go to foster care."

"Relax. You'll be booked and released on bail," he said with quiet confidence, watching her closely to make sure that she was okay. "You'll be back home today."

Was that possible? "I don't have bail money."

"We'll figure something out. And if Jen can't watch the girls, my mom would jump at the chance, if that's all right with you. You know her."

She did. Susan Merritt was one of the women who kept Broslin ticking, involved in organizing just about every event, involved with every charity. She loved kids. She sponsored the Great Broslin Easter Egg Hunt and coordinated the neighborhood Halloween events.

She had more energy than ten other people put together. She talked a mile a minute too, and in the past Luanne had wondered if Chase was so taciturn because he hadn't been able to get a word in edgewise growing up.

As far as personalities went, Susan was a lot like Mia, and Luanne had no doubt they'd get along. But Mia and Daisy didn't know her that well. "Let's see first if Jen can do it." Depending on how long it was before Luanne returned.

Chase nodded. "Ready to go?"

"No," she said sincerely. "But I don't suppose that's going to stop you from taking me."

"I wish I didn't have to." He looked at her for a long time, maybe to make sure that she was really okay and wasn't going to throw up in his cruiser.

"One more thing," he said. "I need the clothes you wore Friday night. I have to send them to the lab."

* * *

Luanne opted for a public defender after Chase strongly recommended a lawyer, and one came out from West Chester to sit in on the interrogation. Latoya Jefferson, a young woman in a crisp blue suit, sharp and quick, took copious notes as Chase questioned Luanne. The three of them about filled up the small interrogation room.

Chase was watching Luanne but speaking toward the recorder on the table between them. "What was your relationship to the victim?"

He knew that, she thought, but then realized he probably had to have it for the record. "Earl was my supervisor at the Mushroom Mile Motel."

"How would you describe the victim? Was he well liked at work?"

"No." She clutched her hands on her lap under the table. Chase hadn't handcuffed her, for which she was incredibly grateful. The whole process was plenty scary already.

"Why?" he asked.

"He was hard on the employees."

"Maria Gonzales, another maid, attested that Earl Cosgrove underpaid his employees by adjusting their hours unfairly. Was that your experience with him?"

"Yes." She stared at Chase. Instead of going after her big-time, he was establishing that Earl wasn't such a great guy. This wasn't what she'd expected from an interrogation.

"Allegations have been made by other employees that the victim also engaged in sexual harassment in the workplace. Do you have knowledge of this?"

"Yes."

"Were you sexually harassed by Earl Cosgrove?"

She could have made it sound worse than what it'd been, might have been better for her case, but she shook her head. "He made some advances."

"Did he touch you?" Chase's face remained expressionless. He'd offered to be her friend before, but now he was here in an official capacity. The facts and nothing but the facts.

"Just on the arm," she said.

"Did you know that he walked home behind Finnegan's late at night?"

"Yes. Everybody at work knew it."

"Could you describe your activities on the day in question?"

She started with telling him about work, then her afternoon with the girls, going to the bar after she'd dropped off Mia and Daisy at Jen's.

"Could you state the name of your date for the record, please?" Chase asked.

"Brett Bellinger."

"How long have you known Mr. Bellinger?"

"Three months. We met in an online group for dog lovers." She shifted on her seat. "I mean, virtually met. Friday would have been our first face-to-face date, but he wasn't able to make it."

"Did you talk to anyone while at the bar?"

"Tayron, and Gregory. I don't know Gregory. His date stood him up, and he bought me a drink."

"To the best of your recollection, how many alcoholic beverages did you have during the course of the night?"

"Two cocktails."

"Were you under the influence when you left the bar?"

Latoya stepped in with "You don't have to answer that."

Luanne's gaze cut to the attorney, her chest tightening. She didn't know how to answer that. She wouldn't have driven drunk. Growing up with an alcoholic father made her detest intoxication. "I only had two drinks," she said.

Chase watched her for a long moment before moving on with "What time did you arrive at the bar?"

"Nine p.m."

"What time did you leave?"

"I'm not sure."

"Did you leave with Gregory?"

"I'm not sure."

His deep-blue gaze held hers. "Are you on any medication that alcohol might have interfered with?"

"No."

His posture stiffened. "Did anyone have access to your drink?"

"No." She paused. "Tayron."

Chase waited a long beat, watching her closely. "So your official statement is that you don't remember what happened after you left the bar?"

That didn't sound like a serious defense. She winced. "Yes."

The interrogation went on for another half an hour, then Chase left the room, and Luanne had a brief talk with Latoya, who told her roughly what to expect next.

She was charged, booked, released on a twenty thousand dollar bail—set so low because Chase told the judge she wasn't a flight risk. Mildred and Harold Cosgrove posted bail for her. The incredible generosity put tears into Luanne's eyes. She could go home to the twins, take care of them while awaiting trial, make arrangements—although what arrangements, she couldn't fathom.

Mildred drove her home from the station, and they picked up the twins from Jen on the way. Luanne invited Mildred in to thank her again, offered her tea. So they sat in the kitchen while the twins, oblivious to the upheaval, watched *Snow White* on TV.

Surrounded by the soft scent of lilacs, the older woman was shorter and rounder than Luanne, her gray hair fashionably styled. Her eyes held regret. "What else can I do to help?"

"You've done so much already. Thank you. I can't tell you how grateful I am." Luanne set a steaming mug in front of Mildred, and another in front of herself.

Mildred sighed as she wrapped her fingers around her mug. "Chase told me about Earl. I asked the other girls too." She shook her head. "I'm sorry. I wish we knew how badly he was treating everyone."

"None of this is your fault."

"Harold and I hired him because he was family. Harold's second cousin's son." She pursed her lips, anger and regret flashing in her eyes. "He'd managed a restaurant before. We should have checked up on him more. But nobody ever complained. We had no idea. Believe me, he would have been fired if we did. We never knew how hard he's been on you girls."

Luanne took a big swallow of her tea. "Are you hiring a new manager?" Not that it mattered to her now. As a person charged with murder and out on bail, no way could they employ her. She'd been generously put on paid leave.

But Mildred shook her head. "We're listing the motel for sale. We've been thinking about it for a while now. This thing with Earl... Harold's heart can't take this kind of stress. The thought of having to find another manager, worrying about getting a bad egg again who might not do right by the employees. We don't have the energy to be involved on a daily basis anymore. If this tragedy taught us anything, it's that we're not cut out to be absentee owners."

Luanne nodded, her heart sinking when she thought about her friends losing their jobs from one day to the next.

"I feel bad about letting you girls go." Mildred drew her mug closer. "We'll call in everyone tomorrow to officially announce that we're not taking any new reservations and canceling everything beyond this month. Everybody will get severance checks. The place never worked with a huge profit, but we can swing a month's wages. Hopefully that's enough time for all of you to find other work. And there'll be unemployment benefits."

She reached across the table and patted Luanne's hand. "I'm sorry, honey."

Brushing her worries aside, Luanne forced a smile. "You're doing something few people would do for their employees. We're grateful. And I'm so grateful for the bail."

Mildred nodded. "Don't you worry about all the police nonsense. I told that detective, anyone who's working hard and raising two kids she loves isn't going to lose her head like that, even if Earl was a jerk. The maids who're short on temper get weeded out on the job fast."

She rolled her eyes. "Some guests would try a saint's patience. A woman who can smile through that year after year is clearly not easily provoked." She glanced at the twins. "And a mother, I know you're not their mother, but you are... A mother who loves her kids wouldn't do anything that would separate her from them. A mother would put up with demons from hell. I know you didn't do it."

The vote of confidence felt so nice, it brought tears to Luanne's eyes all over again.

Mildred flashed an encouraging smile. "That detective will figure it out. And when the motel sells, hopefully fast, maybe you'll all be rehired."

Luanne nodded, even if she wasn't exactly riding a wave of optimism at the moment.

Mildred glanced down for a second. "I'm embarrassed to say this, but it's a relief to pass on the place. We won't have to worry about whether it makes a profit or deal with taxes. Or worry about Greg, Harold's son. We each have a child from previous marriages."

She sipped from her mug. "When my daughter got married, Harold and I were finally in a financial situation where we could help. We bought them a house and paid for it outright so they wouldn't have to carry a mortgage. They had plenty of monthly payments with their student loans and car loans. And Suzy was pregnant with her first."

She sipped her tea, then set the mug down. "Since we gave her all that money, we promised Greg that he'd get an equal share once we sold the motel. He's a good boy. Never brings it up. But he has his own car shop over in Jersey that hasn't done well since the recession. We know he could use the money. Now we can help him out." Her mouth turned down. "We're so sorry about how this will affect you all."

Luanne shook her head. She didn't want Mildred to feel guilty. "The motel is your business. You don't need to explain your decisions to anyone."

Mildred sighed. "I just wish this all hadn't ended so badly."

Luanne nodded. So did she. Dear Lord, she did.

Mildred stayed for another five minutes, just long enough to finish her tea. After she left, Luanne fed the girls a snack, played some alphabet games with them—she wanted them to be ready for preschool—then she set them up with their dolls and horses while she did laundry in the hallway-closet laundry room.

Mildred's words played in her head, over and over. *"I know you didn't do it."*

Could that be true? So okay, she'd fantasized about maybe running some nasty guest's feet over with the vacuum cleaner, but she'd never done it. She hadn't hit the trucker with her spray bottle. She'd thought about it but kept her cool. She had excellent impulse control, in fact. She was very conscientious and dependable.

She'd thought about scaring Earl in the alley, enjoyed fantasizing about him covered in garbage like a pig. He *had* behaved like a pig. But it didn't mean she would act on those thoughts. And she'd never thought about running him over. *Never.*

Yet, according to all evidence, she had.

But what if she hadn't?

She'd heard the news about Earl Saturday morning, seen the damage to the car, and her semifunctioning mind made the most obvious connection. But her brain was finally out of that horrible fog and back to full speed again. At first, stunned, she'd simply accepted the blame. She was used to having her mother blame everything on her, and she always accepted the blame to keep the peace.

She drew a deep breath. She was so done with that. She wasn't a bad person. Time to stand up for herself and start fighting back.

She really didn't think she'd killed Earl. Not that she could come up with another explanation for the blood on the Mustang. *Yet.*

Maybe Gregory could tell her what happened when they left the bar. Unfortunately, she had no idea how to reach him. Why didn't she get his number? No new numbers on her cell phone. She'd checked.

Of course, if she could make herself remember, she wouldn't need Gregory. But her brain kept drawing a blank on that night, she thought as she loaded the dishwasher.

Definitely as if… But it didn't seem possible. How would someone even get pills like that in Broslin?

She didn't know much about roofies, just what she'd heard on

TV about men who put drugs into a woman's drink to knock them out so they could have sex. A shudder ran down her spine.

She didn't remember Gregory touching her drink. But could she be positive that she hadn't looked away, not even for a second?

Except, she hadn't had sex Friday night. She would have known the next morning. She hadn't had sex in over a year. She would have been sore. And she'd woken up in her own bed, which meant she'd driven herself home. Gregory wouldn't have known where she lived.

Why would Gregory drug her if he didn't have sex with her?

Maybe he'd roofied her, but she'd kept it together enough to get into her own car instead of his, and she'd driven away. Maybe, in that altered state, she'd driven by the alley, saw Earl, and gone for it.

The hell of the thing was, in her mind's eye, she could clearly see Earl staring into the headlights of the car, panic on his face. But did she see it because she'd fantasized about it earlier that night, or because, under the influence, she'd run him over?

She turned on the washer and walked back into the kitchen, dark thoughts zooming around and around in her mind like Evel Knievel in the Dome of Death.

If she could track down Gregory, if he would confess to giving her a roofie, her charges might be reduced from murder to involuntary manslaughter. Not that even the lesser charge didn't make her head swim and her heart race. If she could prove that she'd been drugged out of her mind... She might even get probation and not serve any time at all. Maybe the twins wouldn't be taken away from her.

She hung on to that hope with both hands.

She drank a glass of water to calm herself, then went to Mia and Daisy, sat on the floor with them, drew them onto her lap, and kissed them, hugged them. "I love you, chipmunks."

"I love you too." Mia immediately threw her little arms around her, all enthusiasm.

Daisy just quietly nestled against her but radiated unconditional love as only four-year-olds could.

"Are you sickie?" Daisy asked after a minute. Because she was the quiet one, mostly observing from the sidelines, she tended to notice a lot of things other kids her age didn't.

"Of course not." Luanne kissed the top of her head, the silky hair that smelled like baby shampoo. She should have known that

Daisy would pick up on the tension.

Daisy put her arms around Luanne too. "Are you going to go to heaven like Mommy?"

Luanne's heart just about stopped. Did the girls worry that she'd leave them too? She hugged them against her chest. "No way. Not ever. Sisters together forever. It might not look like that to you, but I'm pretty young. I'm practically a spring chicken."

Mia giggled.

Luanne kissed the top of her head too. "I'm sticking around until we're all old women."

"Will we be older by then than you are?" Mia asked. The girls didn't have a firm grasp on time.

"No," Luanne told her. "But the age difference will seem much smaller. We'll probably look like triplets."

Both of the girls looked up at her, eyes wide with amazed disbelief. But they had ear-to-ear smiles. They clearly liked the thought.

And Luanne swore to do whatever she had to so she'd be able to stay with them. They were her sisters, her flesh and blood. They were not going to be taken by the government and given to complete strangers.

After lunch, once they were down for their nap, she called Finnegan's and asked for Tayron.

"I heard about the arrest," was the first thing he said. "How are you holding up?"

She cut straight to the chase. "I don't think I did it."

A small pause. "You don't *think*?"

"I don't remember anything after you brought me that second drink. Was there a third?"

"No. You left. Didn't say bye either."

"Left with Gregory?"

"I don't know. I was serving drinks at the other end. I looked back, and you were both gone. If that little jerk dropped a pill in your glass, I'm going to seriously kick myself in the ass. I usually keep an eye on things like that."

"You can't watch every drink you serve, the entire night."

"I can try. We've never had problems here. When I tended bar in the city, sure. But not in Broslin."

"You didn't catch his last name, did you?"

"I barely caught the first."

She rubbed her eyebrow. "Ever see him before?"

"Not before and not since. I asked around. Nothing so far. I'll keep asking."

"Thanks, Tayron."

"No problem. You hang in there."

"Yeah." Hanging *in there* was preferable to hanging somewhere else. Pennsylvania had the death penalty. Did they still execute people by hanging in this day and age?

She shut down that line of thought. She was not going to obsess over worst-case scenarios. She was going to do whatever it took to make sure that this didn't end badly.

* * *

Catching a ride with Jackie, Luanne took the twins to the motel for the meeting with the owners the next day. Job loss and legal expenses looming large in her future, she could no longer afford a babysitter.

Mildred and Harold were great. They gave their employees the news straight, apologized that they weren't keeping the motel, offered to help any way they could, including glowing references. Then they handed out checks, a full month's wages rounded up to $1,200 for the maids, the most money the majority of them had ever had in one sum.

An even bigger windfall came from Jackie, whose boyfriend was away in the army. She offered his truck to Luanne until the police released the Mustang. That put tears into Luanne's eyes. Not a single person treated her like a criminal. The staff stood one hundred percent behind her.

She stayed a bit, asked the others if they knew a guy called Gregory, and described him. Nobody remembered a guest by that name, but so many people passed through the motel, it would have been a miracle if anyone had recognized him based on her description.

It'd been a wild thought anyway, thinking that maybe Gregory had lied at the bar, maybe he'd seen her before, at the motel, had recognized her at the bar and specifically targeted her for the roofie. She was desperate, coming up with desperate theories.

Luanne and the twins went home with Jackie, accepted the Ford pickup with gratitude, and drove straight to the police station. They nearly bumped into Susan Merritt, Chase's mother. As Luanne was walking in with the twins, Susan was heading out, perfectly put together from her nude leather pumps to her peach, summer silk suit.

She greeted Luanne, asked her how she was doing, nothing but sympathy in her eyes. Broslin was a small town. Everybody knew about the arrest.

"Could be worse," Luanne told her. If Mildred hadn't paid her bail, she'd be in jail.

Chase, two steps behind his mother, flashed a wide smile at the twins. "Hey, ya, tootsies. Robbed any more candy stores lately? Because if you did, I want some of the loot."

Mia giggled. Daisy did too, but one beat behind her sister.

Susan flashed an unfathomable look at Chase, then at Luanne, her gaze settling on the girls. "Who wants to check out the vending machines?"

"Me!" Mia squealed with excitement. Daisy simply lifted both hands in the air.

Chase shot Luanne a questioning look.

She nodded.

"I'll return them in a bit," Susan said and walked the twins to the break room in the back.

"Should we go into the interview room?" Chase asked, looking strong and sure as always, dark dress pants, white shirt, blue-patterned tie that matched his eyes.

He probably thought she'd come to confess.

Luanne shook her head. "I'm here to ask a favor. Is there any way I could talk to a sketch artist about Gregory? The man I had a drink with at the bar. I'd really like to find him. My memories of the evening are still pretty hazy. Maybe he could fill in some gaps."

Chase considered her. "It's your lucky day. We have the guy out from West Chester PD in the conference room right now with Harper and a robbery victim. They should be done in a minute. How are you holding up?"

"I'm okay. I'm not the type to lose it and kill someone," she said with tremendous relief.

Nobody knew her better than she knew herself. She wasn't a killer, not unless she was cornered and acted in self-defense. Or if all her abilities had been impaired, a theory she wasn't ready to share with Chase yet, until she had actual proof. First, she wanted to find

Gregory, somehow force him into admitting the roofie.

Chase watched her. "Everybody has their breaking point."

"I wasn't there yet with Earl."

He nodded. "Come sit by my desk for a second."

He walked her back, pulled a chair over, his desk piled high with files. He waited for her to sit, watching her. "Your car hit the victim. That looks pretty bad."

She nodded. She knew how it all looked. Honestly, things looked so bad that at first even she'd believed she was guilty. But she knew better now. In her heart of hearts, she knew she wasn't a killer. She just had to prove it.

He leaned back in his chair. "Have you found a good lawyer yet?"

She shook her head. "I'm staying with the public defender." The severance check from the motel wasn't enough to hire an attorney.

He hesitated for a moment. "So I have a second cousin who's a criminal defense lawyer."

Of course he did. "Who has second cousins? I don't even have first." She tried to lighten the mood between them, because he was looking at her in a way that she didn't know what to do with. "Frankly, that just feels like bragging."

A ridiculously hot smile turned up the corners of his lips. He tugged open his desk drawer and pulled out a business card, handed it to her. "Just in case. He could cut you a deal on the fee."

Even as she thanked him, the conference room door opened, three men coming out, Harper Finnegan in the lead.

Chase rose. "All right. Let's see about a picture."

The process didn't take as long as she'd thought, and by the end she had a pretty good likeness of Gregory. She could only hope it would help her find him. Gregory had to know *something*. She had no other lead. Zilch.

"Do you need a ride home?" Chase asked once the artist left. He'd been in and out of the conference room, doing his job while keeping an eye on her.

Maybe he was observing her for clues, hoping she'd slip up and say something incriminating. But his attention didn't feel like a setup. She could swear he actually cared. About her. She wasn't sure what to do with that conclusion.

"I have a car," Luanne told him. "A loaner."

Interest glinted in his deep-blue eyes. "From?"

"Jackie." She headed toward the break room for the twins.

His phone rang, so he didn't follow her, just sent her on her way with a wave.

The twins were munching on pretzels and singing songs from *Cinderella*, Susan joining right in. Luanne watched them from the doorway for a minute without interrupting, thinking how different Chase's childhood must have been from hers.

Then she shook off her old longings for a big, happy family. She had the girls. And she would keep the girls. She was *not* going to prison.

She thanked Susan for her help, then headed home with Mia and Daisy.

Things to do, people to see. For one, she wanted to give a copy of the sketch to Tayron so he could show it around at Finnegan's. She was going to take a copy to the motel too. Maybe seeing the face would trigger a memory the guy's name hadn't.

She had a month until her trial to track down Gregory.

* * *

The first suspicious incident happened the following Saturday. Luanne was coming home from her library job—they hadn't fired her despite the murder charges, miracle of miracles. At the intersection at the end of her street, a yellow moving truck barreled by her, not stopping for the stop sign, nearly wiping her out. Only some quick maneuvering saved her, landing her on the sidewalk. The jerk didn't stop to make sure she was okay. Everything happened so fast, she didn't even see the driver's face.

Thank God, Jen had the girls. She'd volunteered to watch them for free on Saturday afternoons until Luanne could afford to pay for babysitting. Jen was a good friend. She might not have kept Luanne's confidence with the whole Chase-is-bad-in-bed thing, but they'd been teenagers at the time. She'd apologized a hundred times, and Luanne had long ago forgiven that misstep. God knew she'd made plenty of mistakes of her own.

Not at the intersection, though. She had the right of way there, the moving van clearly in the wrong. But, at the time, she didn't think much of the almost accident. She'd been driving for over a decade. Plenty of bad drivers drove the roads. She'd had other near misses.

But two days later, when she walked to her car in the morning, half-asleep, for her cell phone she'd forgotten in the car the day before, she nearly fell into the sewer opening next to the curb. Somebody had stolen the grate. She could have broken her neck for sure. The thought that Mia or Daisy could have fallen down into the dark hole made her break out in a cold sweat. She called the township to complain.

The idea that someone was trying to kill her didn't occur to her until the following day at the supermarket, where a soda tower of twelve-packs fell on her, knocking her to the ground. She banged her head on the floor, getting knocked out for a second.

At least her health insurance was still good until the end of the month, so she could go to the emergency room and get checked out for a concussion.

"You're lucky one of those twelve-packs didn't bash your head in, falling from ten feet high," the nurse told her, an older Hispanic woman, Juanita, according to her name tag.

The display *had* been massive, Luanne thought. It'd appeared well built and completely steady, but obviously it wasn't. She *had* been lucky.

And with the sewer grate too. And the moving van at the intersection.

Oh God.

In a split second, sitting in the ER on a hospital bed behind faded green curtains that smelled like bleach, the girls playing at her feet, everything fell into place. *Click, click, click.* She broke out in cold sweat. The accidents were no accidents.

Who? Why?

She was in so far over her head here. For a long time now, she'd been treading water, paddling to stay afloat, but this time the waves were truly closing over her head. She felt as if she was sinking into dark, murky waters she could no longer navigate alone. She was sinking fast.

She thought of Chase. He was the detective on the case. He *had* offered to help. Were they really friends? She had to take the risk.

She called him as soon as they were back in her car in the parking lot.

He picked up on the first ring. "Everything okay?"

Just hearing his voice—strong, sure, steady—made her feel a little better. That voice was her lifeline for the moment. Since she'd been on the verge of hyperventilating, she drew a longer, slower breath, allowing her lungs to fill all the way.

"I think somebody is trying to K-I-L-L-M-E." She spelled the words.   She   didn't   want   to   worry   the   girls.

Chapter Six

Chase met her at her house, sat in the tiny kitchen—the TV turned up in the living room for the kids—and listened as Luanne recounted her wild theory. She kept her voice down, glancing at the girls from time to time to make sure they weren't listening.

He wasn't the paranoid type to read danger into everything, but Chase had to admit that three potentially deadly accidents in one week... "Okay, suspicious. Why do you think somebody is trying to kill you? Revenge for Earl?"

He'd yet to meet a single person who liked the guy. In fact, he'd been conducting second interviews with the staff about the way they'd been treated, files he hoped the defense would put to good use at Luanne's trial.

She sat silently, her shoulders stiff, her eyes filled with worry. And she still looked so pretty that he could have just sat there and watched her all day.

He'd tried not to think about her much over the years. Thinking about her either got him horny or wincing in embarrassment that he'd disappointed her back when he'd had his chance. Of course, when you didn't want to think about something, you thought about it that much more. Like when someone said, *Don't think about an elephant*, and all you could think were trunks and tusks. Except, in Luanne's case, it'd been whiskey-color eyes and perfect breasts.

He leaned back in the kitchen chair. "I can't help if you won't level with me."

She pressed her lips together. Which, of course, drew his attention to that sexy crease in her bottom lip.

"Just tell me everything, exactly as it happened."

She stayed silent.

That she didn't trust him frustrated the living daylights out of him. *Except*, he told himself, she must trust him a little, since she'd called him.

He made a point to relax his shoulders, stretched his legs in front of him, in the hopes that she too would relax a little. "I'm not out to get you. I don't want to see you go to prison. Why don't you tell me what happened that night? You've already been charged with murder. It can't get much worse."

"I can get convicted."

"Maybe there were extenuating circumstances."

She sat there silently for several long moments before finally speaking. "I had a drink when I got to the bar. Then I met Gregory, and he bought me another. I can't remember anything beyond that."

"What do you mean you can't remember?" He watched her closely for any sign of insincerity, but he didn't see any. She spoke earnestly, with an open body language, her eyes never leaving his.

"I was having a drink at the bar, then I was home, waking up in the morning."

His muscles tightened. "Roofie?"

"Maybe."

"Did he—" Did the bastard touch her?

"I don't think so, but I don't remember."

And a rape kit would be way too late. More than a week had passed since.

"I wish you'd told me right away." Frustration buzzed through him, along with an overwhelming wave of protectiveness.

"I didn't figure it out right away. I just thought I had too much to drink. My brain barely worked, everything fuzzy."

"So you really don't remember hitting Earl?" He wanted to believe her, but wasn't sure how much she was doing, saying because she was scared of being convicted, petrified of what would become of the twins. He had no doubt whatsoever that Luanne would do or say absolutely anything to keep her sisters safe.

But whatever she had or hadn't done the night in question, he wished she'd just trust him and come right out with it already. He couldn't help if he didn't know exactly how much trouble she was in.

She sucked in her bottom lip and raked her teeth over it, drawing his attention to the crease in the middle once again. He seriously had to get over that.

"I don't remember anything." She held his gaze, her eyes holding desperation he didn't think could be faked.

Okay, she was telling the truth about that. His fist clenched as he finally accepted the idea that she'd been drugged. He wasn't a violent man, but he sincerely wanted to punch something, preferably Gregory's face.

"Maybe I hit Earl under the influence," she said, biting her lip now, the small gesture sending heat to his loins. "I didn't mean it, I swear."

Chase considered her words for a second. "So you were under the influence but remembered what time Earl went home at night and what route he followed, you planned how, when, and where to run him over, executed the hit without clipping the garbage containers, then drove home and parked nicely by the curb, let yourself in? I'm not buying it." A couple of new ideas readily presented themselves. He rather liked them. "Maybe you weren't driving."

"Who was?"

"My best guess is Gregory. The guy who gave you a roofie is usually the last guy you remember offering you a drink."

"Why would Gregory want to kill Earl?"

"Could have been an accident. He put you in your car, drove you to the back alley to have some fun. Maybe he was paying you so much attention, he didn't see Earl in the dark. Or maybe Earl saw him doing something to you, so Gregory ran Earl over, not wanting a witness."

"And then he drove me home?"

"It's not half-bad as a frame for a murder. Worked so far. You've been charged." He was going to get the bastard. Luanne wasn't going down for this.

"How would he even know where I live? I just met him."

"You keep your registration and car insurance papers in your glove compartment? Have your driver's license with you?"

She braced her elbows on the table and buried her face in her hands, her golden hair sliding forward, hiding her from him. "I feel so stupid." Her voice came out muffled.

All he felt was mad. "Don't," he told her. "Somebody set you up for rape, and then he set you up as a murderer."

She drew big gulps of air, as if trying to stave off hyperventilating. He got up and filled a glass with water, set it on the table in front of her, placed a hand on her shoulder for support.

A shoulder that felt too slim under his hand. "How about if I stay for a while and we strategize a little? Would you mind if I ordered some food again? I'm starving."

When she shook her head, he ordered pizza and breadsticks, enough for the two of them and the girls. Then he sat back down across from her.

She looked up. "So Gregory killed Earl for some reason, framing me. But why come after me now? *If* he's behind the accidents."

Chase thought for a few seconds. "Have you been asking questions about him?"

She nodded, suddenly pale. "I've been showing the police sketch around."

"Me too. Nothing so far." He folded his hands on the table. "So maybe he was counting on you not remembering, that you'd assume you hit Earl drunk, then drove home. The police would have plenty for an arrest. The court would have enough for a conviction. He didn't count on you figuring things out. He needs to silence you before you finger him."

Her gaze filled with a whole new level of desperation. "Can the girls and I get some kind of police protection?"

"I'll talk to the captain. Protection won't be easy to justify. We have pretty severe budget restrictions. I believe you, but other than your say-so, we have nothing to corroborate your three accidents. Even if I can get you protection, first round's twenty-four-hour surveillance. If nothing suspicious happens, the captain has to call it off. Budgets these days don't spring to longtime protection unless there's proven, imminent danger."

She nodded, casting a worried glance toward the twins in the living room. Her entire heart was in her eyes, the love she felt toward those little girls practically radiating out of her. She took very good care of them. But who took care of Luanne?

He followed her gaze. "I can hang out in my car outside your house and keep an eye on things. If somebody comes to do you harm, I *will* catch him."

"You can't put your entire life on hold for me."

He made some noncommittal noises. He could and would make sure that nothing happened to Luanne and the twins. Damn right, he would. He was going to keep them safe. And she was going to trust him, and not do anything else stupid like hitting the hydrant to destroy evidence.

They were going to have to address that at some point, but not now, not when she'd just realized that someone was trying to kill her. She had enough stress for today.

She linked her fingers together on her lap. He wanted to take her hand. He wanted to take more than her hand. *Hell.* He pushed to his feet. "How is your security? I'll walk around and make sure the locks on the windows and the doors are up to snuff."

He had to get moving before he pulled her into his arms or did something equally idiotic.

* * *

Chase wasn't halfway to his car when Luanne began packing.

If she'd learned one thing over the years, it was that she could count on nobody to save her but herself. She'd never been able to count on her father. Her mother had been flighty at best. No family had ever been there for her. She was used to having to solve her own problems.

She rushed for the giant cloth grocery bags they used to avoid plastic, and started filling the first with what food she had in the cupboard: bread, peanut butter, animal cookies.

Gregory had killed already. And had almost gotten away with it. Obviously, whoever he was, he was good at this. For all she knew, he was some serial killer, rapist.

Maybe the police could protect her. But for how long? *A day,* Chase had said. And he couldn't sit outside her house forever. For one, if he was on duty and got a call, he'd have to leave.

She did trust him, she realized. She'd told him everything she knew about the night of Earl's death. But trusting him with her life, and the twins' lives, trusting him to save them...

Keeping her sisters safe was her job, nobody else's. She had to do whatever it took. Bottom line—she couldn't keep them safe here.

At least she had her severance money.

She closed her eyes against the feeling of impending doom that threated to drown her. Was she really so desperate that she was considering skipping out of town?

Yes, she was, she decided. Better to disappear than to be killed.

* * *

The blue Ford pickup Luanne had on loaner wasn't in front of the house. Chase walked up to the front door anyway and knocked. No response. He walked over to the window and looked in, saw one of the couch pillows on the floor, a couple of kitchen cabinets open in the back.

He dialed her cell phone. He'd missed Bing at the station, and he wanted to talk to him in person about setting up protection. So while he was waiting for Leila to let him know that Bing had returned, he'd come back to convince Luanne to move to his place with the girls for the time being.

He had better locks, for starters. His windows actually locked all the way. And he had a security system. Plus, nobody would think to look for her at his place. She'd be safer there. He wanted her and the twins safe.

He held his phone to his ear, but the call didn't even ring out. Luanne's phone was out of service.

If he didn't know that someone was after her, he wouldn't have thought much of her absence and her house being out of order, her not picking up the phone. But as it was, he looked for a key, found it under the second flower pot he tried, and let himself in.

"Luanne?" The open kitchen cabinets stood empty. Unease crept up his spine.

Either she was even lower on groceries than he'd thought, or someone had taken food. None of the kitchen chairs were turned over. Nothing spilled. No sign of struggle.

He tried to keep that in the forefront of his mind as he headed back to the bedrooms. He walked around slowly, examining everything carefully. The girls' room was about as spacious as a bunk bed on a submarine; even the scant furniture filled it to the brim. Dresser drawers open. The basket of clean clothes he'd seen earlier when he'd walked around to check windows was now missing. So were the dolls and horses from the bed.

His neck muscles tightened. He didn't think a kidnapper would pack toys.

She'd run.

His concern switched to anger and disappointment in a millisecond. *Dammit, Luanne.*

Did she plan on skipping bail? If she didn't show for her scheduled court appearance, she'd be in bigger trouble than ever. Didn't she understand how much worse she was making her situation? Why in hell couldn't she just trust him?

He called the station, got Leila on the phone. "Hey, I'm going to need a cell phone triangulated for location." He rattled off Luanne's number, then repeated it. "Call me as soon as you have something. Thanks."

He left the house and drove down the road to Jen's place.

She answered on the first knock. "What's up?"

"Have you seen Luanne?"

The smile slid off Jen's face. "No. I'm not watching the girls every day now. Just when she goes to clean the library. Isn't she home?"

"No. Where could she go?"

"Grocery store? Playground?

Chase watched her for any sign of lying, covering up for Luanne. Didn't see any tells. "Where would she go long-term?"

Jen's eyes widened. "You think she ran?"

"I need to find her. Anything you could think of would be helpful."

"Let me try her cell." She pulled a phone from her back pocket and dialed, concern drawing her brows together.

Chase waited. Luanne might not be taking his calls, but maybe she'd take Jen's. But a few seconds later, with her phone to her ear, Jen shook her head. "The subscriber can't be reached at this time."

She shoved the phone into her back pocket, her body language clipped, her voice tight as she said, "Why would she run? How could she even think that going on the run with the girls would be a good idea?"

Chase could understand the anger. Watching a friend mess up big-time was no fun when you cared about them. "Family?"

As far as he knew, Luanne had none, at least not around town.

"Her mom died," Jen said. "Well, you know that. She doesn't know where her father is."

"You think he got back in touch?"

Jen shook her head. "I wouldn't think so. He was..." She gave a pained shrug. "You know."

Yeah. An abusive alcoholic. Chase thought for a second. "How about the library job? Any close friends?"

"She cleans after hours. Nobody's there but her. You can't run a vacuum cleaner in the library when it's open. It's supposed to be quiet."

"You think she might be there now?"

"She only cleans on Saturdays."

Dammit, Luanne. "Call me if she gets in touch with you. It's pretty important to get her back here before things get out of control." She had to show up for her court date.

"Of course I will. I'll keep calling." Jen sighed, then pressed her lips together, her fingers fidgeting at her side. She clearly thought Luanne was making a mistake.

Chase couldn't agree more.

He was halfway to his car when Jen called after him. "Wait! She has a great-aunt." She stepped out onto the front stoop. "Aunt Hilda or Tilda or something like that. She lives somewhere near Richmond, Virginia."

"You don't know exactly?"

Jen bit her lips. "Sorry." She shook her head. "They don't have a relationship. Nothing beyond exchanging Christmas cards. That's why I didn't even remember it at first. Luanne never really talks about her."

"Thanks."

He went back to Luanne's place and looked around one more time, hoping to find an old-fashioned address book that might hold information on the great-aunt, but he didn't come across anything like that. He checked around for the Christmas card too, a slim chance having that still lying around in the middle of June. He searched anyway, but found no trace of that either.

He called Leila at the station. "Do you remember June Mayfair's maiden name?" He knew about half the town. Leila knew at least three quarters.

"Luanne's mother? Let me think." A moment of silence. "June Desiree."

"Thanks. I need an address for a Hilda or Tilda Desiree near Richmond, Virginia."

"How near?"

"Don't know."

She grumbled something about the amount of work that was going to take.

"Or I could ask Robin to look into her crystal ball," he suggested, tongue in cheek.

Robin was their part-time dispatcher, Leila's nemesis, currently off at a psychic conference in Lily Dale, New York.

Leila promptly hung up on Chase at the mention of her name.

He drove to Jackie's house next and asked for the blue Ford pickup's license plate number. But he didn't call in a three-state APB.

For one, Luanne wasn't officially wanted. She hadn't skipped bail. Yet. Leaving the state didn't look good, but maybe she'd come to her senses, call him, and explain herself.

He tried her phone again, got the number unavailable message, so he drove back to the station.

"Anything on Hilda Desiree?" he asked Leila as he walked in.

She looked up from her computer. "Not yet." She picked up some printouts from the counter and held it out for him. "But we just got the report from the medical examiner."

"Thanks." He read it on his way to his desk, didn't even sit down, turned around and strode straight to Bing's office, stopped in the doorway. "The ME report is in. According to the coroner, the vehicle that hit Earl was going at least fifty miles an hour. That's the speed that would be consistent with the external and internal damage to the body."

The captain raised an eyebrow. "Luanne was gunning for him?"

"Not Luanne," Chase said, and explained about her memory loss, her suspicions of the date-rape drug, which he fully believed. "At first I figured Gregory was just rolling into the back alley for a quiet moment, ran Earl over by accident, panicked, and ran."

"Fifty miles an hour doesn't sound like rolling. It sounds like whoever was driving the car might have been gunning for Earl."

Chase nodded. "Maybe Earl saw them. Maybe Gregory didn't want a witness."

Bing thought for a second. "And Luanne remembers nothing?"

"Nothing after Gregory bought her a drink."

Bing considered all that, then flashed him a level look. "You and Luanne have history."

Chase winced. *Oh Jezus*, did everybody know? "Not a problem."

"If she's the perpetrator, she's the perpetrator. We can't twist things around just because we like her."

"She's not the perpetrator."

Bing rubbed the back of his neck. "Do you have the lab results on the clothes she wore the night of the murder? The killer dragged the body to the side and covered it in garbage bags. There ought to be residue."

"No results yet."

Leila walked up in a pair of dazzling purple sandals that had silver horns, and handed Chase a sticky note with an address on it, then hurried back to her desk, calling back, "There's a Hilda Millman, maiden name Desiree, in Petersburg," before she picked up the ringing phone.

"Who's Hilda Millman?" Bing asked.

"Luanne's great-aunt in Virginia."

"How is she involved?"

"Luanne might have gone to visit her." Chase explained the near accidents, his neck muscles tighter by the minute when he thought how badly she could have gotten hurt.

Bing's eyes narrowed. "Is she thinking about skipping bail?"

"I'd like to drive down and talk to her about that. If you don't need me here."

Bing watched him, his expression growing unhappier by the second. "You go and talk her into coming back."

Chapter Seven

By lunchtime, Luanne was seriously rethinking whether she'd made the right decision. The girls had slept through most of the long drive, so they were on a tear, full of energy, racing through the narrow tunnels of Aunt Hilda's town house. For them, the maze of stacked-up boxes and newspapers was a playground.

A diminutive woman in her mideighties with natural white hair, Aunt Hilda sat in her overstuffed recliner, wearing a pink sweat suit with white sneakers, her four-pronged fancy cane close by her side. Enough furniture crowded her living room to fill a whole other house. Or two. Or three.

She had Luanne's straight nose and brownish eyes. So weird. The twins inherited their father's darker coloring. How strange to suddenly have a visible connection with someone. Luanne liked this newfound link very much. But she didn't like the realization that her great-aunt was a hoarder.

Aunt Hilda ducked her head when she caught Luanne looking around again. "I haven't been able to clean much since the knee replacement."

The dust was the least of the old woman's problems. She wasn't a completely out-of-control hoarder who would have required a TV-type intervention—no leftover food or bugs or anything like that. The floor was still visible, but only in carefully created pathways.

Furniture occupied every available space, not to mention stacks of papers and boxes, packed knee-high or even higher. A very orderly mess—everything squared away, no threat of avalanche, or Luanne wouldn't have let the twins out of her sight, but a giant mess nevertheless.

"Where did all the furniture come from?" she asked.

"Some came from the farm when it went under. Then, well, your uncle was the youngest of four children," Aunt Hilda said. "His father had a brother who never married. When that brother died, he left everything to his nieces and nephews. My Arnold got his share." She rubbed a hand over her knee. "Then Arnold's parents died and they left behind more to divide among their four kids. Arnold's oldest brother never married. When he died, everything went to the three remaining siblings. Arnold's sister died of breast cancer. Her husband went before her. All their possessions went to Arnold and his middle brother. Then Arnold died."

She paused and stared at nothing in particular for a moment. "Then Arnold's middle brother died. His two girls asked me if I wanted to take any of the family picture books, furniture from the grandparents." The old woman shook her head. "It didn't seem right to throw out all that history. Madison lives in a tiny apartment in New York City. She couldn't take a thing. Ursula doesn't even have a place. She travels for business. Right now she's in Japan. She'll be there for at least a year. After that..." Aunt Hilda sighed. "Wherever the company will send her."

Luanne hoped she'd meet Madison and Ursula someday, two brand-new relatives she'd never even heard of before. "Is anyone still around on the Desiree side?"

"Dead or moved," Aunt Hilda said in a depressed tone. "After the farm was auctioned off, the family pretty much scattered."

"Mama used to talk about the farm. How she met my father."

Aunt Hilda narrowed her eyes. "My sister, your grandmother, was none too happy about that. Her only daughter running off with a farmhand. Your mother was after that boy from day one. First, he wanted nothing to do with her. But she kept after him, got pregnant on purpose so he'd take her with him when he moved back up north. She wanted to see the world."

Luanne stared. Her mother had always blamed her for having to marry her father. So she'd gotten pregnant on purpose, had she? For some reason, it felt strangely liberating to know that.

"So everyone's gone?" she asked, to be sure.

Aunt Hilda nodded.

Cripes. No Desiree homestead, no abandoned cabin in the hills where Luanne hoped to hide from whoever was trying to kill her, gain some time to figure out how Earl had really died and clear her name.

Aunt Hilda gestured at the crowded room. "All I have left of the family is what you see here."

85

Generations' worth of possessions. Luanne shook her head, more than a little stunned by the aggregate results. She wasn't sure what she'd expected, but it wasn't this.

"I have to do something with it now," Aunt Hilda said weakly, clearly upset over the prospect. "I'm not going to be able to take care of myself much longer. I haven't been upstairs since the knee surgery last year. Even going down the front steps is a struggle. I need to go into a home. I've had the house listed for almost a year, but nobody wants to buy it."

Luanne could see why prospective buyers would be wary. They probably took one look from the front door and fled.

Her life was a giant mess that needed some serious figuring out. But Aunt Hilda needed some quick solutions too.

Luanne drew a deep breath. "What if I helped?"

Aunt Hilda stared at her with surprise and disbelief. "Help how?"

Good question. "I'm a professional cleaner. And I can list stuff on eBay like nobody's business." Saturday afternoons she cleaned the library, but Saturday mornings she scavenged garage sales for things she could sell on the Internet. In a lucky month, she could make an extra hundred bucks that way. "We could start by listing the furniture online, so people can start looking at that while we're dealing with the rest."

Hilda shook her head. "I asked the mailman about that. Burt says furniture is too big to ship. I'd pay more to the post office than what I'd get for the pieces."

"You can mark items for local pickup only. And then there's Craigslist."

Aunt Hilda still looked uncertain, small and lost in the oversize chair. "If you're sure."

A sudden, overwhelming sense of connection rushed Luanne. They'd never seen each other before, but the old woman was family. Luanne looked at the twins sitting on the floor in the kitchen now, playing with some antique wooden blocks. They needed these kinds of connections, the sense that they weren't alone in the world.

So she nodded, with a lot more certainty than she felt. "I'm sure." She glanced at the old computer on the antique desk in the corner. "Do you have Internet?"

"I do. Ursula talked me into it. Sometimes she sends e-mail from

Japan. Last time she visited, she showed me how to find recipes and knitting patterns."

"Mind if I look around?"

"Of course not. Go ahead."

Luanne told the girls to stay where they were, then quickly checked through the house. The downstairs consisted of living room, kitchen, a dining room that had been converted into a bedroom for Aunt Hilda, and a handicap-accessible bathroom, all overcrowded.

The upstairs situation was better. The narrow stairs and the turn in the stairs had probably prevented larger pieces of furniture from being dragged up there. Three small bedrooms and a bathroom. Lots of dust, but not a hoarder's nightmare.

She came downstairs. "Would it be okay if we stayed a couple of days?"

"You would?" A stunned expression rounded the old woman's eyes for a moment before they welled up with tears.

Luanne hurried over and hugged her. "Hey. Everything's going to be just fine. I can handle this." Keeping busy would leave her less time to obsess over her own situation.

Aunt Hilda sniffed and hugged her back tightly. "I know I'm a mess." She pulled back and smiled through her tears. "You're an angel."

Not really. More of a suspected murderer, but that wasn't something Luanne wanted to discuss within hearing distance of the twins. "Let me start snapping pictures."

She opened the windows for fresh air, then found a feather duster in the laundry room and got the girls involved. Of course, they wanted to be in every picture. They were both hopeless hams. Luanne took two photos of each piece of furniture, one with the girls for Aunt Hilda for later, then one without the girls to post online.

They stopped for a midafternoon snack of peanut-butter-and-jelly sandwiches from her stash that she'd brought from home. Her aunt supplied the milk.

Then Luanne finally put the girls down for their very late nap, toe to toe on the living room couch. Normally, they slept after lunch, but the long ride had messed up their schedule. Still, they had to sleep now, or they'd be overtired by dinner, whining and fighting over every little thing.

Luanne settled in by the computer to upload what she had so

far. Aunt Hilda came to sit by her to help with the description of the furniture. She knew more about styles and the age of the pieces. She had no idea about prices, however, so Luanne looked up similar items to get a feel. They were both surprised that the pieces were worth a lot more than they'd expected.

Luanne entered the twenty or so items she'd photographed so far, local pickup only. "Now we wait."

Aunt Hilda patted her hand. "You made that look easy. Wish I knew ten years ago how this worked."

"Never too late." Luanne turned to her aunt and took her frail hands into hers, glancing at the sleeping twins, then back to the old woman again. "There's something I need to tell you. We didn't exactly come here on the spur of the moment. I mean, it was spur of the moment, but I did have a reason."

Aunt Hilda watched her, nothing but kindness on her lined face.

"I'm kind of in trouble. With the law." She explained what happened. "I didn't do it. Somebody set me up. Are you sure you still want us to stay?"

"Of course, I am." Aunt Hilda squeezed her hand. "You're family."

Luanne's heart warmed from the simple words. "Thank you. Okay, more disclosure. I'm not a fugitive at the moment, but I might become one. I don't know if I'm going back for a trial. I can't go to prison and leave the twins alone. We'll leave before it comes to that. I don't want to get you in trouble."

Hilda waved off the words. "I'm an old woman. They ain't gonna take me out of here in shackles. I've seen most of the local officers run around in diapers."

Luanne was pretty sure that didn't mean immunity. She'd seen Chase naked, and that hadn't stopped him from arresting her. She didn't tell that to Aunt Hilda.

Instead, she said, "Thank you." And gave the old woman a good, long hug before she stood. "I should go upstairs and clean a room and the bathroom for us up there."

"There's linen in the hallway closet." Hilda glanced toward the girls and smiled, looking genuinely happy to have them in the house. "Those sheets have been in there for a while. You might want to wash them to freshen them up a little."

"I'll start with that." Luanne went upstairs to open the windows up there too, grabbed the bedcover, then went for the linen.

The doorbell rang just as she was coming from the laundry room, having turned on the washer.

Her heart thumped. Whoever was trying to kill her couldn't have tracked her down already, could he? She'd kept an eye on the rearview mirror on the whole drive. She could swear they hadn't been followed.

Doubts sliced into her nevertheless. Instead of taking the girls someplace safe, had she just dragged her aunt into danger too?

"I'll get it." She didn't want Aunt Hilda to have to get up. She wiped her hands on her pants as she hurried to look out the peephole, her cell phone in her hand, ready to dial 911 if she saw Gregory's face on the other side.

Chase?

Her heart, already racing, galloped a little faster. If she just ignored him, would he go away? Face stern, shoulders squared, he didn't look like he would. He looked pretty damned determined.

She opened the door slowly, reluctantly, to a gap. "Hi."

Instead of his usual detective uniform of dress pants, shirt, and tie, he wore blue jeans and a plain black T-shirt. He gave her an assessing look, his body language wound up like she'd never seen him, his muscles tight, his gaze darkening. Uncharacteristic anger simmered just below the surface. "What are you doing here?"

"Visiting Aunt Hilda."

He made her nervous, embarrassed—because she couldn't not think of their one disastrous sexual encounter every time she saw him. But he also somehow strangely grounded her. He had that kind of presence. He made her feel…a lot of things, but right now, mostly conflicted. The little pointer in her brain that was supposed to tell her how to feel, what to do, spun around, like when you put a compass on top of a magnet.

"Family visit?" He raised an eyebrow, his voice tight as he asked, "You didn't think maybe you should tell me?"

"You didn't say I couldn't leave town."

"I didn't think I had to. Imagine my surprise when I walked through your empty house that looked like you all might have been kidnapped."

Oh. Had he worried about her? Warmth spread through her chest unbidden. It'd been a really long time since she had anyone to worry about her. She caught the thought and bit back the groan that followed. Oh God, was she needy or what? Was she actually glad that somebody thought she'd been kidnapped? What was wrong with her?

She swallowed. "I just wanted to be safe."

He looked past her. "The girls?"

"Napping." Thank God, the doorbell didn't wake them.

"Your aunt here?"

She nodded.

"Can she watch the twins for a while?" he asked. "I'd like to talk to you someplace private."

She wasn't sure if she wanted to talk to him, but if her case did go to trial it'd be better not to alienate the police. "Hang on. Let me check."

She left the door open and stepped back to turn to her great-aunt. "Would you mind if I ran out for a while? The girls usually sleep at least two hours. They shouldn't be any trouble."

Aunt Hilda eyed Chase in the doorway.

Chase nodded at her. "Ma'am. I'm Chase Merritt, Broslin PD."

Aunt Hilda scowled. "She didn't do it."

"I know, ma'am."

"You keep my niece safe, you hear?"

"Yes, ma'am."

"All right. You two go talk. I'll keep an eye on the little ones."

Luanne grabbed a piece of paper from the sofa table and wrote down her cell phone number. "In case you need to reach me."

"I watched other people's kids for decades at the church nursery. I can handle these two little angels."

Luanne thanked her, then walked outside with Chase.

Who stopped and turned to her, too close, too big, too intense, towering over her. His wide shoulders darn near blocked out the sun, making her throat go dry. "Don't ever run from me like that again," he said quietly.

But those quiet words were more effective than if he'd yelled and shaken her. Which he might do yet, she reflected, since he wasn't moving away. Or he might kiss her. The wild thought hit her out of nowhere when his gaze refused to leave her face.

She could swear she could see the chemistry arch between them like an electric charge. Okay, that was just stupid. Of course Chase didn't want to kiss her.

She gathered herself and ducked around him, then hurried down the front stairs. Better get away from him before he read her idiotic thoughts on her face. "What do you mean you know I didn't kill Earl?" she asked once she put a safe distance between them.

He strode to his black SUV, for once his gait stiff instead of relaxed. He didn't look half-bad in blue jeans, she acknowledged, then wished she hadn't noticed how the denim stretched over his powerful thighs as he moved.

He opened the door for her. "I believe you."

Her heart leaped. "Did something change? Are the charges dropped?"

"Not yet. First we actually have to prove that you didn't do it." He walked around and slipped in behind the wheel. "The ME's report came in. Whoever hit Earl did it on purpose, not by accident."

She tried to process that, found that she couldn't, set it aside for later. "Where are we going?"

"Saw a decent-looking diner driving in. I'm in the mood to try some good Virginia food."

They always seemed to be talking over food, she reflected. Then something clicked, and she narrowed her eyes at him. Was he feeding her on purpose?

Embarrassment flushed her cheeks. She might not have been swimming in money, but she didn't need Chase Merritt's charity. "Or we can sit in the car by the curb and talk right here."

"I drove straight down, didn't stop for lunch."

Argument closed.

She didn't argue with him, but once they were at the diner and the waitress came around to ask what they wanted, she said, "Thanks. Nothing for me. Just a glass of water."

Chase watched her for a moment, then ordered some peanut soup, salmon cakes, and hickory-smoked pulled pork BBQ. Marble cake for dessert. He grinned at her as the waitress left. "That drive worked up my appetite."

She grabbed a complimentary biscuit and said nothing.

He watched her eat with a suspiciously satisfied expression. "Is your aunt all right? The house looks a little rough."

"I had no idea what I was walking into," she confessed. "She's been living alone for a pretty long time. I think she's completely overwhelmed. She needs to go into a home, but first she has to sell the house. I think she put off clearing things out because she doesn't really want to go." Luanne couldn't blame her. "She's lived in that house with her husband for fifty years. All her memories are there."

Chase nodded. "How long has she been living alone?"

"Over a decade."

"Jen said you weren't close."

She grabbed another flaky biscuit. Damned things were addictive. "When Mama married Daddy, her family didn't approve on account of him being a no-good drunk and a Yankee. She told them if they couldn't be supportive of her choice, she had no room in her life for them, and she cut them off. Aunt Hilda sent Christmas cards, but Mama never answered. After Mama died, I started sending cards back." She shook her head. "I should have looked Aunt Hilda up sooner."

"You had your hands full with work and the twins."

She nodded, relieved that Chase understood her instead of judging her for being a lousy relative.

He pushed the basket of biscuits closer to her.

She shook her head. But then she took another biscuit anyway.

He grinned. "So, what are your plans?"

She chewed. Swallowed. "Once the real killer is caught, I need to go home and start looking for another job. Not as a hotel maid."

Now that she made it, the decision felt right, filled her with excitement. "It's not that I hate the job. But if I'm doing something where I'm fantasizing about doing things to guests who grab me and about running my boss off the road... I used to do that, you know, daydream about just running Earl off the road and into the gutter. All of us girls at the motel talked about things we'd do if our jobs didn't depend on it. But I don't want to be that person anymore."

She pulled her chin up. "I can do more. I can do better. I'm going to find a job that I enjoy. Something challenging."

Rather than lecturing her on being grateful if she got any kind of job, he said, "Excellent idea. But whether we catch Gregory in the next few weeks or not, it'd be better if you didn't skip bail. Skipping looks bad. And Mildred Cosgrove would lose her bail money."

Luanne winced before she buried her head in her hands for a second, then looked up, her mouth twisting. "Obviously, I didn't think this trip over." She hadn't been able to think past the fear that whoever was setting up her little *accidents* would succeed, that the twins might get hurt. Once again, she'd acted on the flight part of the fight-or-flight instinct.

"You panicked," Chase stated without reproach. To her relief, the anger he'd shown up with seemed to have dissipated. "You thought somebody was trying to kill you."

"Somebody *is* trying to kill me."

"I'm not going to let that happen."

His words felt reassuring. Honestly, the man inspired feelings of safety. He was the biggest of the guys working at the station. Not fat but large-framed. He was like a rock. She had a feeling little could move him if he didn't want to be moved. She had no doubt he could protect her from just about anything, *if* he was there when somebody put her in the crosshairs. But he couldn't watch her 24/7.

"I promised Aunt Hilda I'd help her clean the house." She let out a puff of air. "I'd really like to do that."

His lips twisted into a lopsided grin. "So you're on the run, and you thought you'd take time out to clean generations' worth of stuff out of the house of a relative you just met for the first time. Don't you have enough to worry about?"

"She needs help. Did you see that living room?"

He watched her for a long moment. Drew a deep breath. "I have tomorrow and the day after off from work."

She stared, not sure if she understood him. "Are you volunteering for housecleaning? Isn't that against some manly code or something?"

He held her gaze. Flashed another lopsided smile. "Obviously, you have me bamboozled."

That smile made her catch her breath. He was bamboozled? By her?

She gave a strangled laugh, her head spinning from the sudden change of direction in the conversation. Thank God the waitress arrived with the food before things could get more out of control. The purple-haired twenty-year-old kept putting food in front of them until the plates fairly covered their small table.

"Okay, you have to help," Chase said when she left. "I had no idea how big these dishes were. I can't eat all this."

She narrowed her eyes. "I know what you're doing."

"What?" he asked, eyes wide with innocence.

"You're feeding me."

"You're perfectly capable of feeding yourself. I hate wasting food. I could take the leftovers home, but I'll be honest, my stomach has a thing against reheated food. One spoonful and it's heartburn city."

Luanne considered resisting. Wasting food was the biggest sin in her house. Even the twins knew that. Either you ate what was on your plate, or it went back into the fridge for later. But here it'd be thrown out. Chase had her in a trap. He looked very pleased with himself on that score too.

She grabbed a fork. "Thank you. I'll have a taste. For the record, I know that you totally set me up, and I don't appreciate it."

He smiled and lined the plates up between them so they could share. But he barely took a bite before his phone rang. He glanced at the display, picked it up. "Chase."

The entire call lasted only two minutes, his face darkening as he said nothing else but a tight, "Thank you," at the end.

He looked at her, hesitated.

She put down her fork. "What is it?"

"You were right about the roofie. The lab found traces of flunitrazepam on your clothes. You must have spilled a few drops."

She sucked in her breath. Here was the proof she'd been waiting for, the step forward that might exonerate her. "So Gregory drugged me." She wrapped her arms around herself. "He wanted to rape me, but he didn't go through with it."

Chase held her gaze. "Are you sure, he didn't…"

She nodded. "I'm sure." Paused. "So we're back to the 'he drugged me, drove me to the alley in my own car, Earl saw us, and Gregory eliminated him' theory."

"Or he just wanted Earl and needed your car, needed someone to take the fall for the hit," Chase said thoughtfully. "The whole thing could have been premeditated. He might even have selected you specifically, because he knew you worked for Earl." He thought for a moment. "The drug is illegal in the US, but available from any number of dealers."

Great. "Why would Gregory want Earl dead?" She racked her brain. "Okay, he was Earl's enemy for some reason. But how would Gregory even know that I'd be at Finnegan's that night?"

"He wouldn't. Unless he made sure you'd be there."

"But I only went because of Brett."

"Have you had contact with Brett since the date he skipped?"

"We chatted on the library computer for a few minutes on Saturday. He fell and broke his leg. Can't drive for the time being with his cast."

Chase pinned her with a sharp look. "The Brett you never met in person. The Brett you only know from Facebook photos."

She stared, her mind racing as her brain made the connection. "You think Gregory was posing as Brett online?"

"Can you think of any reason why they couldn't be the same guy?"

"They don't look alike at all—" She snapped her mouth shut. Those pictures of Brett could have been copied off the Internet. God, she felt like a naïve idiot.

"How about his voice. Did it sound familiar?"

She rubbed her fingers against her temple, filled her lungs. "I never talked on the phone with Brett. We were FB buddies. Chatted online. I thought he was kind of taking things slow, the old-fashioned way. Then out of the blue he sent a note that he was going to be near Broslin Friday night. He wanted to get together." Chagrin filled her. "I can't be that stupid, can I? How could I fall for this?"

"You've been very carefully targeted. You had no reason to suspect anything. Millions, tens of millions, of people fall for Internet scams each year. Even people with PhDs. Even cops."

She nodded, feeling dumb as a rock nevertheless. Her brain churning, she finished off a salmon cake on autopilot.

Chase leaned back in his seat, seemingly content to just watch her eat. "One more thing. The lab found no traces of Earl's blood on your clothes, or residue from the garbage bags he'd been covered with."

She froze with her glass halfway to her mouth, her heart suddenly beating in her throat. "Does this mean that the charges will be dropped?"

"Probably, although you can never predict with the DA. It'd be better if we had an alternate suspect to charge and hand to him." He paused. "What's the connection between Gregory and Earl? Could he be the boyfriend of one of the maids?"

She shook her head, swallowed. "Half of them are married. I know their husbands. Veronica doesn't have a boyfriend. The other two who do, I know the guys. They come in sometimes."

He nodded. "Could be someone from the past. Earl forced someone into something terrible. She left. She just confessed it to her boyfriend. He decided to take Earl out of commission. Do you know anyone who used to work at the hotel but quit?"

"Jen, for starters. But her husband, Billy, is not the type to carefully plot revenge. He would just march over and beat the shit out of Earl if Jen told him anything bad. I can think of two other women who left last year, off the top of my head." She rattled off their names.

Chase pulled a pen from his shirt pocket and wrote the names on a napkin. "Earl might have been an abusive jerk to other people too. Outside of the motel. I'm going to check into that."

He put the pen away and picked up his fork, ate in silence, but a few moments later, the fork stilled in his hands. He had the look of a man who'd just thought of something important.

Luanne leaned forward. "What is it?"

"I've been thinking about something on the drive up here. Have you ever met Mildred and Harold's son?"

She sucked her bottom lip in as she thought back. "Heard about him, but no. I don't think he's ever come into the motel. Why?"

"He'll be receiving the proceeds from the sale of the motel. Mildred told me she and Harold had given money to their daughter a few years back so she could buy a house. To be fair to the son, they promised to give him the money that would result from the motel's eventual sale."

She nodded. "I knew that." Then suddenly cold spread through her chest. *Wait.* "Maybe he thought his parents would sell if something horrible happened."

"They *are* selling."

Luanne's stomach clenched. "I don't even remember what his name is."

"Greg Cosgrove."

The air got stuck in her lungs. "Gregory," she whispered.

"Could be something, or could be just coincidence." Chase pulled out his phone and dialed. "Hi, Leila. Could you please do me a favor? Could you ask Mildred and Harold Cosgrove to e-mail you a photo of their son? Their number is on a sticky note on the top of my desk. And then could you please forward the picture to my phone? Thanks."

Luanne stared at the food, trying to wrap her mind around the idea that Mildred and Harold's son was trying to kill her. "Now what?" she asked Chase.

"Now we wait." He pushed the pulled pork toward her. "Might as well eat while we do that."

She shook her head. She'd suddenly lost her appetite.

"You think you'll ever go back to college?" he asked out of the blue.

Took her a moment to figure out what he was doing. He was trying to distract her from her troubles. Another couple of seconds passed before she could reroute her thoughts. "If I win the lottery on the twins' eighteenth birthday."

"I heard you were good. Minus that one test you failed."

Advanced statistics. Her mother had just been diagnosed. Luanne hadn't been able to focus. She knew that she'd be leaving her classes anyway. "Hey, my grades are my private business," she said with mock outrage. She didn't want him to think that she was stupid.

He gave a one-shouldered shrug and flashed a sheepish look. "Everyone knows everything about everybody else in Broslin. It's the small-town curse."

"Not everything."

"All right." A slow smile tugged up his lips. "Tell me something about yourself that I don't know."

"So you can use it against me in court? If this is some fancy interrogation technique, I can see right through you, buddy."

His smile widened. "Tell me your middle name."

She hesitated. He could have asked worse. Like, 'do you fantasize about me naked?'

Before he could get there, she quickly said, "Lucinda. After my Polish grandmother."

His right eyebrow slid up his forehead. "Luanne Lucinda Mayfair?"

"Call me Lulu and die." That'd been her mother's nickname for her, and she'd hated it all her childhood with a red-hot passion. "I have a black belt in swinging spray bottles."

"That's threatening a police officer."

"Glad you got that. Would hate to have to explain."

He laughed a deep belly laugh that for some reason filled her with warmth. He raised a hand, palm out. "Hey, who am I to judge?

My middle name is Mortimer."

She'd just taken a sip of her drink and promptly spewed it half across the table. "Mortimer?"

"Don't say it," he warned morosely. "We're not ever going to mention each other's middle names again."

As she mopped up the water with her napkin, she bit her lip so she wouldn't laugh.

He edged the pork toward her. "You should really have some more of this."

The man was more stubborn than a red-wine stain. "Only because I think wasting food is a sin," she said tartly.

"Yes, it is," he agreed with all seriousness.

They ate and talked some more, about his work and about the girls. Somehow, for a while, he managed to scatter the cloud of stress that had been floating around her.

They took home the leftovers, plus the extra servings of salmon cake Chase ordered to bring back for all of them for dinner.

Mia and Daisy were just waking up when they got back.

They both greeted Chase politely, but Mia gave up on the ladylike restraint right after that and ran over. "Are you going to play with us?" she demanded.

"Potty first." Luanne took them to the bathroom while Aunt Hilda thanked Chase for dinner delivery. They talked about the diner for a minute, apparently Uncle Albert's favorite, then about family.

"My father was a lawman. Deputy sheriff." Luanne heard through the door. Then the girls were done, running back out and begging for attention.

Chase looked at Luanne, then back at Mia. "What do you want to play?"

"Horse race," she said and ran for her horses in her overnight bag.

Daisy, always a ready accomplice, followed to help. The two girls lined up the horses in front of Chase, and he got right down on the floor to play with them.

Luanne went to sit next to Aunt Hilda, who was back in her recliner. "Thanks for watching the girls."

Aunt Hilda looked at Chase playing with the twins. She was smiling as she turned back to Luanne, but her smile was bittersweet. "He's here to take you back home."

"Yes," Luanne said after a moment.

"Not tonight?"

"No." She wasn't up for another four-hour drive today.

While Chase had the girls distracted, Luanne told her great-aunt about the developments in the case, finishing with "I still want to help out around the house. I'd love to get to know you a little. Give the girls a chance to get to know you. They never had a grandmother."

Tears flooded Aunt Hilda's eyes. "I'd like that. But you don't need to work while you're here. Take a break."

"I don't know if I know how to do that." Luanne gave a rueful grin. "Truth is, I'm not comfortable if I'm just sitting down. I don't know what to do with myself."

Aunt Hilda patted her hand. "I used to be like that. Then my knees went. I put off things around the house, thinking I'll do them when I got better, but I never got better. Can't walk without the cane. Sure as anything can't bend to lift anything."

"I bend and lift two thirty-five-pound girls a dozen times a day," Luanne reassured her. "I'm a champion at lifting. And boxes don't even wiggle. Easy as pie."

After a long moment, Aunt Hilda nodded. "If you're sure. Maybe we'll find the photo albums, and I can show you the rest of the family."

"That would be lovely. And, yes, I'm sure."

Chase laughed at something Mia said, a throaty, relaxed, warm laugh that reached all the way to Luanne's heart.

Aunt Hilda was looking at him too. "He likes you more than a little."

The declaration left Luanne speechless.

"Well, he didn't come to arrest you," Aunt Hilda reasoned. "A man doesn't drive hundreds of miles just to say howdy doody."

Luanne filled her lungs. "I had some near misses at home. Accidents." She hadn't mentioned that before, didn't want Aunt Hilda to worry. "He wants to stay to protect us."

"What accidents?" Hilda's gaze snapped to her, sharp for the first time.

"Near misses. Car almost hitting me on the road, that kind of thing."

Aunt Hilda pressed a hand to her chest. "You think someone

wants to hurt you?"

"It's possible."

"Chase is welcome to stay here. I have plenty of linen for another bedroom."

"I'm sure he meant to go to a hotel."

"Nonsense. He can't protect you from a hotel. He'll stay here."

"Thank you, ma'am," Chase said quietly from across the room.

And Luanne flushed to her roots, wondering if he'd heard everything, even the part about him coming after her for more than a howdy doody.

Before she could wish for a hole to sink into, his phone pinged. He glanced at it, brought it over. The picture of a slightly balding man in his late thirties filled the screen. "Is that Gregory?"

Her heart sank. "No."

"I didn't think so. Doesn't look like the police sketch." But he kept holding the phone out for her. "Are you a hundred percent sure? That's Mildred and Harold's son. Are you sure he wasn't the guy at the bar?"

"I'm sure."

And just like that, they were back to square one. They had absolutely nothing.

* * *

Next time he took a load of garbage to the dump, Chase called his mother from the car. "I'm staying the night in Virginia," he told her.

"Why?"

"To help out a friend."

"A woman?" Her voice immediately filled with dismay.

"Yes."

"How do you know a woman in Virginia? Are you doing this to me on purpose?"

"It's Luanne Mayfair. She's visiting her great-aunt," he said before his mother could have a coronary.

"Oh." A small pause. "Didn't you just arrest her for murder— Never mind. She's such a lovely girl. Local."

Chase grinned. Apparently, in his mother's view, being local was more important than criminality. "She didn't do it," he said, just to be clear.

"A hard worker, that one. Betty and I were talking about that when the arrest report was printed in the paper. And raising those two sweet little babies." She practically cooed the words.

The last thing he wanted was visions of grandbabies dancing before his mother's eyes, so he interrupted with "I might stay a couple of days."

Normally, his mother hated when he was out of town. But now she responded with "Take your time. You just make sure you help Luanne with whatever she needs."

He intended to, Chase thought as he ended the call.

And that wasn't all he intended.

Seeing Luanne again, spending time with her. The more they were together, the more he got this funny feeling that something had gotten interrupted between them years ago, something wasn't quite finished yet.

He was an investigator. When he had a funny feeling, he investigated.

Chapter Eight

For reasons she couldn't fully, or even partially, explain, after a pretty exhausting day, Luanne didn't seem to be tired. In fact, she found sleeping impossible.

Her insomnia could have had something to do with the fact that Chase was right next door. He'd come after her and stayed.

What did that mean?

The gesture didn't seem like a cop thing. It seemed like a friend thing. He was staying to help on his own time. Of course, he'd been telling her all along that he was her friend. Why?

At the diner, he'd said she bamboozled him. Bamboozled seemed more than friends.

Bamboozled.

In a good way or a bad way?

Luanne groaned and squeezed her eyes shut. She refused to regress to a teenager. She was *not* going to spend all night thinking about Chase Merritt.

And then, of course, she did.

Since she didn't fall asleep until toward dawn, she woke late the next morning, which was okay, because the twins slept in too, exhausted by the previous day. She took care of them first before going downstairs for coffee, bleary-eyed, dressed in old sweatpants and a faded T-shirt.

Aunt Hilda was already in the kitchen. Chase was just coming in with rolls of garbage bags under one arm, a big box of bagels under the other, plus carrying a department store bag too. The bagels were all made-up, Luanne saw when he set the box on the kitchen counter and opened it—some with eggs and ham, others with cream cheese.

"Good morning," he said, all bright-eyed and bushy-tailed. "I figured we shouldn't waste time on cooking. We have plenty to do today."

Mia and Daisy raced to the table, where Aunt Hilda was setting out paper plates.

"What's in the other bag?" Mia wanted to know.

"Got myself a change of clothes." He dropped the bag by the stairs. "Those bagels are still warm. Better eat up." He glanced at Luanne.

She narrowed her eyes at him. He was definitely feeding her. Maybe it was some weird fetish. What did she really know about Chase Merritt anyway?

"Thank you." She moved the box to the middle of the kitchen table. "How about I get everyone drinks?"

"Thank you, dear." Aunt Hilda thumped onto her seat with relief.

Luanne poured milk for the girls, water for the adults, as requested, then sat next to Chase. Only five chairs surrounded the kitchen table. The sixth sat in the corner, piled high with newspaper. Something she meant to take care of next.

She put a cream cheese bagel on her plate, then dropped her hands on her lap and linked her fingers. "What do we do?" she prompted the girls.

They snapped their backs straight and chanted in unison, Mia at the top of her lungs, Daisy a little quieter. "God is great! God is good! Let us thank Him for our food. Aa-men!"

Aunt Hilda reached out to pat their little heads with a shaky hand. "You girls are treasures."

Of course, they both beamed. They ate up attention.

"Aunt Hilda said we're a treasure," Mia bragged immediately. "Can we go outside after breakfast?"

Luanne bit into her bagel. The backyard was fenced. "What are you going to do out there?"

"Look for ants." Mia always had a ready answer for everything.

Daisy thought for a moment before whispering, "I'd like to sing with the grass."

Daisy was more of a contemplative child with ideas that often confounded Luanne. When Luanne and Mia used to play the "what does the cow say," "what does the dog say," "what does the rooster say" game in their younger years, Daisy had always wanted to know what the turtle or the butterfly said.

Neither Aunt Hilda nor Chase batted an eyelash now at her latest unusual comment, for which Luanne was grateful.

"I'll go with them," Aunt Hilda offered.

"Sounds like a great idea," Luanne agreed immediately. If her aunt stayed inside, she'd insist on helping like she had the day before, and she really needed to be sitting down and resting.

So, after breakfast, Luanne moved the kids outside with their dolls and horses—in case the great ant hunt didn't pan out. If the toys got dirty, they could be washed in the sink.

"Where do you want to start today?" Chase asked once they were alone in the house.

Luanne glanced around at the piles. "Let's bag up everything that can go to the recycling center. We need to separate the paper from the plastic and the glass."

He grabbed the first roll of black plastic bags. "Once the garbage is out, we'll have more room to move around."

She nodded. "Then while you drop off the bags, I can vacuum, dust some more, then Aunt Hilda and the girls could come in for lunch under improved circumstances."

"Sounds like a plan."

"If we finish down here this morning, after lunch Aunt Hilda could sit in her recliner and decide what to do with all her boxes."

Chase strode over to the chair piled with newspaper and began bagging it. "We can finish the upstairs tomorrow. Is there an attic?" he asked warily.

"And a basement," Luanne said, trying not to be intimidated as she tackled the empty glass jars in the pantry.

He took the first bag from her when she was done and carried it out, a bag of glass jars in one hand, a bag of newspapers in the other, his biceps bulging in interesting ways.

He didn't have a photo model's body, but he had a very masculine presence that was real and definitely sexy. Not that she was looking for sexy. But as he walked to the front door with the bags, she couldn't help noticing his long stride and the way his blue jeans molded to his backside.

Better not let him catch her ogling. Luanne blinked, then went back to work. She filled a second bag and set it by the door. Wiped her brow. Aunt Hilda didn't have air-conditioning, and the air was getting pretty hot and dusty.

They worked for a solid two hours before the twins came in for a drink and snack. Aunt Hilda served them apple wedges and baby carrots that she let them frost with peanut butter. Of course, they were over-the-moon happy about being officially allowed to make a mess.

"How are you holding up out there?" Luanne asked her aunt.

"Most fun I've had in years." Aunt Hilda smiled. "There's a good breeze in the deep shade. Air's nicer than in here. It's lovely to be near so much youthful energy. They don't rest for a second, do they?"

"Not if they can help it." Luanne pressed a kiss on the top of each girl's head, then went back to work.

The kitchen and pantry were just about finished by the time Aunt Hilda took the girls back outside. Luanne and Chase tackled the living room next.

They found the expected: old books, shoes, knickknacks. Then there were surprises. They found at least two hundred empty soup cans under the couch and the love seat, hidden by the skirted upholstery. At least the cans were clean.

They gathered up four bagsful of those, working side by side, on their knees, sometimes on their bellies. She was painfully aware of Chase's hard body next to hers, muscles flexing. She could even smell his soap, Irish Spring, then later his sweat, which wasn't unpleasant, just made him smell like a hard-working man.

They grabbed their bags and headed for the door at the same time. He went through first, dropped one bag, and reached back to hold the door open for her. She held up one bag in front of her, one behind her to fit through. Then the door began to close, and he had to step closer.

For a second, as she stepped forward, her breast dragged across his chest. The instant electricity that zapped through her, the immediate sexual tension, had her looking up at him in surprise.

His gaze darkened as it held hers. And just like that, she could have sworn the temperature hit a hundred degrees. *Major* chemistry. Way more than she was comfortable acknowledging.

She hurried by him, heat flushing her face. Ridiculous. She was not going to fall for those ocean-deep blue eyes again. She was an accused murderer. She was *not* going to fall for a lawman.

When they came back in, she headed for the laundry room, feeling the need for some separation. Still, she couldn't completely ignore him. They kept bumping into each other coming and going, somehow always jockeying for space.

By the time noon rolled around, she was emotionally exhausted, and…aroused. From housecleaning! Well, housecleaning with Chase. He had cobwebs in his hair. She had dirt streaks all up and down the front of her shirt. They were both covered in dust and grime, for heaven's sake. Something was definitely wrong with her. The whole murder-charge stress had driven her batty.

"I'll drive this last load over to the dump," he told her, sounding strained, probably from the heat.

"I'll vacuum and mop, then I'll start lunch." Aunt Hilda had taken a big chunk of ground beef out of the freezer last night. "How do you feel about french fries and hamburgers?"

"Enthusiastic," he said before he walked away, his easy gait on the slow side, almost as if he was reluctant to leave.

She cleaned up downstairs, which went pretty quickly without all the stacks, then cleaned herself up upstairs before starting lunch. The girls came in, hopping with excitement, which was pretty much their standard setting.

"Aunt Hilda said we can call her Grandma Hilda if it's okay with you. Can we?" Mia begged.

"Sorry." Aunt Hilda ducked her head. "I should have asked you first before saying something like that to the girls. Now you're put on the spot. If you're not comfortable—"

But Luanne smiled, something warm and sweet filling her heart. "I think Grandma Hilda would be great."

The girls broke out in wild cheers. They'd never known either of their grandmothers, so this was a big novelty. "Grandma, Grandma!" The twins kept saying the word as if they needed to practice it.

The pleasure that spread over Aunt Hilda's face in response made the entire trip worthwhile.

Luanne patted Mia, who was, of course, the loudest, on the head. "Why don't you two let Grandma rest for a second? How about you two help me?"

After a thorough hand-washing, Luanne let them flatten out the hamburger patties, which they loved doing. As far as they were concerned, the messier a job was the better. They were done in a few minutes.

"Okay, now let's wash your hands really good with soapy water again. You don't touch anything after you played with raw meat. You got it?"

"Got it!"

"God bless you for doing that." Aunt Hilda sat by the table, watching them all with a fond expression. "My knees are so bad these days, it's getting hard to stand by the stove. I really appreciate you cooking for me."

"I'm cooking your own food. I think we're getting the better end of the deal," Luanne assured her, making a mental note to buy the next round of groceries. She didn't want to take advantage of her aunt's hospitality. "Is there anything else you'd like?"

"I have some canned corn in the pantry," Aunt Hilda said after a second. "I'd love to have some if you don't mind making it. It's getting hard to open cans with these arthritic fingers."

Luanne headed for the pantry, wondering how old the empty cans under the couch had been.

When Chase came home, they sat and ate—after the twins rattled off their prayer. A speed prayer meant they liked dinner. When she served vegetable soup or, God forbid, something with broccoli or spinach, they could drag that prayer out for an eternity.

While they ate, Chase entertained them with stories about police dogs. Apparently, at the police academy, at one point he'd trained with a canine unit. The twins listened with openmouthed fascination. He was animated, funny, showing sincere interest in the girls. Even Aunt Hilda hung on his every word.

Luanne looked around the table, and a sense of family hit her so hard it stole her breath.

Anyone walking in would have seen a normal, everyday family, mom, dad, kids, grandmother. She couldn't even imagine what it must be like to tackle life's challenges as a team, as a family unit.

Better not sink too far into that little fantasy. She swallowed the last of her hamburger abruptly and stepped over to the sink to start on the dishes. For some stupid reason, her eyes were suddenly burning.

* * *

Tall and lean, Luanne's body hadn't changed much since she'd been a high school athlete, running track, Chase thought as he watched her standing by the sink. But she was definitely a full-grown woman, if too thin. Just the thought of her breast brushing against him earlier in that doorway sent a rush of heat to his loins all over again.

He wanted to walk up to her from behind and put his arms around her slim waist, cuddle her against his chest. He would turn her in his arms and taste those lips he'd been thinking about all morning, kiss that sexy crease in her bottom lip. He couldn't have been more aware of her long legs and perky boobs, having spent the night under the same roof. Every dream he had began with her appearing at his door. She'd said dirty, dirty things to him in that velvety voice of hers.

He turned from her, back to the kids and Aunt Hilda. He had to stop thinking about her in his bedroom, her blond locks barely covering her perfect breasts, or he'd be getting up from the table with a bulge in his pants. No need to embarrass himself in front of everybody.

"May I have some more milk?" Daisy asked very politely, very quietly.

Since the carton was nearest to Chase, he poured for her.

"Thank you," she said immediately.

Luanne had raised the girls right, whatever hardship she had to go through to do it.

"Do we have to nap?" Mia skipped her milk refill and went straight to negotiating. "Can we help with cleaning? We like cleaning."

"Nap first, fun second," Aunt Hilda said. "I want you rested. You'll be helping me sort through boxes of old toys later."

"Really?" The girls giggled with excitement.

"We'll see how strong you are when you wake up." Aunt Hilda winked. "Some of those toys are pretty big. I do recall a rocking horse. You better get plenty of sleep."

Mia was off her chair already. Daisy gulped the last of her milk.

Chase stood too and walked to Luanne at the sink. "Why don't you take the girls up and settle them in? I'll finish here."

She stared at him with surprise for a second. Blinked. As if no one had ever helped her with dishes. And then the very real possibility occurred to Chase that nobody ever had. Because she'd been doing everything all alone pretty much.

"Go on," he said brusquely, not comfortable with the overwhelmingly grateful look on her face that replaced the surprise after a moment.

"Are you sure?"

He nodded. "I might be just a man, but I think I can handle a couple of plates."

She picked up the girls, who had a million questions about the toys. "Are there dolls?" "How about little horses?" "Do you think there's a water slide in the boxes?" "Or a puppy!" Daisy suddenly yelled with a volume that was unusual for her.

One on each hip, Luanne carried them to the stairs. "No puppy."

"How do you know?" Mia challenged.

"We would have heard him yipping."

The girls seemed to take that as a reasonable explanation and moved on to the next on their wish list: rubber snakes.

"God bless those girls," Aunt Hilda said at the table. "They sure bring sunshine, don't they?" She waited until Luanne was upstairs. "Is she in a lot of trouble?"

"I'm going to help her fix that."

"You care about her."

It didn't seem right to lie to someone who'd taken him into her house. "Yes, I do."

"Good. She needs a strong, honest man in her corner."

He wasn't sure what to do with the unconditional approval, so he stepped to the table to pick up the last of the plates.

"Those girls love you," Aunt Hilda added, and Chase felt his heart turn over in his chest.

"Great kids," he said brusquely.

He hadn't much thought about children before, but he was beginning to understand why his mother was so desperate for grandkids close by. They did grow on you after a while, he willingly admitted.

He'd been living on his own for a long time, so all the people in the house should have made him long for solitude. Yet, for the first time, his life felt oddly complete.

He was going to think about that sometime in the near future. After Luanne was exonerated and safe.

When she came back downstairs, they began sorting out more of the excess furniture and the piles of boxes that held second, third, fourth, fifth, and sixth sets of dishes, utensils, dozens of cookie jars, homemade knickknacks, even art.

Soon the first calls from the online listings began to come in, then a steady procession of people to pick up their purchases. One was a dealer who took three dining sets all at once. Suddenly, the house was beginning to feel roomy.

Aunt Hilda sat quietly in her chair. "I feel like I'm throwing out people's memories."

Luanne hurried over, crouched next to the recliner, and patted her hand. "Their memories are in your heart. And you're not throwing out any of this. You're giving some lovely furniture to people who will keep using and cherishing these pieces. Instead of sitting here, gathering dust, those extra tables will be surrounded by kids eating dinner. Lots of new memories being made."

Aunt Hilda patted Luanne's hand in turn. Sniffed. "You're right. I'm a silly old woman. I'm so glad you came."

Chase could practically see their emotional connection deepen as they smiled at each other. Luanne was good at this, he thought, at knowing what to say. She was good with the girls too, loving but firm, fun. The more time he spent with her, the more he liked her, in a way that went way beyond his horny teenage crush on her.

"If you think you can use something from here," Aunt Hilda said, then looked at him. "You too, Chase. It's the least I can do for all your help. You can take home whatever you'd like."

"Thank you. I think I'm good. You know men. All we need is a couch and a TV stand." He smiled as he looked around. "All right. What do we tackle next?"

Hilda's forehead pulled into an overwhelmed frown for a second or two, but then she squared her shoulders. "How about the kitchen? The extra dishes could go to the thrift store. It'd be nice to have some room in the cabinets. But I feel bad giving you more work. You both worked so hard and so much already. You already made a big difference."

"Not the type to sit around." Chase needed to keep moving. His hands were itching for Luanne. Better occupy them with something else, he decided, and began loading the SUV with boxes Hilda had already designated for charity.

Luanne went to the kitchen and opened the first cabinet door, looked back to her aunt. "All right. Just tell me what goes and what stays."

They worked all afternoon, Hilda taking the girls out back after they woke. Chase carried several large boxes of antique toys out for them.

Luanne vacuumed and mopped again when they were done for the day, while Chase took down the curtains she insisted on washing.

"I'm taking you all out to dinner," he announced as the girls and Hilda came in. They'd all been stuck at home all day. Time to get out of the house.

Of course, the girls squealed with glee.

Luanne shook her head. "Do you eat out all the time?"

"Just when I'm hungry." He shrugged, then grinned. "It's my prerogative as a bachelor."

"Oh dear. I better get dressed." Aunt Hilda patted her hair, suddenly energized. "Come on, girls, let's pretty up. A handsome man is taking us out to dinner." She winked at Luanne.

Was Luanne blushing?

They were all suddenly in such an excited female tizzy, Chase decided he was going to take them out again tomorrow.

They ended up at Chuck E. Cheese, at the girls' request. He had more fun than he ever remembered having. Every once in a while, he caught Luanne watching him. Every once in a while, he caught himself watching Luanne.

She thanked him a hundred times while there, then again when they ran into each other in the hallway upstairs as they got ready for bed, finally at midnight. The girls and Aunt Hilda had been long asleep. Luanne had decided not to go to bed until she'd cleaned out the decade-old ashes and cobwebs from the living room fireplace, and he'd stayed up to help her. Luanne was leaving the bathroom from her shower; he was heading in.

"Thanks again for dinner. That was a real treat for all of us." She flashed him that smile he was getting familiar with, half-grateful, half-worried. Because he'd done something for them, and she wasn't sure how she was going to pay him back. He had a suspicion she was keeping some kind of tally in the back of her mind.

He was proven right when she said, "As soon as I get a new job, we're taking you out."

He didn't protest. One, it would have been futile. Two, he wanted to go to dinner with Luanne and the girls again. "I'll ask around for job openings when we get back home. But first, let's figure out who's trying to hurt you, so your life can go back to normal as soon as possible."

She was standing too close to him in the narrow hallway, her face freshly scrubbed, her blond hair pushed back, still wet from the shower. She wore a sleeveless pink cotton nightgown that ended an inch above her knees.

Suddenly the air thickened between them. Tension built. He was painfully aware that they were the only two people still awake in the house, alone in the hallway, only the night around them.

He wanted her. Who wouldn't? She was sunshine. She was sweet but strong. She could be shy about some things, but funny. Enough contradiction to be interesting. She had a heart that kept stretching to include everyone who needed her.

"I'm sorry," she said.

He blinked. "About what?"

"You know." She looked down at her toes, then looked up again, her cheeks coloring. "After high school. For telling people you were bad in bed."

They were talking about sex? He felt his body harden. "And that I was a bad kisser." As long as they were on the subject...

"That too." She looked genuinely chagrined. "I only told Jen. She was supposed to keep it a secret."

He watched her as she shifted from one foot to the other. "Don't worry about it. I forgive you." It had been a major pain in his behind at the time, all the guys ribbing him. They hadn't let him live that down for years. But faced with Luanne practically naked and just a short foot from him in the hallway, he found it surprisingly easy to forgive.

He flashed a teasing smile. "You were just too inexperienced to appreciate what I had to offer. You shouldn't blame yourself for finding my high school charms overwhelming. Could have happened to anyone."

He'd been her first. She'd been his second. He'd had no idea what he was doing. He only knew that it was considered bad if it ended in three minutes. So he'd tried his best to make it last for her.

Her eyes narrowed. "I don't think—"

He was *not* going to discuss his single worst sexual failure. He dipped his head and sealed his lips over hers.

Need exploded inside him as soon as they touched. Last time, he'd gone slow and gentle—she'd been a virgin—and left her disappointed. This time, he let her have all the heat and passion that

112

had built up inside him since he'd gotten here. He sneaked one hand around her waist and pulled her flush against him, and as she opened her mouth—maybe to say something—he deepened the kiss.

Suddenly, she was clinging to him.

All right, then. He really liked that.

Now that he'd convinced her that he was *not*, in fact, a bad kisser, he would have dearly liked to set her memory straight on a few other things. He wanted her, right then and there, against the wall, with her long legs wrapped around his waist, his erection buried to the hilt inside her. Which wasn't going to happen, for various reasons. For one, the girls could wake up and come out of their room. And he was dirty from the day's work.

Kissing was it, for the time being. He made sure he did a thorough job of that, paying special attention to that maddening crease in her bottom lip.

Technically, now that she was no longer a suspect, the possibilities were endless. She *was* a person under his protection, but the guidelines there were fuzzier and more lenient.

He kissed her again and again, then, as he pulled back, he let himself get lost in her eyes for a moment.

"I love your lips. I love those whiskey-color eyes of yours," he murmured. "They remind me of my father."

Her eyebrows shot up, a teasing smile hovering over her lips. "You like kissing me because I remind you of your father? That's just so wrong."

Yeah, said that way... He smiled back. "Once a year, after Christmas dinner, my father would let me drink one sip of his treasured aged whiskey and take one puff of his cigar. You remind me of something special that made me feel like a man, something I was excited about, looked forward to all year."

Her eyes softened. She lifted her lips back to his.

She tasted like mint and smelled like Irish Spring, the soap Aunt Hilda gave them. She felt right in his arms, if on the skinny side. Her boobs really were as perfect as he'd remembered.

His hands were clean enough, he reasoned, and went for second base.

* * *

How could she have been so incredibly, utterly wrong?

Luanne's head was spinning as she held on to Chase's shoulders for support. Dear Lord, the man could kiss. He could kiss every coherent thought out of her mind, in fact.

His warm hands cupped her breasts, and her nipples immediately drew into tight buds, poking against his palms.

He shifted her, trapped her between the wall and his great body. He took her like a man who expected full capitulation. Where was sweet, hesitant Chase? Left behind in high school, apparently.

He felt like a man, and he smelled like a man, and he sure as anything kissed like a man. And then some.

All the good-night kisses and necking in cars she'd missed because of the twins, this kiss made up for them within the first minute.

He completely filled her senses and mastered her body, and they still had all their clothes on. She was melting from the inside out.

Chase.

She wanted him to lift her up so she could wrap her legs around him. She couldn't have cared less that his clothes were dirty. A little dirt never hurt anybody.

She'd never been a sex-crazed teenager. Or a lusty adult. After a full-time job, plus a part-time job, and the twins, she didn't have the energy. She shouldn't have had the energy now, after a full day of cleaning. But desire buzzed through her, and she wanted more, desperately.

Of course, they couldn't. This was crazy. The twins were just a few steps away. They were in Aunt Hilda's house. Yet she hung on to him until finally he drew back, breathing hard, his dark gaze raking her face.

An amused smile twisted his lips, and he raised an eyebrow, as if asking, *Now, was that terrible?*

She gathered herself. Cleared her throat. "I'm not going to feed your ego."

He laughed as he stepped away from her.

Chapter Nine

He shouldn't have kissed Luanne. At least not until the case was closed and she was safe. But Chase couldn't regret it.

The following day, as they worked upstairs, he wanted to kiss her again. While she made lunch, he drove another carload of garbage to the dump. He called the captain on his way back.

"I'd like to take some time off."

"In the middle of a murder investigation?" Bing didn't sound angry, just caught off guard.

"Maybe Harper could step in. His parents and the employees at the bar have been cleared." The murder had to be investigated in Broslin. Luanne had to be protected here in Petersburg. Chase couldn't do both at the same time, and he chose Luanne.

Yeah, he wanted to see the case to the end. He wanted to be the one to snap the handcuffs on. But he didn't want it to the exclusion of everything else. He didn't have that kind of relentless drive to always win. Or maybe he defined winning differently. His priority was Luanne. If she and the girls were safe, that was enough of a win for him.

Bing asked, "You sure?"

"Sure."

"I take it you'll be staying in Virginia?"

"Yeah."

"All right. I'll let Harper know. You better call him and brief him."

* * *

"I can handle the rest," Luanne told Chase over the dishes after lunch, mostly because she couldn't handle being so close to him that their arms brushed together.

Hilda rested in her room while the girls were napping in theirs, not a peep so far.

Sometimes Daisy had fears when she slept and called for

Luanne. She often woke at night and at nap time. As soon as Luanne went in and gave her a kiss, the little girl would go right back to sleep. But Daisy had been sleeping like a log at Aunt Hilda's place.

What was the difference? And it suddenly occurred to Luanne that maybe Daisy was scared of losing her, of her disappearing like their mother, and then the girls would be all alone. But the extra adults here made her feel safer, more protected.

Chase's quiet "What is it?" interrupted Luanne's thoughts, and she realized that she'd stopped washing and gotten lost in her thoughts for a second, dripping water on the floor.

He was searching her face. "Did you remember something?"

She shook her head. "Just thinking about the girls. I don't want them to be all alone."

"You're not all alone," he said firmly. "Harper's taking over the case. I'm staying." He set down the dishcloth he'd used to dry the plates.

She stared at him. "Why?"

"To make sure you're safe. If I figured out that you came here, so can the killer."

Her heart thumped. He was right. And beyond herself, she had the girls to worry about too, and Aunt Hilda now. So even though she already owed Chase more than she could ever repay, which made her uncomfortable, she didn't try to talk him out of his decision. "Thank you."

He held her gaze for a moment and nodded. "I'm going to clean up the front garden. I don't want to go back upstairs to work and wake up the girls."

He didn't have kids, hadn't been around kids a lot, as far as she knew, yet he considered Mia and Daisy in everything before acting. Her heart softened. "I'll come and help when I'm done here."

The rest of the day went like that, the two of them working together, mostly in companionable silence, like a well-oiled team. When the girls woke, they watched the kiddie shows on PBS in the living room with Aunt Hilda while Luanne and Chase finished up upstairs.

By that night, the bedrooms and the bathroom up there were purged of all piles and old dust. The upstairs looked light and spacious again. The house gleamed.

Chase took them back to Chuck E. Cheese for dinner, spent

most of his time playing with the girls. Even Hilda played a few games. She was laughing, downright energized, looking ten years younger than when Luanne had arrived in town with the twins.

Luanne watched them fool around with a smile on her face. She felt happier too, lighter, safer. Being surrounded by two supportive adults was wonderful, the first time in a long time that every decision didn't fall on her shoulders alone, the first time she had somebody to share the work with.

She liked that. A lot. And she liked having fun as a big family. She liked the way Chase would forget his gaze on her, a sexy half smile on his face as if he was remembering last night's kiss rather fondly. The evening was perfect in every way.

When they were at the car outside in the parking lot a while later and Daisy remembered that she'd left one of her prizes on her chair, Chase had Mia on his neck, so Luanne ran back to retrieve the plush rabbit.

She hurried into the squat building, passing a man standing by the bushes next to the entrance with his back to her, smoking a cigarette. She walked inside, found the bunny, and hurried back out.

But the man was suddenly right there, next to her, grabbing her arm. Brown hair, brown eyes. Panic slammed into her as the guy flipped her around. Gregory? She didn't catch enough of a glimpse of him to tell. Cold fear raced through her, freezing her immobile.

She expected... What? A knife in the ribs?

Then adrenaline rushed her, and she finally had the presence of mind to jab back hard with her elbow, but didn't have time for anything else because the next she knew, Chase was at her back, sending the guy flying. After one thorough, dark look to make sure she was all right, Chase stepped over to the jerk and hauled him up, then secured him by twisting his right arm behind his back, moving quickly and smoothly. The whole time, he used his body to shield most of what was going on from the girls.

He shoved the guy to the light by the door so Luanne could take a good look. "You know him?"

Scrawny twenty-year-old, eyes wide, the wild look of a heroin junkie. He was in rough shape, she realized now that she could see him better—clothes unkempt, hair like a feather duster.

She shook her head. Definitely not Gregory.

"Why did you attack her?" Chase demanded as the kid

whimpered.

"I didn't attack her, man." The kid shrank, neck pulled in, shoulders hunched as if he expected a beating. "I just wanted the purse," he whined. "I'm hungry."

For drugs, most likely, Luanne thought, even as the manager burst through the door behind them, a blur of black suit and bald head.

He directed his red-faced anger at the attacker. "I told you to get out of here, Joey. I called your mother. She's on her way."

The young guy looked like he might start crying.

The manager turned to Luanne and Chase. "Did he bother you? I'm so sorry." He handed them coupons for free meals from his suit pocket, worry marring his face, probably the fear of a lawsuit. "You go on and have a good evening. I'll take care of this." He clearly didn't want trouble. Police cruisers lining the walkway to his front door for the next couple of hours would probably have been bad for business.

From the way he talked, it sounded like Joey was an ongoing problem around the place. Chase hesitated only a second before he released the kid.

"The police can't really charge him. They can, but he'll never get convicted," he told Luanne on their way back to the car, taking her hand, squeezing it for a second, then releasing it.

Amazing how good such a small gesture of comfort could feel. "He didn't get my purse. I don't want to press charges." She filled her lungs. "He just scared me for a second."

She didn't want to make a big scene and have the girls worry. Most of all, she didn't want to spend the rest of her evening in the parking lot, talking to the police. It'd been a five-second scare. She was over it.

Aunt Hilda was standing by the car, looking between Chase and Luanne, smiling. The girls stared at him as if he was Santa, the Easter Bunny, and the Tooth Fairy all rolled into one, the most impressive mythical creature of all.

"You beated up the bad man." Mia's voice dripped with awe.

"I didn't. I just made him move back a little. Fighting is not good," Chase told her as Daisy hugged his leg first, then Luanne's.

"Did he say he was sorry?" Mia wanted to know.

"He did."

Mia nodded. Then Daisy nodded too. Chase opened the car door for them, and they climbed into their car seats. Luanne snapped them in.

"No popcorn for him," Mia said, the last word on the bad-man subject, then she asked Aunt Hilda what her favorite game had been at the restaurant.

They were all laughing in the car on the way home at Mia's dramatic retelling of how she won a pile of prizes, the happiness palpable in the car. And Luanne thought, *Chase did this*.

The girls were completely in love with him. All the way, nothing held back. So was Aunt Hilda. And, Luanne realized, a little stunned, she was more than halfway there.

Too fast. God, she was in no position for romance. She was out on bail, charged with murder.

That melted the smile right off her face, just as Aunt Hilda said, "I wish you all would stay forever."

She sat in the back with the twins, because, of course, they wanted to sit with Grandma. They greeted her suggestion with a chorus of "Yay!"

Luanne filled her lungs, wishing life was that easy. "We're really going to miss you," she told her aunt. "We'll come back to visit as much as possible."

She spent the evening looking at old family photos with her aunt and the kids, Hilda telling stories about various relatives Luanne had never heard of before. With every story, the family bonds tightened. The girls ate it up. They loved being part of something big.

Chase was up in his room, on the phone with Harper, running through ideas, strategizing, talking over the case to make sure they didn't miss anything.

Because she was thoroughly confused about her feelings about him, she made sure they didn't meet up in the hallway that night. She didn't need another knee-buckling kiss to cloud her head.

And then she lay in bed, thinking about kissing him.

And then her knees went weak from *thinking* about kissing him. She flopped over and groaned into her pillow.

She couldn't sleep. Of course, every time she tossed and turned, her bed creaked. Since she'd heard Chase's bed creak earlier, she was pretty sure he could hear hers. She tried to stay still. She didn't want him to know that he was giving her sleepless nights.

But five minutes later, she was flopping onto her back again, seeking a comfortable position that might lull her into sleep.

Her door opened, slowly. Chase stepped inside, the moonlight outlining his impressive body. Her mouth went dry at the sight.

He strode to her without hurry and effortlessly scooped her up into his arms, walked out of the bedroom with her. "You were going to wake up the girls," he whispered when they were in the hallway.

He took her straight to his bed, laid her down, then walked around and got in next to her, turning so they would face each other.

Could her heart beat any harder? She could barely eke out a simple "Good night."

But he had other plans, it seemed, because he reached out, his strong hand cupping her cheek. "We're not going to sleep," he said mildly, in his own easygoing way.

She felt lightheaded.

And then he shifted closer, nuzzled her nose with his, and kissed her.

Last night's kiss had been a sudden rush of passion. This time, he was all slow and measured. He dragged out every nibble, every touch of the lips. Definitely the old Chase. *Here we go again.* He kept playing with her, minute after endless minute. And slowly, her bones turned to liquid.

She wanted to have sex with him, even if her memories of the last time they'd tried that, the summer after high school, were less than stellar. She'd been a virgin, embarrassed, uncomfortable, one of the few girls among her friends who hadn't *done it* yet. She'd snuck out of her bedroom to meet Chase in the middle of the night more from peer pressure than anything else.

He'd been incredibly tender, agonizingly slow, in the back of his old Chevy out by the reservoir, when all she wanted was to have it over with. The experience had been nothing like in books and movies.

She could live without sex, she'd decided, and focused on studying instead of dating when she was in college. She had two years of that before she came home to take care of the twins.

She'd had one on-and-off relationship since, with her ex-neighbor, Luke, who was a drug rep for a major pharmaceutical company, on the road most of the time. When he was home now and then, he'd come over. They'd chat, watch TV, maybe have sex. Just as uncomfortable as it'd been with Chase, but at least with Luke it was over much more quickly. Honestly, she barely noticed.

But Luke had moved last year, and she'd had nobody since.

Luanne forgot all about Luke when Chase reached for the bottom of her nightgown and slowly tugged it up, pulled it over her head, and tossed it to the end of the bed. His gaze raked her body, and he licked his lips, as if ready to eat her up.

She was filled with need, but at the same time, so nervous she was ready to jump out of her skin. She might have inadvertently spread a rumor about him not being good in bed, but the truth was, she was pretty sure the problem was her. For her, sex had just never been all that great. Other women seemed to enjoy the act. Jen loved it when Billy threw her on the bed and had his way with her.

Luanne swallowed. She didn't want to disappoint Chase.

"Okay," she said, breathless. "But just be quick about it. Please."

He looked up from her breasts to her face. "Stamina is usually considered a good thing in a man."

She tried to catch her breath. "It's...uncomfortable. I'm not good at this," she confessed. "I don't like to drag things out."

His eyebrows slid up a fraction, his voice deepening to a silky smoothness. "Is that so?" And then ever so slowly, ever so carefully, he licked a lazy circle around her nipple.

A small moan escaped her throat, taking her by surprise and embarrassing her.

His lips twitched. Then he licked the nipple itself.

She moaned again, startled by the pleasure.

Then he took her nipple into his mouth, sucked hard suddenly, and she felt moisture gather between her legs. When he moved to the other nipple while rubbing the first between his thumb and index finger, she reached down to run her hands over his back and wide shoulders, over his hot, smooth skin, wanting to touch him as much as wanting to hold him in place.

He looked up. "For someone who's not good at this, you're amazingly responsive."

He must have approved, because she could feel his erection pressing against her thigh. But he didn't pick up the pace to get to what men really wanted. Oh no. He took at least half an hour just to play with her breasts. Who did that?

Chase tantalized her nipples into throbbing, begging buds of pleasure, then finally-finally!—moved down her body, his warm lips trailing kisses, nibbles, nips, setting her on fire. She moaned, she arched, she very nearly begged. First for him to get to the point already, then to stop, stop, stop when his mouth reached the edge of her sensible cotton panties.

"Chase?"

He didn't respond. He simply peeled off her underwear and went to work on her with his questing lips instead of going for his own pleasure. Every touch, every lick took her further and further away from sanity. She dug her fingers into his hair.

Every time she was on the edge, he'd back up, trail kisses down her inner thigh, then up again. Then lick her. Then back away again when she moved. Freaking for-e-ver.

Her brain fogged from all the heat, but she was still able to put two and two together. He was punishing her for that stupid rumor. He was going to have his revenge, torturing her to death. But it was such sweet torture, she couldn't protest.

Then he drew back and blew on her throbbing clitoris, bending back to it the next second and sucking it into his hot mouth sharply, scraping his teeth against the engorged nub.

He brought her to a shattering orgasm, then, before she could recover, he eased a finger inside her, then another, and built the tension back up all over again, pushed her over the edge again, leaving her spent and limp, dazed, dazzled, confused, and utterly conquered.

What just happened here?

Twice! When she hadn't even had one orgasm before. Ever.

Slow was good, apparently. Slow was brilliant. A smile stretched her lips.

"You?" she asked, languid and beyond content.

"No protection." His voice was tight. He sounded like he was doing breathing exercises. He came up and lay next to her, an arm over his eyes. "I'll go shopping tomorrow."

She liked sex with Chase. She gloried in the thought that he wanted to do this again. "I could—"

But he said, "This is more than enough." And tucked her against him.

Within minutes, she slept like a brick. Better. Like an entire pile of bricks. Like a brick factory, in fact.

His ringing phone woke her in the morning. While he took the call, she pulled on her nightgown and went to check on the twins.

They were still sleeping soundly. She dressed in silence, then left the door open to a crack when she went downstairs to make coffee.

Chase joined her in a few minutes. He grabbed her by the waist, pulled her to him, and kissed her silly.

"We're going back," he said as he drew away with a happy glint in his eyes.

"We are?" she asked, dazed and breathless.

"The lab was able to lift three usable fingerprints off the hundred-dollar bill Gregory paid with at Finnegan's. One belongs to a Gregory Jorde. We have him. Almost," he corrected. "Harper's staking out his place right now. The guy isn't home, but we know where he'll be at 1:00 p.m. today. He gives a computer class at the West Chester library on Wednesdays. I want to be there at the takedown, and I don't want to leave you here, in case we somehow miss him. In case the reason he's not home is that he's figured out where you are and he's on his way here. Any number of complications can come up. Until he's behind bars, I want to make sure that you're safe."

And she'd need to be in Broslin to positively identify Gregory as the man who'd bought her that second drink in any case, she thought and nodded. "When do we have to leave?"

"The sooner the better."

Aunt Hilda was shuffling forward from her bedroom. "Good morning."

Chase filled her in while Luanne went upstairs to wake the girls.

Chapter Ten

After a teary good-bye with Aunt Hilda, and promises to visit again as soon as possible, Luanne drove home with the twins, Chase right behind her in his own car the entire trip. He followed her straight to her house, went in first to make sure it was safe, then helped her move her bags and the girls in.

He took Luanne's hands and made her look at him. "I want you to stay at my place. If we don't catch Gregory today, I'm going to ask the captain to put me on around-the-clock protection detail," he said. "If that happens, I want you guys to move in with me. Bigger house, better security system, meaning that I actually have one. I'd like to take you there right now, after you pick up clean clothes. I want you to stay until the takedown is over. And if we don't catch Gregory today, I want you to stay with me until we do."

He glanced at the threadbare, narrow couch. The house had only two bedrooms. At his place, at least he could sleep in his own bed. And he wouldn't have to fight her about buying groceries. He had a full fridge and full kitchen cabinets, while hers were mostly empty.

She didn't look excited about his plan. She watched him, completely still as she considered his words, the twins running for the TV, ready for their cartoons after the long drive.

He stepped forward. Brushed his lips against Luanne's. "I'll call my mom to come over while I'm in West Chester. She'll love the girls. She knows where everything is. And I don't want you to be alone. Just in case. Not that I think anyone would look for you at my place."

"It seems weird," she said at long last. "Not that I don't trust you," she added quickly. "But what would people think?"

"They'd think I'm trying to protect you." He raised a challenging eyebrow. "Or I could take you into protective custody."

She put her hands on her hips, staring him down. "I'm not moving to the police station with the twins."

"Then move in with me. For good. Or just until the danger is over. I'll take what I can get."

* * *

Luanne couldn't even think about the *for good* part at the moment. So she focused on the rest. "All right. If Gregory doesn't show up for his class and you don't take him into custody today, we'll move in with you until you catch him."

A slow smile spread on Chase's face. Then he reached for his phone. "I'll call mom so you won't be alone while I'm gone."

"Wait." She was so not ready to spend an afternoon with Chase's mother. She could only imagine the questions about their time in Petersburg.

"We'll go to Jen's while you're at the takedown," she said quickly. "Billy will be home. He works the night shift this week. And the girls missed Bobby."

Chase took her hand, his gaze suddenly gentle. "Don't run from me again."

"I'm not running. I just need girlfriend support. I swear."

He didn't look happy about her choice, but he nodded. "All right, let's go."

The twins protested when Luanne turned off the TV, but as soon as she told them they were going to see Bobby, they were ready to roll. Chase drove them over, left her on the front stoop with a brief but thorough kiss, then headed to West Chester.

"Oh my God, is it hot in here?" Jen grinned and fanned herself with her hand when Luanne walked inside. "I saw that. When did this happen?"

"I don't even know what's going on." Luanne shook her head.

"I want details. Sex?"

Luanne glanced at the kids, already at the toy chest at the far end of the living room, lost in play. "I'm not going to discuss it."

"No fair!" Jen cried. "Just because I said something that *one* time! I said I was sorry. Good grief, years ago. I'm begging you."

"Amazing." And that was all Luanne was going to say about that. She stuck to her guns, even as Jen tried to pump her for information for the next half hour while they had coffee.

When she realized she wasn't going to get details, Jen switched to another topic. "So what's with the running off and the coming back? Any progress in the case?"

Luanne wasn't sure how much she was authorized to say. "They found Gregory in West Chester. If all goes well, they're going to grab him this afternoon."

Jen pressed a hand against her chest, listening in fascinated horror. "Wow. Just like on TV."

"What's like on TV?" her husband asked from the stairs. Billy was padding down barefooted, hair sticking up every which way. He must have gone straight to bed after his night shift and was just getting up for the day.

"The police got the guy who killed Earl. I mean, they're getting him today." Jen shot to her feet. "I'm glad that's over. It's been nerve-racking to think there's a killer out there, right in the neighborhood."

Her husband grabbed her ass and squeezed as he passed her.

Jen smiled at him. "We don't have any butter. We'll need that for dinner."

"I'll run out," he volunteered immediately.

"Thanks. And grab some milk?"

Jen came back to Luanne on the couch, while Billy went to the door to pull on his sneakers. "Anything else? Last chance."

Jen flashed him a brilliant smile. "That's it."

"Are you nervous?" she asked Luanne once Billy left.

Luanne thought for a second before answering. "Not for myself. I don't think Gregory knows that I'm even back in town. I'm nervous about Chase and the other officers. What if there's a shootout?"

Jen patted her knee. "They train for that. Come on, I'll distract you. I want to show you something. Come upstairs with me for a second."

Luanne carried her coffee mug as she followed her friend up the stairs, into the master bedroom. "New curtains?"

"That too," Jen said and opened the top dresser drawer. Then she pulled a gun and pointed it at Luanne. "Close the door behind you."

"What? Wait…" Luanne set the mug on the dresser next to her, shock making her movements stiff. "What are you doing? If this is a joke—"

But Jen's hard expression said she wasn't joking. The harsh lines on her face transformed her from a friend to a stranger. "I'm sorry. I don't have another choice. You have to be dead before Gregory is captured. That way the cops can think that he killed you. Like he killed Earl."

"What are you talking about?" Luanne wanted the world to stop for just one darn second until she could catch up to what was happening.

Jen pressed her lips together. "You were supposed to go to jail. Just for a few years."

The thought slamming into Luanne's head was wild and crazy, but nothing else made sense. "You killed Earl?"

"I had no choice," Jen said matter-of-factly, as if murder was completely normal.

"Can we talk about this?"

"I have to be done by the time Billy comes back." She was as calm as if they were talking about dinner.

"Why did you kill Earl?" Luanne still couldn't make any sense of anything. She felt like she'd been sucked into a parallel universe.

Jen's eyes turned cold. "He threatened to take Bobby away if I didn't sleep with him again."

"You had sex with Earl?" Jen had quit the motel after Bobby was born. "Did Earl push you into sleeping with him?" Luanne's heart sank. "You never said anything."

Jen looked away for a split second. "I couldn't. I didn't want Billy to find out. I got pregnant. We've been trying for so long. Billy was so happy."

She swallowed hard. "I ran into Earl at the store a couple of weeks ago. He took one look at Bobby and figured out that Bobby was his. He followed me to my car in the parking lot, told me if I didn't sleep with him again, he was going to sue for custody of *his* son." Pain filled her voice. "It would have broken Billy's heart."

Even with Jen holding a gun on her, Luanne's heart went out to her friend. "You have to talk to the police. He raped you. He blackmailed you. There are extenuating circumstances."

But Jen shook her head stubbornly, her mouth set in a narrow line.

Luanne couldn't think. So she blurted out the screaming question that banged around in her mind. "Why me? Why did you set me up?"

"For the girls." Jen's expression softened a shade as she put her other hand on the gun, keeping it aimed. "I wanted babies so much, for so long. I wanted daughters. And there you were, two perfect little girls dropped on your lap without you having to do anything for it. No hormone injections, no painful fertility treatments, no surgeries. No difficult pregnancy, no twenty hours of labor."

Luanne stared. She'd never known how much all that had affected Jen. She'd never even suspected.

"If you went to prison, I would have offered to raise Mia and Daisy. You wouldn't have wanted them to go to the foster system. I would have adopted them." Jen smiled confidently, her eyes remaining cold. "I'm going to adopt them now. They already know me. Social Services is going to take that into consideration."

Luanne was still half in denial as her brain churned. "You put a roofie in my soda Friday night before I went to the bar."

"I didn't want you to remember what happened."

"How did you know Brett wouldn't show?"

"I made up Brett." Jen gave a smug smile. "Fake Facebook account."

The sense of betrayal was staggering. Luanne had a hard time catching up with reality. Come to think of it, she'd been doing that a lot lately. She stared at the woman she'd thought was her best friend. Just... Unreal... No other word for it.

All those times she'd spent talking about Brett to Jen, getting her hopes up that she'd found a decent guy. While Jen was probably silently laughing her ass off.

Behind the fear and betrayal, anger gathered. "Where did you get the drug?"

"Billy got it for his back injury when we went to Ireland to visit his grandmother."

Such a simple answer. Why hadn't she thought of that? Then another question popped into Luanne's head. "You left the kids home alone and came to the bar after me?"

"I would never leave the kids home alone," Jen shot back with her voice full of heat, clearly offended at the suggestion that she was a bad mother. "Billy had the night off."

And, of course, Jen knew about Luanne's little back-alley fantasy about Earl. She'd mentioned it a time or two when Earl had pushed her to the edge. "I thought you were my friend."

Jen snorted. "Yeah. A good friend you are. We were supposed to go off to college together. You chose your loony mother over me and stayed home. Then when I came home, married Billy, and had Bobby, needed your support here, you skipped off to college. You only came home because of the twins."

Jen's voice grew colder with each word as she continued. "I just want the girls. If you got convicted, you would have gone away for a few years. You've worked so hard for so long. It would have been a break. People can even go to college while they're in prison."

Okay, so the woman was completely delusional. Her best friend was seriously off her rocker, and Luanne had so little time to socialize, so little time and energy to spend even with her best friend, that she'd never noticed.

How much had they even talked? Five minutes when she dropped off and picked up the girls. Less if she was running late.

"Don't do this," she begged. "We can explain Earl. The police already know he abused the staff. But you're not going to be able to explain away killing me in cold blood."

"I want the girls," Jen repeated, her eyes unblinking, her hand dead steady on the cold, unforgiving weapon.

* * *

Harper had a search warrant for Gregory's apartment, so the quickly put-together joint Broslin PD–West Chester PD team went there first. They had time before the 1:00 p.m. class at the library.

Gregory still wasn't home. And they couldn't find anything incriminating at his place either—nothing to tie him to Earl, nothing to tie him to Luanne. As far as Chase could tell, the suspect was a single guy, between jobs, volunteering once a week at the library.

No history of previous violence. The only reason he was in the fingerprint database was that he'd taught computer classes at various summer camps, and he'd had criminal background checks to qualify for that.

They sealed the place anyway. One of the West Chester officers—round, bald, serious as a sledgehammer—stayed behind in case Gregory showed up here instead of going to class. The rest of the team went to the library and waited in the community room.

When Gregory arrived, ten minutes early, they took him into custody without a hint of trouble, transported him straight to the Broslin police station, with West Chester PD's full cooperation.

"Why did you kill Earl Cosgrove?" Chase grilled him when he finally got the man in the interrogation room with Harper.

129

In his midthirties, brown hair, brown eyes, Gregory was sweating bullets, had already sweated through his tan, button-down shirt. His eyes, filled with confusion and fear, darted from Chase to Harper, then back. "I swear I don't know what you're talking about."

Hell of a thing was, Chase could swear he was telling the truth. The man displayed none of the telltale signs of lying, his gaze frightened but direct, the desperation in his voice authentic. Chase exchanged a glance with Harper.

"Why did you set up Luanne Mayfair? Why her? How do you know her?"

"Who?" Gregory squinted.

"You targeted her at Finnegan's two weeks ago, drugged her drink so you could take control of her car," Chase snapped, losing his legendary patience at last.

"That blonde at the bar?" Gregory shook his head frantically, his eyes begging them to believe him. "No way. I talked to her for like ten minutes. She was completely wasted. Looked good one second, then cross-eyed the next. When I walked up to her, I didn't realize how far gone she was. She wanted to go home. The night was a total bust. I left a minute after her."

"And grabbed her by her car in the parking lot?" Harper demanded.

"No, man. I swear. Her girlfriend was driving her home. I was actually glad to see that. Luanne was in no shape to get behind the wheel."

Chase exchanged another look with Harper. "What girlfriend?"

"Tall redhead. She was waiting for her in the parking lot. Roundest ass you've ever seen. I was thinking I wished she was in the bar earlier."

"Jen," Chase told Harper, and took off running.

* * *

Luanne could see the handle of a baseball bat under the bed, probably Billy's. She took half a step that way, her heart trying to beat its way out of her chest as panic filled her. She was seriously close to hyperventilating.

"You tried to kill me. The moving van, the grate, the grocery store. How?"

"Billy was watching the kids. I told him I had to run out for something." Jen shrugged. "I didn't do the grate. Someone probably stole that for scrap metal."

Luanne had no idea how to handle the situation. What did you do when your best friend turned into a homicidal maniac?

What would Chase do?

He'd stay calm, for starters.

"I want the girls to know about me." She stalled. "I don't want them to forget me. You'll be their mother, but I want them to know that I was their sister. They should have roots."

"Of course."

"We got a box of family pictures from Aunt Hilda."

"I'll bring those over."

"And you can't let Mia run roughshod over Daisy. Daisy has to be heard too."

"I already know that. I spend as much time with them as you do," Jen said defensively.

That she was right filled Luanne with guilt. She pushed that aside. She was done with people bullying her with guilt. She needed to concentrate on survival. "Do we have to do this here? The shot will scare them. I don't want them to be scared. Couldn't we do it in the garage? You don't want that kind of mess in your bedroom."

"Why would you be in the garage? This makes more sense. You had a headache. You lay down. Gregory came in through the window."

"How did he find me?"

"He followed you from home."

"Chase would have seen him."

"Nobody is infallible." Jen was surprisingly calm, making it all up as she went. She was determined to get the girls and had committed to the cause.

Stall. "How did he get up to the second-floor window?" Luanne asked, shifting another half a step closer to the bed.

"I'll put up the ladder later." Jen adjusted her finger on the trigger. "I don't want to drag this out. Billy will be back in a minute. I'm sorry," she said again.

Luanne dove for the bed in the same second as Jen squeezed off a shot.

Chase's voice filled the house the next instant, coming from outside, magnified by a bullhorn: "Jen O'Brian, come out with your hands in the air. We already have the children here safely."

"Leave my kids alone!" Jen screamed and ran out of the room, thundering down the stairs.

Luanne stayed where she was, heart racing, limbs shaking, half under the bed, clutching the baseball bat. *Sweet Jesus. Did that just happen?*

"Drop your weapon! Drop your weapon!" multiple voices shouted outside.

Then, a minute later, footsteps on the stairs, then Chase skidded into the room, dove for her, pulled her onto his lap, checked her over, his hands moving over her, following his darting gaze, his voice thick as he asked the single question: "Are you hurt?"

His gaze hung on her face as if his life depended on her answer.

"Only my pride." Her heart pounded. "The kids?"

He touched his forehead against hers, grunting with relief. "Sitting in the back of my car, playing bank robbers."

The last of the tension ran out of her. *Oh, thank God.* Her knees began to shake. How stupid was that, now that the scare was all over? Yet when she tried to push to her feet, she couldn't quite stand.

Chase stashed his gun back in his shoulder holster and stood, pulling her up, then tugged her into his arms, against his mile-wide chest.

She snuggled her face into the crook of his neck, her heart still beating wildly.

"That little adventure just shaved ten years off my life," he said, his tone rough. "Don't ever do that again."

"I promise not to be held at gunpoint by a psychopathic friend." She groaned. "I can't believe I missed all the signs. How could I suspect nothing?"

He pressed his lips to the top of her head. "It's not how your mind works. You're not criminally insane."

His radio crackled, a disembodied voice telling people to stand down. They had the suspect in custody.

Luanne wrapped her shaking arms around Chase. "Thank you for coming for us." Drew her lungs full. "It's over now, right? All the way. I'll be cleared of the charges?"

He nodded. "I still want you and the girls to move in with me."

"We're not in danger."

"In a proper family, the mother and the father live together."

Her head snapped up, and she stared at him.

"I like your voice," he said with a lopsided smile. "It's all velvety and stuff. Gets under my skin. Makes me think dirty thoughts, to be honest."

"You're marrying me because you like my voice?"

"You have other positive attributes."

"Such as?"

"Fantastic boobs."

She narrowed her eyes at him. "Chase Mortimer M—"

He kissed her. Lingered endlessly because, hey, when did he ever do anything in a hurry? He didn't pull back until her brain was mush.

"I love you. We're getting married," he said mildly in that easygoing way of his. "I've already waited nearly an entire damned decade. I'm a patient man, but I'm not going to wait endlessly."

"But…" She stammered.

"But what?"

"It's so fast."

He growled. "When I went slow, you wanted fast. Now I'm going fast, you want slow. Luanne Mayfair, are you trying to drive me crazy on purpose, or is it just a lucky side benefit as far as you're concerned?"

Good grief, this day was turning out to be a doozy. She kept staring at him, her brain just plain overloaded.

He muttered something about "womanly mysteries."

"We haven't even dated yet." She frowned. "You haven't even proposed."

A lazy smile twitched the corner of his lips. "I thought you didn't like to drag things out."

Huh. She drew up an eyebrow. "If we're getting married, you better not get into the habit of using my own words against me."

"Definitely not on my list of habits I'm aiming to develop," he promised.

"What habits *are* you aiming to develop?"

He leaned forward and dragged his lips against hers. "The habit of seducing my wife daily." He picked her up into his arms. "The habit of spoiling her rotten." And as he walked down the stairs, he listed a few more titillating others.

Epilogue

They were married at Broslin Chapel, two months later, the first Saturday the chapel was available. Jen was in jail awaiting trial. The judge had refused bail. Billy's mother had moved in with them to take care of Bobby, the entire family bewildered by Jen's actions.

They didn't come to the wedding, but half of Broslin was there. Mia and Daisy sat in the first row, between Chase's mother and Aunt Hilda, beaming from one woman to the other. Two grandmothers! For them, it was an embarrassment of riches.

Of course, Mia and Chase's mom were talking to each other in hushed tones, keeping a running commentary. Anyone who didn't know better would think they were related. Two peas in a pod. Daisy was holding Aunt Hilda's hand, a beatific smile on her face, radiating quiet happiness.

Behind them, the Broslin PD filled up the entire pew, with girlfriends and spouses. Quite a few men in the chapel kept their eye on the new officer, the only female on the force, Gabriela Maria Flores, an inner-city cop Captain Bing had recently brought in.

She looked ridiculously beautiful without makeup and in a shapeless uniform. Seriously, with her height and cheekbones, the woman looked like she could sell Armani on a runway and kick ass while doing it.

"You may kiss the bride," the minister said, and that was the last thing Luanne heard for a while, because the next second Chase's lips sealed hers, and the world disappeared.

The man didn't do anything halfway. Or hurried. She had no idea how much time passed before whistles and catcalls and shouted suggestions to get a room finally reached her consciousness. She pulled back, her face flushing. Chase didn't seem the least abashed, on the other hand. A satisfied expression filled his handsome face.

"I love you, Mrs. Merritt," he said.

"I love you, Mr. Merritt." Her heart was full of him to bursting.

Before she knew what was going on, they were outside, showered with cheers, well-wishes, and rose petals. She'd vetoed the rice. Just couldn't see food going to waste.

Chase escorted her to his decked-out police cruiser, the hood covered with white roses. Instead of rattling cans, somebody had tied two dozen handcuffs to the bumper.

She winced. She'd come too close to those for comfort. It'd be a while before they were funny for her. The judge had only recently decided not to try her for tampering with evidence. Crashing the Mustang hadn't been her brightest idea ever. Her all-around exemplary behavior and volunteer record had luckily been considered as mitigating factors.

Chase was grinning at the handcuffs. Of course, he would be.

"Put them to good use!" a voice called from the crowd, Joe Kessler, Broslin's very own ex-football-hero, now another detective at the Broslin PD.

"What do you think I am, a centipede?" Chase called back, and the crowd broke out in laughter. Then he added, "If you have to tie your woman down so she doesn't run away, you're doing something wrong, buddy." And people laughed harder.

Then she was finally in the car, and Chase was pulling away from the curb, the whole scene like a fairy tale. Well, minus the rattling handcuffs. The Grimm brothers had somehow missed that.

Luanne was ridiculously happy, the kind of happiness she hadn't even known existed, looking at Chase more than at their surroundings, all choked up and giddy. She kicked off her shoes that pinched a little, then gave a contented sigh. Her happiness was perfect.

"Sexy shoes," Chase observed, stealing a glance at her bare feet. Every toenail was a different color, the twins' contribution to getting her ready for her big day.

"Leila helped me pick them out." Four-inch heels, the color a silvery, shimmery wonder that made her feel like she was wearing glass slippers. Unfortunately, they were about as comfortable. "I think they're giving me blisters."

Chase shook his head. "Word to the wise. Leila isn't exactly an expert on sensible footwear. Steer away from her, or you'll be wearing something pink and furry someday with a hammer claw for heels."

She laughed at the image.

"I'm not joking."

"I know. That makes it even funnier."

He drove to their new home, a splendid four-bedroom Victorian bought from Murph Dolan, a former Broslin police officer. The house had a brand-new kitchen, brand-new flooring, new bathrooms, new everything. Murph had begun the renovations, then one of Chase's contractor friends finished it.

"Murph is so going to regret that he sold this house when he sees it," she said as Chase turned off the engine.

Murph had followed the woman he'd fallen in love with into the witness protection program.

Aunt Hilda bought the fixer-upper when she'd moved to Broslin. The deal was, instead of going to a home, she'd get to live with Luanne and the girls. She insisted on buying a house, however, for them. Chase insisted on paying for the renovations since he was to live there as well, his bachelor pad not suitable for a large family.

"Murph is going to have his hands full," Chase said as he came around and lifted her out of her seat so she wouldn't have to put her shoes back on. He strode up the path with her to their gleaming new front door, with a little more hurry than his usual speed. "I'm glad he could come back. And that's the last we're going to talk about him today."

With the assassin eliminated by Interpol, Murph and Kate were returning to town. They'd purchased twenty acres from Captain Bing's old family farm and were building a rehab facility for soldiers with PTSD, called Hope Hill Acres. Big news for a small town like Broslin. New jobs. The facilities were already being built, along with housing for Murph and Kate so they could be in the middle of it all, overseeing the operations.

"Maybe I can get a job at Hope Hill when they get going. You think you could ask Murph?"

Chase opened the door and carried her over the threshold. "If you say Murph one more time, I'm going to be seriously jealous."

Luanne grinned, loving the feel of his strong arms around her. "Can you give me an example of what jealousy might make you do?"

He stepped inside, his eyes narrowing. "It could make me lose my mind and mercilessly ravish you this instant."

"That Murph sure is a handsome fellow," she said.

He carried her forward without another word.

"The kitchen island? Wait!" She squealed as he deposited her in the middle, pushed her knees apart, and stood between them, catching her face in his large hands.

"It's a great island," he said, his voice thick. "Nothing wrong with it. For any purpose. Hell of a nice kitchen. We're going to have all our family meals here."

"Right after I disinfect the counters," she whispered, her voice suddenly weakening from his intent gaze.

"Yeah, well." He flashed a lopsided smile. "We all know what a terror you are with the spray bottle."

"Don't you forget it." She stared at his lips, inches from hers. "This house will be sanitary or else."

His blue gaze deepened to nearly black. "I don't suppose I could talk you into one of those little French maid outfits." His voice was a ragged breath.

She couldn't breathe at all, thinking about him peeling that French maid outfit off her. "We could negotiate."

He growled.

She swallowed. "The girls and I have been talking about a puppy."

"Pound. Eight a.m. tomorrow morning. It's a date." And then he held her face with one hand while he ravaged her mouth, his other hand shoving her dress all the way up to her waist.

Ooh.

The next second, his large hands were on her butt, and he pulled her hard against him, her most sensitive parts pressed against the impressive bulge in his tuxedo. And then the next second after that, everything was tingling, heat and need flooding through her body in waves.

His mouth mastered hers, claiming everything she had to give, while she peeled off his jacket and the cummerbund with fumbling fingers.

He didn't fumble whatsoever. He pushed the straps of her wedding gown down her shoulders slowly, tracking kisses over to the crook of her neck, then lower.

He had this maddening hot method where he'd drag his lips over her skin first, lick it next, then rake his teeth against the sensitized skin while nibbling and tasting her. Her nerve endings were approaching total sensory overload with frightening speed.

Then he gently pushed his questing fingers into the cups of her dress, and with one smooth move popped her breasts free, the material supporting them from below lifting them for his lips. He looked, his dark blue eyes more intense than they'd ever been, for an endless moment, then he buried his face between her breasts and inhaled. "God, I love you. Just in every possible way."

She kissed the top of his head and made unintelligible noises, way past the ability to form words.

He seduced her left nipple with his hot mouth while he teased the right nipple with his fingers. His free hand worked on pushing his pants down. Then his erection sprang free and pressed between her legs, and she felt her body grow moist and ready for him.

She tried to wiggle out of her scrap of white lace underwear, but she had trouble reaching the silk, the voluminous folds of her dress blocking her efforts.

"No," Chase said, pulling back a little. "I want to see that thing before we get rid of it." He gently pushed her onto her back.

Her boobs bare and pointing to the ceiling, her legs hanging off the edge of the kitchen island with a very naked and hard Chase between them, she was so aroused she thought she might come just from him looking at her. And, oh, he was looking, his gaze darkening as he reached out to trace the lacy silk.

Shivers of pleasure ran through her. His lips twisted into a slow, lopsided smile. He placed his warm palm between her legs and cupped her, rubbing, applying pressure. She gritted her teeth so she wouldn't beg him to hurry, because she was beginning to understand just how good slow could be.

When he had her so worked up that she was writhing under his hand, he removed it, then pulled her panties off at last. *Oh, thank heaven. Now,* she thought. She wanted to feel him inside her, his hard length stretching her.

Instead, he caught her feet, brought them up, kissed her toes, kissed, licked, nibbled his way up her inner thigh. Then he licked deeper and gave her release at last, pleasure pulsing through her in waves.

"Look at me," he said roughly, and she did, melting from the heat in his gaze, her body still contracting.

He lifted her legs, resting her heels on his shoulders, then took care of protection and positioned the tip of his erection at her opening at last. She wasn't sure if she had it in her to go for another ride.

Impossible. Not so soon. She needed a few days to recover.

Or not, she thought as he slowly pushed inside her and stretched her, filled her, setting her nerve endings afire all over again.

He held her gaze, fierce concentration on his face. The love and passion in his eyes made her heart sing. And then he moved, and she lost herself to him completely.

Much later, when she lay breathless and naked on the kitchen island, Chase came up on his elbow next to her. "You can't work for Murph."

She rolled her eyes. "You can't be seriously jealous."

He kissed her brow. "I could be, but not because of that." He hesitated. "I'm going to tell you a secret. But when my mother and Aunt Hilda bring it up, act surprised."

"Should I be worried?"

"They bought the motel."

"What?" She bolted to a sitting position.

"Mom's been itching to invest in something locally. Aunt Hilda jumped on board as a silent partner. She'd had her husband's life insurance money stashed away all these years."

"That much?" Luanne couldn't even visualize anybody having enough money to buy an entire motel. Ever.

"They want you to be the general manager. Since you know how the place is run. If you ask, probably all the old employees will come back."

She stared. She seemed to be doing a lot of that around Chase. Just once, she wanted to have him say something and have herself respond with her intelligent face instead of gaping.

"The job comes with tuition reimbursement," he said.

She blinked, completely overwhelmed. Didn't look like she was going to find her intelligent face anytime in the near future.

"You can finish that business degree right here at WCU if you want. We have a bushel of grandmothers eager to babysit the girls." He grinned. "They didn't want to tell you before the wedding so you don't start worrying about details and can just focus on our big day. Mom wants to babysit the girls while you work. She's jealous that Grandma Hilda lives with us and has more access to Mia and Daisy."

Her head spun. "I need to think about this."

"Not today you don't. We have a tight schedule." He picked her up and carried her up the stairs. "I'm planning on seducing you at least one more time before the reception."

And he did. Slowly and deliberately. All the way. And then some. As only Chase could. Making it last forever and ever.

And when he was done liquefying her bones, and Luanne jokingly asked, "That was it?" he did it again.

THE END

--Thank you so much for reading my books! I really hope you enjoyed Murph and Luanne's story. If you have a second, would you please consider leaving an online review? Even a sentence or two would be hugely helpful to me. Thank you!!! Dana

www.danamarton.com
First Edition: June 2014

BROSLIN CREEK SERIES
Deathwatch
Deathscape
Deathtrap
Deathblow
Broslin Bride

GUARDIAN AGENT

A Novella

BY

DANA MARTON

I dedicate this story to Jenel Looney, a truly extraordinary person and the best friend anyone could ever wish for.

Agents Under Fire

GUARDIAN AGENT

AVENGING AGENT

WARRIOR AGENT

"... started with a bang and the tension never let up. Marton is an accomplished thriller writer, and it shows. Every time I promised myself I'd stop and turn out the light, I kept reading just one more page..."
Paula Graves, national bestselling author (about GUARDIAN AGENT)

Chapter One

Dark waters lapped the century-old palace's foundation, eager to claim the forgotten building on one of Venice's backstreet canals. At four in the February morning, tourists still partied on in the distance, drunk on love, youth and full-bodied Italian wine.

Gabe Cannon could hear both the water and the faint beat of the music, but he couldn't hear the half dozen men in the building with him. His new commando team spread out like ghosts moving through the night.

"Target on the roof," the team leader's voice whispered in his earpiece.

He stole up the crumbling stairs, ready for the rogue soldier who needed to be brought in before he caused more damage. He'd known Jake Tekla ten years ago in the army--a decent guy back then, but war could change a person, could even twist a man's mind.

Static hissed in his earpiece before the words, "Kill order authorized. Repeat, authorized to shoot on sight."

His instincts prickled. Standard procedure called for an attempt to capture first, and see what information they could gain during interrogation. Usable intelligence trumped a quick kill, every time. Then again, he worked for a private security firm now: XO-ST. Xtreme Ops Shadow Teams. They did things differently than his previous employers, the U.S. Army and the FBI.

Gabe reached the roof. Plywood patches formed a psychedelic pattern in the moonlight—an unexpected break. Not having to sneak around on crumbling Mediterranean roof tiles would make this much easier. He stole forward and eased into the cover of a crooked chimney stack.

He caught a silent shadow at the door he'd come through--Troy, one of his teammates, joining him. Odd how Gabe had been last into the building, but first on the roof. Maybe the others had pulled back on purpose, testing the new guy. Another person might have been annoyed, but he'd expected this much. He wasn't afraid of having to earn his stripes.

Dormers, chimneys and ridges blocked visibility. Clouds kept drifting across the moon. *Scan. Move forward._Take cover.* A night game of hide and seek in a labyrinth, with a fair chance that the ramshackle roof could open up under his feet any minute.

Then he stole around a dormer and spotted the target at last. Jake Tekla blended into the night in black fatigues, similar to Gabe's, black ski mask in place. He looked much slighter than Gabe remembered. Being on the run had taken its toll on him. The man crept toward the edge of the roof, his focus on the jump he was considering.

No visible weapons.

Yet another thing that didn't add up. Not for a government-trained, seasoned soldier.

Gabe inched closer, watching for a trap. He flicked the safety off his gun. *Come on. Turn.* He moved another step closer then stopped with his feet apart, gun raised, silencer in place.

His target sensed him at last and spun around.

Oh, hell.

Gabe caught the curve of a breast in the moonlight, and his finger froze on the trigger as he stared at the *woman*.

She could be a trap--Tekla's accomplice or a decoy.

He had a kill order.

Most of the men he worked with squeezed the trigger each and every time, preferring to err on the safe side. He'd been like that once. A muscle jumped in his cheek. He pushed the North Village incident from his mind.

The woman stared at him for a moment, then her instincts kicked in and she ran. Or tried. He lunged after her, caught up in three leaps and brought her down hard. She was lean, yet soft, every inch unmistakably feminine. But none of that feminine softness showed in her fighting spirit. She shoved against him with all she had. She had to know she was conquered, yet she refused to yield, stirring some of his base instincts.

"Stop," he hissed the single word into her ear as he did his best to subdue her.

Plywood gave an ominous creak on the other side of the ridge-- the team moving into position to cover the roof and inspect all its nooks and crannies. Something stopped Gabe from calling out even as the woman did her best to scratch his eyes out, fighting in silence. Enough small things about this op had triggered alarms in his mind for him to want to see what he had here before he called the rest of the team in.

He patted her down one-handed, although if she had a knife she would have probably used it on him by now. He kept his voice low. "Did Tekla send you?"

She tried to buck him off. He managed to hold her down with one hand and ripped her black mask off with the other. Wavy dark hair tumbled free, eyes going wide with panic even as her full lips snarled. Despite the semidarkness, he couldn't miss her beauty, or the fact that she had Tekla's eyes and nose.

"Who are you?" he asked, even as the answer was already forming in his mind.

The man had two sisters, the younger one a teenager and the other somewhat older. The one under Gabe now was all woman and then some. *Definitely not the teenage sister.* He'd met both once at the airport when he and Tekla had gone home on a short leave over Christmas, back in their army days. They didn't have parents, he remembered suddenly. Tekla had enlisted so he could support what was left of his family.

What in hell was his sister doing on the roof? No way his team's intel could be so bad on an op like this. They weren't fighting in the chaos of some distant battle field. The target's sisters were supposed to be living with a distant aunt in Arkansas, according to the op files.

His mind ran all the options as he pressed her down a little harder to keep her still. He wanted to believe that Brent Foley, the team leader, hadn't known who she was when he'd given the kill order, but being naïve didn't pay in this business.

But if Brent did know... Eliminating one of Tekla's sisters might push the guy over the edge, bring him out into the open as he came in for revenge. XO-ST's small army for hire consisted of ex-soldiers and ex-agents, conducting outsourced ops for the U.S. government and anyone else who could meet their price. Brent wrote the book on how to reach goals by whatever means necessary.

Except, Gabe hadn't signed on to kill innocent women, no matter how badly he needed the money. He motioned to her to stay down and stay quiet, then eased his body off her a little so she could breathe.

"Is he here?" he whispered.

After another spirited minute of resistance, her muscles went slack and she lay there, breathing hard, despair filling her eyes. She shook her head.

He pulled up all the way. Her gaze slid to his gun, and she swallowed, her body stiffening. Fear came onto her face, that wide-eyed look of people who know they are about to die. She didn't beg, nor did she offer her brother's life for her own. She simply met Gabe's gaze and lifted her chin.

She still looked impossibly young, although he figured she had to be around twenty-six or twenty-seven by now. Her slim body might have looked fragile next to his, but her eyes shone with defiance. That attitude wouldn't be enough, not with a kill order in place and a team of mercenaries spread out around them.

"I'll come back." He pulled a plastic cuff and, with one smooth move, secured her to the iron scroll that decorated the roof's edge.

He switched on his mouthpiece as he turned from her, ignoring her silent struggle. "Target escaped the roof. East end."

He ran along the edge toward the other side where a six-foot gap separated the old palace from the next building. Dark shapes materialized from the shadows. He jumped without giving the steep drop below him much thought. As expected, his clear purpose and energy drew the rest of the team behind him.

He dashed forward as if he could see a man's disappearing back somewhere up ahead. He didn't slow for twenty minutes and several rooftops later. Then he braced against the edge of the roof as he stared down onto a dark, abandoned bridge below him. "Lost visual contact."

A four-letter word came through his headset, followed by, "Did he look hurt?"

"No."

"I could have sworn I clipped him before we lost him last week." A moment of silence. "Spread out."

As the team scattered, Gabe made his way back to the old palace, trying to think of the woman's name, not expecting much after ten years, surprised when it did pop into his brain: *Jasmine.*

A simple plan formed in his mind as he walked. She was going to take him to Tekla.

He would bring the man in himself, making sure she didn't get hurt in the process. Things could get out of hand when a cornered person was confronted with an entire commando team.

For all he knew, the other sister was here, too. His jaw muscles tightened. He had no respect for a man who would use his sisters as a shield. Gabe vaulted from roof to roof, watching out for crumbling edges.

If he could complete the mission without bloodshed, he wanted to give it a try. Maybe saving a few lives, after having taken so many, would even the scales a little.

Except, he found the palace roof empty.

He stared at the sawed through plastic cuff next to a shattered roof tile and its sharp shards. He should have thought of that, dammit. Anger coursed through him as he moved to look over the edge, not seeing her anywhere below.

A few hardy tourists strolled the sidewalks, out doing the whole 'Venice by starlight' thing. He considered going down among them, even as he knew it would be futile. She could be anywhere by now.

Closer to the city center, St. Mark's Square and the areas around the major hotels, would be even busier. A lot of visitors had arrived for the famous Carnival that would start next week. They enjoyed taking their fancy costumes out for a test drive. He would never find her tonight.

He'd underestimated her. She wouldn't be easily defeated. Of course, she was trying to protect her brother, which he respected, but he *was* going to bring Tekla in.

He needed the money badly. Lives depended on it.

Chapter Two

Jasmine hurried along the Grand Canal, dodging a group of die-hard revelers, glancing back over her shoulder for the hundredth time. She couldn't see Gabe Cannon anywhere.

Her teenage fantasy man was hunting her brother. She sure hadn't seen that coming. Freaking surreal.

He looked just as good as when she'd first met him at that airport and had fallen instantly in love over pizza and chips. One of those unavoidable pitfalls of life, really. He'd been more handsome than any of her pop idols, and her teenage emotions had been just begging for an outlet.

She cringed in embarrassment when she thought of all the melodramatic drivel she'd written about him in her high school diary.

His dark hair was a little longer now and his face had developed a few more hard edges, but the sight of him could still knock the air from her lungs. He probably didn't even recognize her. Last time he'd seen her, she'd been a gangly teenager with braces.

"Permesso." Jasmine moved around an older woman who held half-dozen poodles on leashes, barely registering the dogs, her mind on other things.

Gabe Cannon could have killed her on that roof.

She reached the next bridge and touched the wing of the carved angel on the right post in a silent prayer, as she did every time she passed through here. She needed a guardian angel and badly. And maybe she had one. Maybe he'd been looking out for her tonight.

That Gabe hadn't handed her over to his team was nothing short of a miracle. She'd broken free, thanks to some quick thinking. "You are never unarmed," her brother had taught her shortly after they'd gone on the run. "Everything around you can be used either as a tool or a weapon."

Of course, Gabe could have meant for her to escape. Maybe he thought he could follow her from a distance. Good luck with that. She'd become a master of evasion in the last few weeks, learned every island, every canal in the city. With her twists and turns and doubling back, she was confident that she'd shaken him.

One final test, then she could go home and get some sleep.

The canal glistened darkly in the moonlight, leading to the harbor a few blocks ahead where U.S. Congressman Richard Wharton's whale of a yacht bobbed on the waves, overshadowing the smaller vessels around it. She didn't go that far, just past the hideously expensive gondolas and the only slightly less pricey water taxis to catch a *vaporetto*. The water buses, used by locals, were the least expensive way to get around in Venice.

A half-asleep teenager asked her something in the local language as she stepped on board.

"I speak very little Italian. Sorry," Jasmine told her.

The girl turned from her and asked another person.

Jasmine went to stand in the back. She never sat. She preferred to be on her feet, ready to leap and run at short notice. Or leap and swim. Hopefully, not tonight. She didn't like the look of the cold, dark water.

She inspected every person on board from her vantage point. No sign of Gabe.

"Bella Signora, you're an American, si?" A young man in his twenties sidled up to her with an exaggerated smile and an I-want-to-ravish-you look.

She ignored him.

"Antonio show you real good time. I'm very special for ladies. Very confidential. Two hundred American dollars. All night," he added with wide-eyed enthusiasm.

If the situation wasn't so sad, it would have been funny. Since... the incident... she couldn't stand the thought of a man touching her.

"No thanks."

"Are you sure?" He dragged out the last word, probably thinking she just needed encouragement. But when he touched her arm and she flinched, jerking away from him on reflex, he finally got that she meant what she said and moved away from her to look for another potential customer.

She got off at the last stop, Soremo, an out-of-the-way island that once had been famous for its salt warehouses. The giant storage rooms had been divided into small flats at one point, now housing teachers, shop assistants and blue-collar workers--people too busy cranking out a living to pay her much attention.

She slipped through a broken window in the back of an abandoned building and listened. Hearing nothing but the water and rats scurrying in the far corners, she moved to the top floor, careful of the rotting stairs. Between the saltwater and the sea winds, anything not paid attention to quickly deteriorated here.

"It's me," she called out when she reached the door in the very back. And as she opened it, she could see Mandy lower the only gun they had left.

"Did you bring food?" The seventeen year old looked her over with sleepy eyes.

"I do what I promise." Jasmine reached into her shirt and pulled a Panini then the small bunch of bananas she'd snatched while weaving through the streets. She gave a third to Mandy before she went to check on her brother.

"I got antibiotics." She presented the small Ziploc bag that held half a dozen white pills.

"What did you sell for it?" Not even the several days' growth of beard could hide Jake's sunk-in cheeks.

"Nothing." She'd stolen those earlier in the day.

Back when her life had been normal, she used to think the line between right and wrong stood pretty clear, the whole black and white thing. These days she lived in gray, moving toward darker and darker tones every day. If she hadn't sold Jake's backup gun for food weeks ago, she might have shot Gabe on the roof before she recognized him.

She wasn't comfortable with that thought, but she couldn't afford to be caught. Mandy and Jake needed her to take care of things until Jake recovered.

"You have to take Mandy and leave," he said under his breath after he swallowed one of the pills. "It's not safe for you here."

Her muscles stiffened. "It's not safe for us anywhere."

A moment of dark silence passed between them, filled with her nightmarish memories.

Guilt made Jake's face look even gaunter. "I never meant for you to get hurt. But this place isn't any better. I should have taken you someplace else. I can't protect you like this."

He'd taken a bullet the week before. She'd removed the slug with a pair of knitting needles she'd lifted off an old lady at a cafe, but the wound was getting badly infected, immobilizing the whole leg and bringing on fever. That he also had a broken arm from a nasty fall didn't help.

"We're not going anywhere without you," Mandy said around the food in her mouth. Then coughed.

She'd been coughing last night, too. Jasmine shot her a questioning look.

Mandy shrugged. "I think I'm allergic to mold. Or rat poop."

They had plenty of both.

"Are the men still in the city?" Jake asked in a casual tone, shifting on his folded cardboard box bed, keeping his right arm out, careful with the makeshift cast.

Jasmine went back to the stained, ancient mattress she'd salvaged from a dumpster and sat next to her sister, pulling the blanket higher around Mandy's shoulders. The temperature wasn't bad for February—low fifties since the sea tempered the city's climate—but they were far from comfortable without heat.

Sometimes, on moonless nights when nobody would see smoke coming from the window, they burned garbage in a steel barrel that stood next to the last window in the back. Mostly they relied on the sun to warm up the south-facing room during the day, and the thick brick walls to radiate that heat back overnight.

"They were out hunting tonight. I tried to lead them away." Doing her best to impersonate her brother. "At least to the mainland." To the airport in Mestre, to be more specific.

She'd wanted them to think that Jake had gotten on a plane, but they'd caught up with her at the old palace. "Gabe Cannon is with them now."

Jake sat up, his forehead wrinkling as he considered the news. After a long minute, he shook his head. "Don't go anywhere near him. We can't afford to trust anyone at this stage. If they caught you-"

She couldn't bring herself to confess that Gabe already had. A miracle that the night hadn't turned out worse.

About twenty mercenaries were currently hunting them. One team searched the city; the other secured the railroad bridge and Ponte della Liberta, the five kilometers long Liberty Bridge that connected Venice to the mainland for car and bus traffic.

Jasmine swallowed her food without tasting it. She needed to find a way to outsmart those men, and she needed to find it quickly. Today's plan had failed. She would have to come up with something better for tomorrow.

Jake finished his meager ration and hobbled over to a window, looking out into the night. Mandy slid down onto the mattress. Normally, she had the most energy among the three of them. And the biggest mouth. But not tonight.

Jasmine reached out to feel her forehead, then squeezed her eyes shut for a second, a sense of hopelessness washing over her. "You're burning up with fever."

"I'll be fine by morning."

"Why didn't you say anything?" Jake's knuckles turned white, he gripped the windowsill so tight. Didn't take a psychic to figure out that he blamed himself for putting them into this situation.

"I didn't want to be any trouble," Mandy said with a small voice.

The sight of her vivacious, chirpy little sister being beaten down like this just about killed Jasmine.

Jake hobbled over to them and sat on the corner of the mattress. Although he would never say it, his leg couldn't support him longer than a few minutes at a time. He pulled the Ziploc bag from his pocket and passed a pill to Mandy who raised her head and swallowed it obediently.

They both needed so much more than that. Her siblings need real medical care, preferably a hospital and the sooner, the better.

Jake lay down and gathered Mandy to him, his own teeth chattering, his face drawn. And as she looked at them, Jasmine had to accept at last that he wasn't going to get better any day now and take charge again. He wasn't going to lead them out of here to safety.

She had to do it.

Gabe Cannon's blue eyes flashed into her mind, the way they'd turned silver in the moonlight. They stood out in contrast to his dark lashes and dark hair, a spellbinding combination of coloring that had wreaked havoc with her teenage heart. Thank God, she was a lot more mature now. She wasn't going to let him bamboozle her this time.

She shoved the last of her food into her mouth and slipped her flashlight back into her pocket as she stood, knowing that what she was about to do would either save them or bury them.

Jake frowned. "Where are you going?"

Better that he didn't know. He might try to stop her. "You both need something for that fever."

Her brother held her gaze for a long moment. "Be careful."

"Take the gun," Mandy offered from under the blanket.

"You keep it. If anyone else but me comes through this door, you shoot. Okay?" She hated putting that kind of burden on her sister, but she could find no other way to make sure they were safe. Jake could barely move his right arm, let alone aim a gun with it. She gave them her most confident smile before she slipped away.

At one point, out of sheer desperation, she'd tracked the men who hunted her brother to the *pensione* they rented on the main island. She'd wanted to know what kind of enemy she faced. She'd gotten the answer to that: overwhelming.

She had promised herself she would stay away from the place.

Of course, back then she hadn't known that one of the hunters was   Gabe.

Chapter Three

Gabe kept his eyes on his laptop, giving no sign that he'd noticed the woman who'd been observing him through his window for the last ten minutes. *Jasmine.*

Brent should have listened to him when he'd recommended setting up perimeter security. But the team leader was too arrogant to think that anyone could ever turn the tables on him.

He made a show of yawning and stretching. His gun hidden in the desk drawer. She would have seen if he tried to retrieve the weapon, so he simply turned the key with a slight motion then palmed it. At least now he knew she wouldn't be able to get to it while he left the room in the hopes of luring her in.

He scratched his chest, stood and headed for the bathroom. Going to the window would have scared her off, and his goal was to make her feel as secure as possible. Maybe Tekla was ready to turn himself in and sent her as a messenger.

He closed the bathroom door behind him, waited two minutes then flushed the toilet. She would be pushing the window open, using the noise he made to mask any possible creaking. After a few more seconds, he turned on the tap. She would use that to move into the room, knowing he'd turn the tap off when he was done, giving her warning before he came out of the bathroom.

He left the water running and put his hand on the doorknob. Then he slammed the door open and burst forward.

He registered the empty room a split second before she dropped on him from the storage shelf above the bathroom door, nearly knocking him off his feet.

"Hey. Stop that." He tried to twist to get hold of her, but his temple caught her sharp elbow and he saw stars. He staggered toward the bed and flipped her down at last, but she managed to hook her leg behind his neck and he ended up on the bottom somehow, with her sitting on his chest.

Her wild, shoulder-length waves framed cheeks pink from effort, her chest heaving as she leaned forward to pin his hands next to his head on each side. She ended up with her fine breasts inches from his lips.

He could have subdued her in two moves, but he liked her on top of him. She might be more likely to answer his questions if she thought she was in control of the situation. If their position sent some heat zinging through him, she didn't need to know about it.

He relaxed his muscles and gave her a thorough once over now that he had her in a lit room and could fully see her. The barely disguised triumph in her eyes, the color of aged Bourbon, amused him.

"Anything I can help you with, Jasmine?"

She looked nothing like the gangly teenager he'd met ten years ago. She had filled out in all the right places and turned into a beautiful woman. A woman who reminded him that he'd been lonely way too long. He would have given a lot right now if she weren't related to his mission and came to him simply to spend the night with him.

She pulled back to search his face. "Why are you chasing Jake? He was your friend once."

Oh, hell, nothing in life was ever simple. "My friends don't turn rogue."

"He was framed." She spoke with full-conviction, her eyes flashing.

"Your brother killed three men. One of them was a U.S Army officer."

Her generous lips narrowed to a thin line. "You don't know the circumstances."

She had gumption, passion and loyalty in spades. He felt a twinge of respect, and a twinge of something else, too, but he was going to ignore that. "So what changed between the roof and now? Why run away if you were just going to come back to me?"

"Now I have the upper hand." She allowed a small smile.

He watched her for a second. "And you think that since I knew your brother at one point, and because I didn't turn you over to the others on the roof, I am the weak link on the team."

She stayed silent, apparently smart enough to know that insulting him wouldn't gain her any favors.

"Does your brother always send you to fight his battles?"

"He doesn't know I'm here." She hesitated for a moment before she went on. "He was set up. He knows something and people want to kill him for it."

"Let me guess, he discovered a vast conspiracy." He didn't bother to keep the skepticism from his voice.

Annoyance tightened her kissable mouth again. "I don't know what he discovered. All I know is that he discovered it in Lahedeh. He thinks the less I know the safer I am."

"Maybe he'd tell me?" he suggested, ready to finish this mission and be back stateside to help his sister for a while with his nieces before the team was given their next assignment. They'd been tracking Tekla all over the continent for an eternity, but they should be done soon now that they had the man trapped in Venice.

"He's not anywhere around here."

"Right. Then why did you do your mama-bird-trying-to-draw-the-snake-from-the-nest imitation and lead us across town tonight?"

Her chin came up. She did have a cute chin. Also very kissable.

He forced his gaze up to her eyes. What in hell was wrong with him? "So what is it, exactly, that you want from me, Jasmine?"

"Distract those idiots you work with so I can get away from Venice and find a safer place."

"You mean you and your brother?"

She held his gaze, her expression giving nothing away.

"He shouldn't have dragged you into all this." An unpardonable act of selfishness as far as Gabe was concerned.

"You don't know what you're talking about."

He gave her a smile to throw her off balance then flipped her, reversing their positions, surprised by the surge of need he couldn't even acknowledge let alone act on. "I know you're not going anywhere until you tell me where he is."

Once Tekla was in custody, the pressure would be off her and she would be safe. Not that she showed any appreciation for him looking out for her.

She fought their change of position, stilling only when someone rapped on the door. Her cheeks were flushed, her eyes wide with alarm, the tip of her tongue darting out in a nervous gesture to moisten her lips.

He stifled a groan.

"Brent wants to see everyone in his room," Troy said outside.

Gabe watched a string of emotions flicker across Jasmine's face. Here came a moment of decision for him, and she knew it. He could turn her over to the others, and they could use her as bait to draw Tekla here. If it weren't for that kill order, he would have.

But Brent had pulled out all stops for this op. Maybe because he was ready to go home, or perhaps because he was starting to lose face over Tekla's ability to evade him this long. He seemed ready to end the op by whatever means necessary, a decision that didn't sit well with Gabe.

Whatever her brother had done, Jasmine wasn't guilty.

"On my way," he called out to Troy.

"Let me go." Jasmine resumed her struggling as soon as the man's footsteps had faded in the hallway.

Gabe only considered the request for a second. He wasn't going to lose her again. He needed her to take him to Tekla. Bringing Tekla in seemed the only solution. A peaceful handover would ensure that the man lived long enough to stand trial for his crimes. Once he was in custody, the pressure would be off his family and they would be safe. And with their mission accomplished, Gabe's team could go home to the U.S. and collect their payment.

The chase needed to end before someone innocent got injured. And for that, he needed Jasmine's cooperation. But to get that, he needed more time with her. For now, restraining her without hurting her was the key.

Of course, she fought him every step of the way once she realized what he was trying to do. He could barely get his belt off to tie her right hand to the headboard. Then he grabbed a curtain tieback and secured her other hand with that.

She kicked at him, her shoe connecting with his solar plexus and knocking the air from his lungs.

He scowled at her. "I wouldn't do that again."

She kicked lower this time, her foot slamming into him way too close to a place it had no business being.

"That's it." Two more curtain ties and her feet were tied, too, each to a bedpost.

Fury burned in her eyes, then desperation as she struggled against her restraints more and more violently. She didn't seem to be aware that she was scraping her wrists raw.

"Stop that." He bent to hold her still, to snap her out of her frenzy. "I'm not going to hurt you."

But she didn't seem able to stop. Panic had pushed her beyond reason. He swore under his breath. She wasn't a trained soldier, conditioned to conquer her fear in a situation like this. But he couldn't let her go. She would flee the second he left.

If one of the others caught her...

And they *would* catch her. Right here, in another minute, if she didn't keep quiet.

"Just hang on for a second." He grabbed for the duffle bag at the foot of the bed and rummaged through it for his emergency kit.

"This is going to help you calm down." He pulled the syringe of sedative and popped the cap, pushed the drug into her arm in the same motion. He tried to control the dosage. The full phial was calibrated for a large-built man, a fighter who might be twice her weight. "Stay still."

But she was beyond following orders. She swore at him violently and jerked forward, causing him to push in more of the drug than he'd intended. *Dammit.*

Boots scuffed outside.

"You'll be safe here. I'll lock you in," he told her as he headed for the door.

Her eyes flashed with fury. "My brother is going to kill you for this."

Chapter Four

Ten of the twenty team members were in Brent's suite, battle-hardened soldiers perching on every available surface. The team leader had them divided from the beginning: Team A searching the islands, Team B guarding all avenues of exit, making sure Tekla didn't slip through and sneak away to the mainland.

Gabe listened to Brent's briefing, his mind only half on the meeting, the other half wondering if Jasmine was all right back in his room.

"Got a call from my local cop. They've been having a wave of unusual petty crime lately. Not the souvenir-filching tourists, which they're used to." Brent opened his laptop and read aloud the list of dates, locations and items. Food, water, a blanket from one balcony, shampoo stolen from an open bathroom window. The list kept going.

A couple of the men snorted when Brent got to *knitting needles*.

He ignored them and went on. "I had my guy look at security camera footage. One woman seems to have been around most of these locations at about the right time. He sent me a headshot. Looks like the photo we have of Tekla's older sister." He didn't sound the least surprised.

"Did you know she might be here?" Gabe asked with all the nonchalance he possessed.

"I had a suspicion." Brent watched him carefully. "I sent some friends to that aunt's house in Kansas. They found nobody there. Not even the aunt."

And when was that, Gabe wanted to ask, but didn't want to seem suspiciously interested.

Oh, hell. A sudden chill ran down his spine. What if they were all here?

Three women in the middle of all this--a sure recipe for disaster. He would have liked to grab Tekla by the shoulders and shake sense into the man. What was he thinking putting his family at risk like this?

"So how do we know Soremo is the right island?" Troy asked, not unreasonably. One hundred seventeen small islands made up the city of Venice.

"Got security camera footage of the woman hopping on the water busses when she's done scavenging on the main island, but no pictures of her getting off anywhere."

"Maybe she swims," one of the guys suggested as a joke.

"She gets off at a station that doesn't have a security camera," Gabe offered.

That earned him a look of approval from the boss. "Exactly. Away from the tourist center. She's hiding somewhere in a residential district. We find her, we find her brother."

"There are other residential islands besides Soremo."

"The water buses she takes when she disappears all have their final stop here." Brent stabbed his index finger at the map spread on the desk, at the red X he'd drawn earlier.

"We've been out all night. Nobody got more than a wink of sleep." Gabe scrambled to think of an excuse to hold them back. If his suspicions were right and Tekla's other sister and his aunt were with him... They didn't deserve to become casualties.

To his relief, Brent nodded. "People are getting up and getting ready for work right now. We'll wait an hour. By then, most of them will be gone and the houses will be empty."

He looked at his men before he continued. "The B Team will be at the showdown with us. I don't want to leave anything to chance on this one. Be ready at oh seven thirty. Better get some sleep until then. I want everyone ready for this."

He paused. "Tekla is considered armed and dangerous. You're authorized to use whatever force necessary."

Gabe shifted in his seat. "What about the sister?"

Brent shrugged. "She needs to stay out of the way if she knows what's good for her. We're facing a seasoned killer here." He swept his gaze around the room. "If she tries to help him and gets caught in the crossfire, I don't think we'll be catching much flak over it."

Brent's need to catch Tekla seemed a little too over the top, he pulled out too many stops. If he had a personal agenda, Gabe sure would have liked to know what it was.

He stood aside and let the others pour out into the hallway, trying to figure out how he could convince Jasmine to trust him and take him back to Tekla, how to convince Tekla to give himself up so his family wouldn't get hurt.

"We'll have him today," he told Brent, buying time until the others cleared out of the hallway.

He didn't want them to catch a glimpse of Jasmine on his bed when he opened his door. "We could be shipping out of here by tomorrow. Not that being in Venice is a hardship. I was expecting battlefield combat when I signed up."

Brent gave him a dispassionate look. "We've seen plenty of battlefield action. I'm sure we'll see more. We take each assignment as they come."

"Afghanistan or Iraq?"

Gabe had done three consecutive tours of duty in the Afghan mountains before he'd joined the FBI. Brent knew all of that. They'd done a comprehensive background check before they hired him. Gabe, on the other hand, had been told very little about the team's previous missions.

"Both," Brent said now.

"Army?"

"Started out as an army medic, but switched to private security pretty quickly. Pays a hell of a lot better than the government."

Gabe understood that difference only too well. When his brother-in-law had died in a crash, leaving his sister with three kids, he got out of the army and in with the FBI so he'd be close enough to help. Then Penny, his youngest niece, had been diagnosed with autism. Promising treatment was available, but cost the heavens. His sister had never stood a chance on her librarian's salary.

All his money had been going to North Village already, and he couldn't abandon that project. Brent had come around, wanting to recruit him, at the exact right time.

Gabe left the man and stepped out into the hallway.

Troy stood bent over in front of his door, wiggling the key in the lock. "Wonder if people here ever heard of WD-40."

He was the only other ex-FBI guy on the team, a pretty decent man. Scars from an explosion crisscrossed his face.

"So how do you like it so far?" His voice sounded raspy, his vocal cords having been damaged in the same explosion.

"Not a big fan of making war on civilians. I think Brent should rethink a couple of things," Gabe replied honestly.

"This is the first op I've been on with the team where we have an American target. Given a choice, I prefer fighting foreign terrorists."

Gabe nodded. "I'm looking forward to this op being over." Hurry up, buddy. The man stood right in line with his door and would get a full view of Jasmine if Gabe opened it.

"Anyone waiting for you back home?"

He shook his head, pretty sure Troy meant a girlfriend and not his sister and nieces. He'd never done well with long term relationships. "How do you expect someone to put up with what we do? Right?"

"Takes a special woman," Troy told him, sadness creeping into his voice. "One in a million." His key turned at last and he disappeared into his room.

Gabe unlocked his own door and pushed inside, strode straight to the bed where Jasmine was sleeping like this was the last chance she was ever going to get.

She had the thickest, longest lashes he'd ever seen, flawless skin and lips that were sure to come back in his dreams. But now was not the time to linger and appreciate her beauty.

"Jasmine." He bent low to whisper. "Wake up. We have to get going."

Her eyes fluttered, but didn't open all the way.

He shook her gently.

She didn't even stir.

"Jasmine?" He pulled her into a sitting position. "You have to take me to Jake. Is your sister with him?"

She blinked one eye open.

Awake at last. He let her go.

She fell back onto the sheets.

He pulled her up again. "You have to wake up. Brent knows where your brother is."

"You drugged me." She tried to punch him in the face, but missed and fell into his arms. Pulled back. "Help me to the bathroom. I need to splash some cold water on my face."

He dragged her over to the sink and leaned her against it, turned on the tap then went back to his desk. Finding out whether Brent was involved in something questionable wouldn't hurt.

Gabe's hand fisted. He made a point to relax it.

He'd just started with XO-ST. One of the smallest private security firms out there, they only had two dozen teams, each working separately under the supervision of someone like Brent on whatever contract came their way. Not easy work, but Gabe could do what they needed. He was good at this. And he needed the money.

He opened his laptop and typed in a URL, then his password when the small window appeared in the middle of his screen. The site that popped up held his digital tool chest from his FBI days. He downloaded one of the programs and, with its help, his screen was duplicating Brent's in another minute.

He could see everything the man was doing. He could also take control and open files on his own, but Brent would see that. The mouse pointer would freeze on the screen while his laptop took Gabe's commands. So Gabe simply watched.

And saw nothing terribly helpful. The man surfed porn sites for a few minutes before turning the Internet off. Then the screen stopped changing.

Maybe he went to sleep to rest up for the takeover. Or was taking a shower. Or just gone to the bathroom. What were the chances that he was sitting in front of the laptop, staring at the blank screen?

Gabe took control and opened the file directory.

Not as useful as he had hoped. Instead of names, the files were simply numbered. Not much he could guess from that. The first held nothing but dates, another listing a long string of numbers. The next held a detailed satellite map of a small village, showing every street, every house.

The name on the bottom was written in farsi, but he could piece it together after a minute. *Lahedeh*. Afghanistan.

"I don't know what Jake discovered. All I know is that he discovered it in Lahedeh," Jasmine had told him earlier.

A cold feeling spread in his stomach. He cut the link. Couldn't risk keeping it open too long and getting caught.

Lahedeh could be the connection between Brent and Tekla.

Or it could be a coincidence.

He needed to find out what was going on, because like it or not, he was up to his neck in this mess now. He glanced at his watch as he pushed to his feet.

"Ready?" He stepped to the bathroom door and pushed it open.

Jasmine sat on the closed toilet lid, sleeping, her head resting on the edge of the sink. She looked incredibly young and utterly worn out, but he couldn't give her a break. They needed to leave.

He turned off the tap, then pulled her up. "Is your sister in Venice? Is she with your brother?"

She opened her eyes. "No." Swayed a little.

"This is not a good time to play games with me. Are your sister and your aunt here?"

She pressed her lips closed.

Which probably meant, yes. He didn't know much about the aunt, but Tekla's younger sister would be about high school age. A kid.

Jasmine collapsed softly against him and went back to sleep.

Dammit. Of course, he had only himself to blame for her state.

He scooped her up and stuck her in the shower, turned on the water. Her eyes popped open as she sputtered, fighting to get out while he tried to keep her in, a task about as easy as bathing a cat. And as hazardous to his health.

He let her out when she looked like she was fully awake and when he thought he might lose an eye if he didn't.

"Jasmine? Jasmine, honey." He tried to make nice. "Where is your brother hiding?"

She was awake, but uncooperative. She simply glared at him. She didn't look ready to forgive the tying down and the drugging. Or the forced waking.

Fine. He could get started without her. They were going to Soremo. And between here and there, he *would* get her talking.

Chapter Five

Despite his best efforts, she slept through the *vaporetto* ride, curled against him. At least she'd stayed awake earlier long enough to take off her own soggy bra and panties and put on the pair of boxer shorts he'd given her and one of his T-shirts. Then she'd passed out again, leaving the rest to him. Gabe had to tie on the sweatpants with a curtain tie. His sweatshirt just about swallowed her.

He helped her off the waterbus at the last stop.

"Left or right?" he asked, turning her face toward the cool breeze that came off the water.

She opened her eyes and looked around. "Where are we?"

Not exactly progress.

Her knees were folding. He picked her up into his arms. People smiled at them, probably thinking he was being romantic.

"What are you doing?"

"Saving you and your family," he said under his breath, keeping a smile on his face for the onlookers.

"Mandy, has a fever."

The younger sister. "We'll take care of it," he promised.

"How do I know I can trust you?"

"You're just going to have to make up your mind about it, honey. I'm here to help."

"You tied me up and drugged me."

"To keep you safe."

She managed to keep her eyes open long enough to pin him with a sharp look. "How do I know you're not a murderous bastard like the others?"

He said nothing. He would have been lying if he said he wasn't.

She interpreted his silence correctly. "Don't you have a conscience?"

"I do."

She blinked. "Tell me one bad thing you regret doing."

"We're not getting into that right now. We don't have time for this."

"One thing," she demanded.

Fine. Okay.

"I once led a team to eradicate a makeshift weapons factory in the Afghan mountains. Small place with an unpronounceable name. We called it North Village. Led the charge, shot the place to hell. We killed most everyone inside this one industrial-looking building. They were classified as enemy combatants in the attack order."

He drew a slow breath. "They weren't. The village was starting some grassroots truck part repair business. Most of the men worked there. Now the village is nothing but orphans and widows."

He paused. "So no, I'm not a good person. But I no longer follow orders blindly either. And no more innocent people are going to get killed on my watch if I can help it."

She looked into his eyes for the longest time, doubts and desperation mixing in her Bourbon gaze. Then she nodded to the right. "That way."

The houses they passed were progressively worse and worse. They reached a ramshackle building at last and she insisted on being put down. She slipped inside through a broken window. He followed her in, the sight of garbage and scurrying rats getting to him for a second. Nobody should have to live in a place like this.

"Up there." She nodded toward a crumbling staircase.

"I'll go. Why don't you stay down here? Rest a little."

"I can handle it."

He did believe that. She'd managed to escape from the roof. And, despite the inherent dangers, she had managed to get his attention and bring him here to help.

"So up the stairs, huh?" He took in the dubious structure with a healthy dose of reservations. "Are you sure?"

She stumbled forward without hesitation, and he followed a few steps behind her, far enough so their combined weight wouldn't bring down the stairs, but close enough so he could catch her if she fell back. She didn't. She reached the top and hurried down a dark hallway.

She stopped in front of the last door. "It's me. I'm bringing someone. Don't shoot."

He went for his weapon but stopped halfway. The sight of a gun might provoke Tekla. Better leave his gun stashed under his shirt, Gabe decided. But he kept his hand ready to draw, not liking in the least that Jasmine stood between him and the man inside.

He glanced at his watch. They still had time before Brent would be here with the teams. Time to convince Tekla to send his family home to safety and give himself up, so nobody would have to die today. If he also wanted to tell Gabe what in hell his connection was to Brent, that would be icing on the cake.

"Okay, we're coming in," Jasmine called out her last warning. But when she pushed the door open, they found the cavernous, ramshackle   room   empty.

Chapter Six

Gabe looked closer at a suspicious lump of blanket on the floor among the stacks of wood, plastic crates and other rubble. The blanket rose and fell slightly then rose again as whoever hid under it breathed. *Ambush*, he thought, and drew his weapon.

At the same time, Tekla stepped from a column to the side, holding a gun in his left hand. A homemade cast covered the right one. His eyes narrow slits, the man leaned his back against the wall behind him, barely resembling the charismatic hotshot he'd once been.

His once chiseled cheeks were now sunk in. He looked twenty years older and twenty pounds lighter than the last time they'd met.

And a lot less friendlier. "What's wrong with my sister?"

"I'm fine." Jasmine stepped forward, swaying on her feet, which pretty much undermined her words.

"Where are her clothes?" Tekla demanded, then went on without waiting for an answer. "Come over here and get behind me," he ordered Jasmine. "What did he do to you?"

Her response came after a long, uncomfortable moment of hesitation. "He drugged me a little. It's okay. He's here to help." She rubbed her forehead. "I think," she added.

Way to go with the endorsement.

Tekla had killed three innocent men, Americans. He wouldn't hesitate to shoot now when his family was in danger and he was cornered. The situation had top potential for going real bad real fast, so Gabe held still. No sense in giving provocation if he could help it.

167

"Brent and his men are coming," Jasmine said with exquisite timing.

Jake swore as he took the safety off his gun.

"I know about Lahedeh," Gabe said the only thing he could think of to defuse the tension.

Tekla froze, a look of surprise replacing the fierce concentration on his face. "You do?"

"I know Brent was there." He bluffed.

"Brent who?"

Oh, hell. Tekla had been to Lahedeh. Brent had been to Lahedeh. That *had* to be the connection between the two.

This op definitely meant something personal to Brent. He wanted Tekla dead too badly. And he didn't care who died with the target. Sometimes he sounded as if he *wanted* the whole family to be eliminated.

Why?

No way would those kinds of orders come from the U.S. government that was supposedly their client for the op. Not when the target was a U.S. citizen.

Gabe kept steady, wanting the op to be over without getting killed, without having to kill anyone unnecessarily. He scrambled for something to say.

But Tekla spoke first, his eyebrows lifting. "Was Brent the other medic?"

Here we go. Brent *had* been a medic. "Yes." Gabe gambled.

Tekla looked him over again. "Where do you come in? You weren't there. How did you hook up with him?"

"Left the Army for the FBI two years ago. Brent recruited me from there. I have nothing to do with what went down at Lahedeh."

"You have no idea what went down at Lahedeh." Tekla sneered.

"I might," he bluffed.

"If you did, you'd be dead already. Everyone else is, except me. And I mean to stay alive."

"Nobody has to get hurt. Let me take you in. The government will give you a fair trial."

Tekla gave a short, sour laugh. "I'll never reach any courtroom."

"We're here on a government contract. You killed people. You're AWOL from the Army. If you have a good reason for all that, they'll hear you out." He did believe that.

"Can I come out? I can't breathe in here." A plaintive voice asked from under the blanket Gabe had been keeping in his peripheral vision.

"Come out and go into another room with Jasmine," Tekla ordered.

The younger sister peeked from her hiding place, then emerged little by little, hair all mussed and cheeks pink with fever, eyes glassy. Jasmine went to her immediately, feeling her forehead and frowning.

"She's in no shape to walk around," she told her brother. "Gabe isn't going to hurt us."

He appreciated the vote of confidence. He scanned the room. "Where is the aunt?"

All he got were funny looks. "The aunt from Arkansas," he clarified.

"Spending the winter with her sister in Florida," Tekla said.

Thank God. The last thing they needed in the middle of this volatile situation was another civilian.

"When are the men coming?" Tekla asked Jasmine.

She shot a questioning look to Gabe.

He glanced at his watch. "In about forty minutes." As a gesture of goodwill, he tucked his weapon away. "She needs help." He nodded toward the younger sister.

Jasmine rolled her eyes at him. "Why did you think I came to you?"

"Didn't have a chance to ask, with you trying to scratch my eyes out and all that."

Tekla shot a dark look at Jasmine.

"I can't do this alone, okay?" She pulled a bottle of water from the rubble and handed it to her sister before looking back at her brother, her eyes begging. "You need as much help as Mandy does. We can't just hang tough. It's gone beyond that. I can't fix this."

The quiet desperation in her voice touched Gabe's heart.

She'd been surviving with no resources, no support, in a foreign country, trying to save her brother and her sister. And the thing was, she'd done it. She'd taken care of them. She'd evaded an entire commando team, risked her life, putting everything on the line when she'd come to him.

"I'll help." Hell, that had been a forgone conclusion probably from the moment he'd caught her on the roof and first faced her spirit and courage, first realized that something might be off with the op.

"You turn yourself in to me," he told Tekla, "and I'll make sure your sisters will be safe."

"Absolutely not." Jasmine shot to her feet with a look of betrayal on her face. "I brought you here to help my brother escape."

"Your brother made some bad choices. He's going to have to face the music for that, but the rest of you don't have to get hurt."

"You don't understand anything!" she yelled suddenly, wrapping her arms around her slim body. She began to pace, throwing desperate looks at her brother.

"Then tell me what happened." Gabe turned to Tekla. "If there's a rational explanation for what you've done, let's hear it."

"The less you know, the safer you are."

"Like your sisters?" he snapped. "Do you know what a miracle it is that they're still alive? How long are you prepared to gamble with their lives?"

Gabe caught himself and toned it down a notch. "If you don't trust Brent and his crew, I have connections I can call on. I can turn you straight over to the U.S. authorities. The FBI, even."

"This thing goes too high. Brent has a backer. Someone in the government."

Gabe considered the possibility and the implications. Brent was one of two dozen team leaders at a fairly small private security company that specialized in overseas missions. The contract to retrieve Jake Tekla had come from the government that couldn't send military forces after the man into a sovereign country like Italy. Maybe they could have justified something like that in the Middle East, but certainly not in Europe.

The U.S. government didn't want to get local law enforcement involved, at least that was the way Brent had explained it to Gabe when he'd been hired on. A rogue American soldier, a killer on the loose wouldn't have inspired much confidence in the U.S.

And the Italians were already wary of military presence in their country, especially since the cable car accident a few years back when a U.S. jet flew too low, cutting the cables, sending twenty people plunging to their deaths.

So sending a private outfit after Tekla and keeping the op under wraps had made sense when Brent had first explained it. But, apparently, Brent and Tekla had a shared past in Lahedeh, and it sure looked like Brent had a private agenda where catching Tekla was concerned. What were the chances that his team just *happened* to get the government contract?

Maybe Brent did have someone somewhere, making sure the contract went his way.

Too many unknown elements. Too much to lose. The op wasn't entirely right, but Tekla wasn't innocent, either. Gabe didn't want the man's family to come to harm, but he drew the line at aiding and abetting a killer.

He looked the guy straight in the eye. "I need to know about those three men you killed."

Chapter Seven

"How about we step out into the hallway?" her brother asked Gabe.

Jasmine opened her mouth to protest, but Gabe said, "I think your sisters have a right to hear this. I think they should get a vote in what happens."

She gave him a slight smile, her heart softening. She liked that he was treating her and her sister as equals. She liked the way he looked at her, a *lot* differently than he'd looked at her ten years ago. As if he actually *noticed* her now. Way too late, but definitely flattering.

Man, she'd been crazy about him. Well, that ship had sailed. She wasn't going back to live on Obsession Lane. She'd embarrassed herself over him enough for a lifetime back in the day. Every email she'd sent to Jake had at least one question about whether he'd seen Gabe again, and if so, how he looked, had he mentioned her.

Thank God, this time around she was a lot more mature and a lot smarter. She was *not* going to develop any kind of crush on him again. Although, if he managed to save them, she might—*just might*—forgive him for tying her down and drugging her.

The two men stared at each other.

She knew how difficult it would be for Jake to trust someone after all they've been through. He had a lot of pride. And he'd always shouldered all the responsibility for the family. He *hated* to ask for help. He always wanted to fix everything alone.

But he also always did the right thing.

"All right." The tight set of his jaw betrayed that he was only doing this because he had no other choice. He lowered himself to a sitting position and set his gun down at last.

Gabe acknowledged the gesture with a nod. "Let's start with what happened in Lahedeh. What were you and Brent doing there?"

"We were still looking for Osama at that point. My team—Brian, Greg, Eric and I—went down into the water cistern. We found two locals down there with these huge terra cotta jars. They got Brian before we got them, and injured Eric. Greg called in the medics. They were there pretty fast. I knew one, but not the other."

"Brent," Gabe put in, his face clouded.

Jake nodded. "Greg and Brian were pretty tight, from the same town and all that, enlisted together. So Greg was ticked that they killed his buddy. He started pumping more bullets into the dead locals. I told him to knock it off before someone got hit by a ricocheting bullet. So then he starts kicking over the jars. Or tried. They were too heavy. He knocked the lid off one... I've never seen that much gold."

"What gold?" she asked the same time as Gabe did.

"Some warlord's hoard. Worth millions."

Her blood pressure spiked. "Our lives were destroyed because of money? That's the big secret you couldn't give up? I thought it had to do with national security. Are you kidding me?"

For the first time in her life, she really, *really*, wanted to hit something.

"Eric was the team leader. He sealed the jars, told us this was all confidential. Word couldn't get out or we'd have the warlord's private army after us, plus all the locals and treasure hunters. He took charge. Later he told us that the treasure was transported to the National Museum in Kabul."

"Except it wasn't," Gabe put in.

Jake shook his head. "Last day I was in Afghanistan, I had a couple of hours to kill in Kabul and a cute private I wanted to impress. I thought I'd take her to the museum, show her the gold and tell her the part I played. See how far that gets me."

She rolled her eyes. Her brother had a way with women, no doubt about it. He definitely had the Casanova gene, and he wasn't afraid to use it. She hated to see him like this, sick and weak. That he couldn't protect them about killed him, too. He was too used to being the tough guy, a warrior.

"They never heard of the gold." He adjusted his bad leg. "So I tried to call Greg when I got back home. He was dead. Friendly fire." He closed his eyes for a second. "Called the medic I knew. Friendly fire again. Couldn't track down the other guy. Figured it was time to get the hell out of Dodge."

He took a slow breath and shot an apologetic look to Jasmine, his eyes filling with regret. "That was a mistake."

* * *

Gabe watched as Jasmine wrapped her arms even tighter around herself and stared at a spot in front of her feet, all emotion sliding off her face.

He wanted to know what happened to her after her brother had first gone into hiding, but Mandy had slumped over while they'd been talking, and that worried him. She didn't seem fully aware of her surroundings anymore. They had to take care of Mandy before they could move out of here.

He stepped forward. "We have to bring this girl's fever down."

Jasmine looked at her sister then launched into action, shaking off whatever dark weight had been sitting on her shoulders. "There's a tub in one of the other rooms. We could bring cold water up from downstairs."

"Do you have any buckets?"

She hurried to the corner and pulled two five-gallon paint buckets she probably had picked up at a construction site.

He took those from her. She grabbed a chipped pot from the windowsill and led the way.

He could tell downstairs that the water service to the building had been shut off at one point but someone, probably Jake, had rigged it. He filled the buckets and she filled the pot, then they started up the stairs. The drug seemed to be wearing off. She no longer swayed with every step.

"What happened back in the U.S. before you came here?" He wanted to help, but to do that, he needed to see the full picture.

She wouldn't look at him.

He knew he should let it go, but something deep inside him demanded to know. He followed her into a smaller room and dumped the water into the tub, caught her by the arm as she turned to go back. "Jasmine?"

She avoided his gaze, a haunted look coming onto her face. "When they couldn't find Jake, they came after us to draw him out."

He waited, cold tension gathering in his stomach as he wished he knew what to do for her, what she needed from him. With the work he did, his relationships with women had been always superficial: quick and easy. But he wanted to give something more to *this* woman, something real, something she could hold on to.

His jaw clenched with frustration. "Jasmine?"

"Mandy had an emergency junior prom planning meeting, so she had to stay after school, thank God. I was home alone." She swallowed hard.

He put the empty buckets down and gathered her into his arms without giving her a chance to resist. "Who?"

"I don't know." Her voice broke. "They took me and kept me tied up in a basement to draw Jake out."

No wonder she'd fought his restraints so violently. If he'd known— "I'm sorry." He bent to rest his chin on the top of her head.

And, little by little, she relaxed against him.

He wanted to ask what they'd done to her, but he was afraid of hurting her by dragging up the past. So he simply held her until she pulled away.

"Jake came. He got us out of the country." She moved toward the door. "We better get Mandy."

He put two and two together halfway down the hallway. "These were the two civilians Jake killed in the U.S.?"

His opinion of the man rose a couple of notches. So there *was* a good explanation for those kills. Of course, the death of that Army captain still remained unexplained.

The empty pot slipped out of her hand, her reflexes still not one hundred percent, and she bent to retrieve it. Her top rode up her hips, revealing a strip of skin. Two half-moon-shaped scars peeked out at Gabe.

"Did you get hurt on the roof?" He winced, hoping he hadn't been too rough on her when he'd brought her down.

She yanked on her top to cover the spot. "Old stuff. It doesn't matter."

He stilled. "Did those two men do this to you?"

A grief-stricken expression came onto her face, making him wish he hadn't asked. "Sorry." He was such a damned idiot sometimes. "You don't have to talk about it."

She drew a shaky breath. "I don't. Not even to Jake." She watched him for a second. "But I want you to know what kind of men Brent works with."

The tone of her voice almost made him wish she didn't.

"One of them liked to come down to me while his buddy was sleeping at night. He would pull my shirt up or my pants down..." She swallowed. "He liked to bite me."

Human teeth marks, he recognized the scars now and the gruesome images in his head filled him with fury.

"He got real excited if he drew blood. Sometimes he touched himself." She looked away.

He didn't know what to say. Murderous rage burned through him, impotent rage since he could do nothing about those men at this stage. He wanted to protect her, but he was too late.

He thought of Brent. Maybe not entirely too late.

He wanted to take her into his arms again, but she didn't look like she would welcome anyone's touch just now. So he simply said, "I'm sorry," and they went on with their task of trying to bring Mandy's fever down.

He carried the girl over to the tub then let Jasmine take it from there. "Call me when you need me to bring her back," he said before he closed the door behind him.

Time to finish his talk with Jake.

"What about the army captain?" was the first question he asked. Jake had killed that man first, before the other two.

"Eric was the captain of the four-man team I went down to the cistern with. Brian, Greg and the one medic were dead. I figured the other medic was, too, but couldn't confirm since I didn't know his name. I figured Eric took the gold and had the others killed. I knew he would come after me, and I knew arranging some friendly fire on the battlefield would be pretty easy for him. So I went AWOL, but left him some leads to follow. I wanted to meet him on my own turf, when I was ready. He came. He didn't want to leave any witnesses."

"So you killed him in self-defense."

Jake nodded. "Meanwhile, my unit shipped back to the U.S. I was heading back home, ready to turn myself in over the AWOL thing, but then Jasmine was kidnapped." His face darkened. "I knew then that the second medic had to be alive and running the show."

"Who were the two bastards Brent sent to grab Jasmine?"

"Hired guns. Brent must have paid them to do his dirty business. I think at the beginning he figured it'd be quick and easy to get me. But I took care of his goons and brought my sisters across the ocean. So Brent stepped up his game, somehow finagling a government contract for his security company to bring me in. That gave him a whole team to order around."

A pretty complicated story, but it all made sense in a way. Gabe rubbed his hand over his face. He could no longer get around the fact that he believed Jake. "Do you think his team knows about the gold?"

"I don't think so. If they did then he'd either have to share with them or kill them for knowing. He's just using them as his private commando team. All they know is that they have orders to bring down a rogue soldier."

Gabe thought for a second. "So back in Lahedeh... The medics had an ambulance, could transport the gold out and stash it somewhere. Then Brent and Eric took out everyone who knew about the gold, except you. Eric failed there, so Brent has to finish the job."

"The way I figure it," Tekla said, "Brent left the army and joined a private security company so he could get back into Afghanistan with less oversight and more freedom to come and go as he pleased. He couldn't exactly bring the gold out in his Army duffel bag."

"Right." Gabe agreed. Military personnel were tightly controlled and supervised. "But as team leader for a private firm, Brent could tell his team they were transporting arms seized from the Taliban, or whatever. One sealed crate looks pretty much like another."

Jake nodded. "Getting the gold into the U.S. would be the next obstacle. How do they get it through customs? Maybe that's where the *high up in the ranks* protector comes in."

Gabe scratched his chin. Sooner or later, they had to figure out who that man was. Otherwise, Jasmine and her family would never be safe.

Chapter Eight

After the cold bath brought her temperature down, Mandy could stand and walk once again, even if her teeth chattered. Jasmine helped her back into the room where Gabe and Jake were still talking. It did her heart good to see the two of them without pointing guns at each other.

Gabe jumped to help as soon as he saw them coming. He seemed to truly care. His being here was helping already. Jake could have never carried Mandy over to the tub with his bad arm and leg, and Jasmine couldn't have done it either. Her little sister was taller than she was and weighed about the same.

But Gabe was here and things were going to turn around. For the first time in a long time, she saw the light at the end of the tunnel.

"Take Mandy and Jasmine. Get them someplace safe. I'll stay here and deal with Brent," Jake told Gabe suddenly.

She gaped for a second, while heat crept up her face. "I'm not going anywhere without you."

As far as she was concerned, they were going to live or die together.

* * *

Gabe watched the dynamics between the two with interest.

"How about Colonel Markowsky?" he offered Tekla after careful consideration. "Whoever is involved in whatever is going on, I can't see the colonel participating in anything shady."

Markowsky had been his colonel, but everyone in the Afghan war theatre knew or knew of the man. He was the toughest son of a bitch there, and the most honest man Gabe had ever met.

Tekla didn't protest.

Progress. Especially since Gabe was sure Jasmine meant what she'd said. She had incredible loyalty to her family. She wouldn't leave her brother. The woman had character. He liked that.

"What if the colonel could get you out of Venice? Out of Italy? You're AWOL from the Army. His men could take you into custody. If you explained yourself to him, he could help."

"What about my sisters? The Army can't help them."

"If the colonel can get them back to the U.S., I can take it from there." He thought of a good friend who was still with the Bureau. Gordy could get the girls into one of the safehouses if Gabe asked. And he would keep quiet about it.

Tekla watched him closely. "I've got your word on that?"

"You do. It's either this or face Brent and the teams when they get here. Which won't be long now." He glanced at his watch. They had about ten minutes left before Brent reached the island. "Even if you can evade them once again, how long do you think Mandy is going to make it without medical care?"

The man looked at his sisters as he struggled to his feet. "All right. Let's do this."

They all looked at each other. Here they were. Last Chance City.

Gabe pulled his phone and identified himself when the colonel picked up on the other end.

"FBI treating you good, soldier? If they aren't, you know we'd welcome you back here. Anytime you want to return to us, just say the word."

He'd saved the colonel's life once from a roadside bomb, his and the lives of four other men in the vehicle, which the colonel never forgot.

"Thank you, sir. I'm not with the Bureau anymore. I work for a private outfit these days. I'm in a situation here, sir."

"Are you in trouble?"

"I'm with people who are in trouble." He thought of Camp Darby, U.S. Army Garrison, at Livorno, a few hours' drive from Venice. The colonel had a reputation for knowing everyone everywhere. "I don't suppose anyone at Livorno owes you any favors, sir?" And then he explained everything.

"I can have a car sent to your location."

"Livorno is a three-hour drive from here, sir. Could you find out if they already have someone out our way?"

The colonel promised to do just that before hanging up. Relief coursed through Gabe. And the news only got better.

"This could help with the colonel." Jake tugged a tattered manila envelope from under his homemade cast.

"What is it?" Jasmine asked, looking as if this was the first time she saw the thing.

"Some documents I've been able to find before we ended up here. It should be enough to get an investigation going."

Gabe reached for it, but his cellphone interrupted. The colonel was calling back.

"A convoy of U.S. troops is on its way to Livorno from the Nato base in Hungary. They'll be passing through near Venice. I'm sending one of the trucks over to Ponte della Liberta. Can you rendezvous with them at oh eight hundred?"

Gabe glanced at his watch. Just enough time to make it. "Yes, sir."

"Help is here." He lunged into action as soon as he hung up, handing the envelope to Mandy, wrapping it up with her in her blanket and picking her up. "You have to help your brother," he told Jasmine. "We have twenty minutes to reach Liberty Bridge."

She tried to prop Tekla up as best she could, but the stairs proved unconquerable on crutches. So after Gabe took care of Mandy, he had to go back up and carry Jake down on his back. At least, Jake could take it from there, so Gabe could go back to carrying Mandy who couldn't move nearly as quickly as they needed to go.

The morning rush was just about over, so they didn't have to fight any crowds. Since they didn't have time to wait for the next *vaporetto*, Gabe hot-wired a motorboat and helped everyone in, hoping to be away before the theft was discovered.

He kept an eye out for the owner, and also for the teams. Hopefully, by the time Brent and his men found the hideaway, Jasmine and her siblings would be getting into the back of an Army truck, heading away from Venice. Gabe drove toward the bridge, grateful that Team B wouldn't be out there today.

Mandy and her brother huddled under the blanket in the back of the boat, one in worse shape than the other. Gabe stood in the front, steering. Jasmine came up to him.

"So what do you do when you're not ducking commando teams?" he asked.

Her maturity, capability and ingenuity had more than impressed him. He tried to picture the life she would be going back to when this was all over, but he couldn't. He knew her heart was in the right place. He knew she was the most remarkable woman he'd ever met. But beyond that, he knew next to nothing about her, and suddenly that seemed intolerable.

"I dabble in SM stuff," she told him.

SM what? He nearly choked on his own saliva. A picture of her in a studded leather choker and thigh high boots popped in to his mind, her slim hand holding a whip. The image nearly knocked him on his behind.

"Social media consulting," she explained.

"Oh." He cleared his throat, his blood pressure slowly returning to normal. "So what happens to your job now that you've been away for so long?"

"I have good people in place." She gave a self-deprecating smile. "Not that I don't worry about them. I check in whenever I can snag some credits at an internet café."

Right. She owned the company.

"You're a good man, Gabe Cannon," she said out of the blue.

"There's a village of orphans and widows in Afghanistan who would beg to differ," he said more to himself than to her.

She tilted her head and watched him for a few seconds. "What are you doing to help them?"

"What makes you think I'm doing anything?"

"Seems to me you're the kind of man who does the right thing if he can."

He gave a sour laugh. "Don't make me into some kind of saint. You'll be disappointed."

"So what are you doing for all those people in North Village?"

She'd paid attention. She even remembered the name of the place. "Trying to refit the truck part factory with sewing machines for the women. A friend of a friend get them a Fair Trade contract if the factory is operational by the end of spring." They were about halfway there. Everything was going great, except he had no idea how he was going to send money after his current gig with XO-ST was over.

"You have a lot of friends," she observed.

"Doesn't mean I'm a good man."

"I think you are." She pressed an unexpected kiss to his cheek, then went to the back to sit with her brother and sister.

His skin tingled. He was a thirty-six-year-old hard ass commando soldier and his cheek tingled from a kiss. He rubbed his thumb over the spot. Somewhere in the middle of his chest his heart turned over. An unfamiliar feeling. He glanced back at her, and she smiled at him, and his heart turned over again.

Something was going on. He just couldn't put his finger on it. He wasn't sure he liked the feeling. Kind of left him off balance a little.

He maneuvered among the water taxis, gondolas and all the private boats that left the harbor every morning, so focused on what he was doing that he barely heard when Mandy said, "I don't have the envelope."

Jasmine searched the blanket. "Where is it?"

"I don't know. I thought I had it with me."

"I set her down when I went back up for Jake. It might have fallen into the rubble then," Gabe said, knowing that in all that mess, none of them would have seen it.

"We have to go back for it." Jake pushed to his feet. "It's all the proof I have. Without those papers, I'll never be exonerated."

"At least you'll be alive and you--"

Jasmine interrupted. "Drop me here. I'll take another boat back and meet you at the bridge."

They just reached the far edge of the harbor, plenty of small boats bobbed unattended in the water around them.

"As long as you can make it to the rendezvous point in time, you can make them wait for me," she added.

He hated the idea, but didn't have time to argue, no time to come up with a better plan. If they all turned around, whoever was bringing the truck might think they weren't coming and take off without them. "Watch out for Brent and his men."

"They know we were on Soremo, but they don't know which building. I'll be in and out before they get that far with their search."

He sidled over to a pier and let her jump up, then pulled away, not liking the way things were going.

They reached the bridge in another ten minutes, a silver ribbon stretched across the water. Gabe followed along and soon saw the

Army truck idling on the mainland end, waiting on the shoulder. He got the boat as close as he could, tied it up, then helped Mandy and Jake.

A corporal met them halfway to the truck, a young African-American man. "Gabe Cannon?"

"That's me. Thanks for coming." He didn't introduce the others, wasn't sure how much information the colonel had passed on. The less everyone knew the better.

The man helped support Tekla who walked with a bad limp, favoring his uninjured leg, while Gabe carried Mandy. They all tried to look as inconspicuous as possible under the circumstances.

"I'm glad you're here on time. We need to leave immediately," the man said.

"We'll have to wait for my other sister," Tekla protested.

"That's a negative, sir. We don't even have official permission to stop here. We only pulled over so one of the men could *check a tire that sounded funny*. We can't wait around and we can't, under any circumstances, enter the city. We can't engage in any local trouble in any way. We are not to draw attention to ourselves."

They were at the truck. The back opened and two men reached down to help Mandy up.

Tekla searched the water, looking sick and desperate, at the end of his rope. "We have to wait."

While he tried to talk the corporal into breaking orders, Gabe ran back to the water's edge to watch for Jasmine, so he could signal as soon as he spotted her. He was sure the truck wouldn't leave if she was in sight.

But instead of Jasmine, he spotted one of Brent's men on the bridge. Then another. And another.

The B Team.

He hadn't been followed when he'd taken Jasmine back to Soremo, he'd made sure of that. He could think of only one other explanation for them showing up here at the exact wrong moment. He patted his shirt, found nothing. Yet it had to be on him somewhere. Brent must have planted a damn tracker on him.

He glanced at the watch the team leader had borrowed a couple of weeks ago. He said he needed it to use the stop watch function for a friendly one-handed pushup competition. Gabe ripped the watch from his wrist and tossed it into the river.

They knew exactly where he was. Brent had probably tracked him on his laptop, radioing his movements to the teams. Which meant he would have seen where Gabe had spent the last hour before heading here. Brent had the location of the house. The A Team was probably there right now--with Jasmine.

He ran toward the boat, just as a bullet hit the fuel tank. The explosion knocked him off his feet. He could see, as he lay there, dazed, the corporal jumping into the back of the truck, pulling a protesting Tekla up behind him. Then the truck shot forward and they booked it the hell out of there.

The corporal and his men could take care of Tekla and Mandy. But Jasmine...

She was all alone against a commando team, battle-hardened men with authorization to kill. A wall of fear hit him.

Gabe dove into the water and swam as if his life depended on it.

Chapter Nine

He only had to make it over to the cement pillars that held up the bridge, and climb one. Everybody was watching the burning boat. Since whoever had shot the fuel tank had used a silencer, no shot had been heard. Nobody had any idea what was going on.

Traffic came to a halt, people got out of their cars to get a better look. Gabe grabbed an abandoned motorbike and flew forward between the lanes of cars.

Glanced back. The B Team weren't pursuing him. They were too busy chasing after Tekla.

Gabe picked up speed, ignoring his wet clothes and the rules of traffic. He had to reach Jasmine before it was too late.

* * *

"Come on out. We won't hurt you," one of the men called out one level below her.

They were herding her to the east end of the building from where there would be no escape. She had to reach the staircase to the roof. This end of the building had no exits. No windows either. The place butted up against a warehouse, the back walls were solid brick.

Her chances of getting out of here were slim. At least Gabe had her family. He was the type of man who set things right. He would help Jake and Mandy.

God, she wanted to stay alive to see them again. Jake and Mandy. And Gabe. Because, who was she kidding, she was falling back in love with the man all over again.

"Your brother gave himself up. All we want is to take you in safely," came the next lie from below.

Jasmine kept low and ducked between fallen beams, trying to steal around the men. She had to find a way to get out. She couldn't engage them and fight them off. There were nine of them. Her gun only had four bullets. She would save those until the very end.

Which seemed to be suddenly here.

She ducked as a man crept into the room on her right. He scanned the rubble. Hadn't seen her yet. She could only seem him through a gap in old wallpaper that hung from the ceiling in the corner where she hid. He turned slowly, gun trained. Then looked right at her.

She took her shot and ran like hell, knowing the sound would draw the rest of them.

She was looking behind her as much as she looked ahead. Steel arms snaked out from behind a column and caught her.

* * *

Gabe heard the gunshot from outside and his pulse quickened. The team would use silencers, so it had to be Jasmine. He found the window she'd brought him through earlier and vaulted right in.

Impulse pushed him to rush to her, but his training held him back. Assess. Plan. Execute. He searched the small area he could see.

No envelope where he'd put Mandy down. Either Jasmine had gotten it or Brent had. He moved on without pausing to search. Jasmine came first.

He stole around a doorway. One man stood at the bottom of the stairs, looking up, watching in case she tried to escape through here. Gabe snuck up on him, shoved his knee in the back of the man's to bring him down. A hard tap to the guy's temple with his gun and he was out for the count.

He didn't want to shoot if he didn't have to, since he didn't think the men were involved in Brent's private agenda. Plus, a gunshot, even with a silencer, could be heard by other team members who were nearby.

He disarmed the guy then crept up the stairs. Saw movement in a doorway. He pulled into the cover of a column and waited.

Troy, the ex-FBI guy, was moving his way. Probably the most decent man on the team, but Gabe had no choice, no time for explanations. He waited until they were in line with each other, then went for it. Beyond a small grunt, nothing betrayed that he brought down another man.

He inched toward the back room where the Teklas had stayed, listening for the slightest noise, the faintest creak. He thought another man or two were ahead, and could hear the soft sounds of others on the level above him.

He reached the door and looked through the open gap. Two men in there. Gabe scuffed his boot on the floor. One of the men came to investigate. Gabe took care of him, then stepped into the room.

The other guy swung and raised his gun. Gabe shot him in the right shoulder and left thigh. That should keep him down for a while. He strode over and ended the man's moaning by shoving his hat into his mouth, then secured his hands with a plastic cuff.

"Jasmine?" he whispered to the piles of stuff strewn around the room in case she was hiding in there somewhere.

No response came.

He stepped back, retraced his steps to the stairs then stole up to the next floor, gun in hand.

A bullet whizzed by his ear at the same time as he heard a small pop. He ducked, rolled and aimed. And didn't miss. A debilitating hit, but not fatal. Nobody rushed to investigate. The others must have been out of hearing distance.

He moved down the hallway carefully, then another and another. Ahead, two men were inspecting a giant room, clearing it section by section. Gabe looked at the sagging beam that barely held the ceiling of the hallway above him, slammed the door shut then shot at the beam until it gave, collapsing the ceiling and sealing the men inside.

Not that he had time to gloat. He was too busy running, since his impromptu demolition worked only too well. The partial collapse in front of the door created a chain reaction. Bricks were coming down all around him as he ran.

A falling beam caught him in the back and knocked him to the floor, an avalanche of bricks half burying him. He had barely begun to dig himself free when he caught sight of Brent through the settling dust.

He had Jasmine by the arm, holding his gun to her head.

"You served your purpose, Gabe. I think your contract is going to end here. Short, but productive. Just as I hoped." He gave a cruel grin.

Gabe controlled his fury. He'd been pegged from the beginning, recruited because of his connection to the target. "Long shot, wasn't it? Tekla and I were never best friends. Last time we saw each other was a decade ago."

Brent had counted on the man to come out of hiding, if he thought he could give himself up safely, to a friend. It hadn't exactly worked out that way, but the stalemate had been broken. Gabe had led them to Tekla's hiding place. Brent had Jasmine because of *him*. Man, he hated the thought of that.

"I didn't bring you here because of your friendship to Tekla," Brent lectured. "You were brought in for your girlfriend here. When the men I hired took her, they searched the house and sent me every scrap of paper. Most of it was crap. But this one little diary..." He gave a mean laugh.

"A teenager's diary from ten years ago. Didn't pay much attention to it first, but I read the damn thing after Tekla took out those men. I figured I might find a clue to where he was hiding. People go to familiar ground when they're on the run and all that. Nothing about Venice in the diary, I tell you that. But there were pages and pages about you." Brent sneered.

Jasmine blushed scarlet and wouldn't meet Gabe's eyes.

He was too angry at Brent, too worried about her being in the middle of all this danger to feel amused. But he promised himself to enjoy the hell out of this little piece of information the second they were safe.

First, he had to get out of this jam. "Tekla got away. He's talking to the authorities right now. Whoever has been protecting you won't take the fall for this. He'll make you the scapegoat."

Brent flashed a grin of pure conceit. "I have enough on the man to be sure he'll never turn against me."

So he hadn't simply bought a politician with the promise of a share in the gold. It all came down to blackmail. "What's next then?" He needed to keep the man talking. His gun hand was almost free.

"I shoot you now, then wait for the B Team to call me with the news that they have Tekla. Once I know I no longer need your girlfriend for anything, I'll have some fun with her before I shoot her."

Jasmine stood frozen—her eyes wide, cheeks pale—looking lost in some nightmarish memory. She was too stunned to struggle.

Come on, honey, Gabe tried to tell her with his eyes. *Do something. Anything. All I need is a second of distraction.*

"You know, reading all those teenage fantasies wasn't as bad as it sounds." Brent leered at her, but was still talking to Gabe. "Let's see what she does with a real man. Maybe I won't shoot you just yet and let you watch. If you say, pretty please."

"Go to hell."

"I take that as a no." Brent raised his gun.

That brought Jasmine out of her frozen fear, and she launched herself at the man who hadn't expected much resistance from her. Big mistake.

"What the hell—" He turned to deal with her.

Which was all Gabe needed. He shook off the rest of the bricks and took aim. He didn't try to go easy on this one. He put a bullet right into the middle of Brent's forehead.

Another shot rang out at the same time, slamming into the man's chest.

Troy stood in a doorway, his face grim as he looked at Gabe. He must have heard it all. "Let's get out of here before the others gather themselves and someone gets killed in the confusion."

His scarred face looked even more haunted than usual as he watched Jasmine, and Gabe remembered the rumor he'd heard from another guy on the team. The same explosion that had messed up Troy's voice and face had also killed the woman he loved. And for the first time, Gabe had an inkling of what that could mean to a man.

"Thanks for the help." He pushed free from under the rubble, ignoring the pain that shot up his leg.

Troy nodded, his eyes narrowing. "Don't you ever knock me out again."

"Sorry about that." But his attention was on Jasmine who still stood in the same spot, her eyes riveted on the blood flowing around her feet.

Brent had grabbed on to her as he'd fallen. His lifeless fingers still circled her ankle.

"I'll make sure we have a clear path out of here." Troy took off.

Gabe kicked Brent's arm away and pulled Jasmine into his arms. Nothing ever had felt more right.

"I have the envelope," she whispered as she lifted her face to his. "Are we okay now? Is it over?"

He wanted to kiss her more than anything he'd ever wanted in his life. And then he did, just a slow brush of his lips against hers. He needed to go easy on her. She'd just been through hell. But she tightened her arms around his neck, and kissed him right back.

A long, life-altering moment passed before they pulled apart.

"I'm here. I'm not going to let anything happen to you," he promised. *Ever.*

Chapter Ten

His room at Camp Darby in Livorno seemed more and more like a cage with every passing day. He'd brought Jasmine here to catch up with her brother and sister after the showdown with Brent three days before. They'd been separated for Gabe's debriefing and he hasn't seen her or her brother since. Nobody seemed to be able to tell him where they went.

He wasn't allowed to leave. He was to wait for the colonel who wanted to speak to him in person and was due at camp any minute.

So when the door of his room opened, Gabe pulled his spine straight and put his heels together out of habit. But instead of the colonel, Jasmine walked in.

"Hi," she said, her Bourbon eyes fast on his face, a small, shy smile on her amazing lips. "How is your leg?"

The rubble that had buried him had done some muscle damage. He'd been limping the last time she'd seen him.

"Fine." He was used to getting banged up, didn't see why everyone wanted to make such a big deal out of it. He'd been checked and rechecked by medical personnel in the camp.

She linked her hands together in front of her in a nervous gesture. "I didn't get a chance to thank you. You saved my family."

"No thanks necessary." He wanted something else, something more. He wanted her not to walk out of his life. He wanted to be able to kiss her again. And again. "How is Mandy?"

"Much better after some IV fluids and antibiotics."

"And Jake?"

"Has a new cast." Her smile grew a little. "Looks like the Army is going to clear him of all wrongdoing."

"Good. Excellent."

They faced each other in silence for a long minute, both of them clearly uncomfortable. He hated all the awkwardness between them.

To hell with that. He smiled at her. "So do I get to know what's in that diary?"

She blushed crimson. "That diary got you into this mess. You could have been killed. How can you joke about it?"

"No joke. I'm sincerely interested." An understatement. He would have given his antique baseball bat collection to know what she'd written about him ten years ago.

"I was a foolish teenager."

"And now?" He stepped closer.

She didn't answer.

He held out his hand. "My life is a mess. I don't know if I have anything to offer to a woman like you. I'm pretty sure you'd be a lot better off without me."

She gave a lopsided smile. "Are you asking me out?"

He held her gaze. "I'm asking a lot more than that."

She stepped into his arms.

"I'm going to kiss you, if that's all right."

She lifted her mouth to his without hesitation.

She was soft and sweet, the most amazing woman he'd ever met. He wanted to know more of her, all of her. Need surged through him to feel those soft curves of hers, to hear her soft breath hitch in his ear as they tangled in the sheets together...

The door's scraping interrupted his fantasy, and they pulled apart. The colonel came in and gave them a narrow-eyed look, his gaze settling on Gabe.

"I just had to sit through a very uncomfortable meeting with some top brass and Congressman Wharton who is visiting the troops here ahead of the elections. They're not happy about the shootout."

"Yes, sir. I apologize, sir."

"Do you have proof of any of your fairytale beyond your report and Tekla's envelope? *Hard* proof. And by that, I mean, do you know where the gold is, soldier?"

Gabe started to shake his head, but then thought of Congressman Wharton's great yacht as it had bobbed in the harbor back in Venice a couple of days ago. Working in pairs, the A Team had searched all larger vessels to make sure Jake Tekla wasn't hiding on one of them.

But Brent had gone to the Congressman's yacht alone. Because of the sensitive nature of the thing, he'd said. He'd gone at night. Didn't want the media to catch him. They showed up every couple of days to snap some photos of the Congressman.

What if he hadn't gone to the yacht to search it? What if he'd carried something with him? Like gold disguised as crates of supplies? The teams had several vans.

He filled the colonel in on his suspicions.

The man gave him a displeased, narrow-eyed look when Gabe was finished. "If there's one thing I hate, it's dirty politicians. You better be right about this." He strode to the door, turned back from the doorway. "Neither of you go anywhere until I say so."

They stared after him.

Then they stared at each other.

"Are we grounded?" she asked, her tone uncertain.

"Welcome to the Army. I'm sure we'll find something to do." He grinned at her, happy to see her, happy that the op was over and they were both safe, happy that she'd come to see him.

That had to mean something, right?

"Jasmine, honey?" He stepped closer to her again.

"Yes?" She stepped closer to him.

"Do you still feel the same about me as you did when you wrote that diary?"

To his disappointment, she shook her head. But then she said, "I feel much stronger."

He took her into his arms. "Thank God. Because I'm pretty sure I'm falling in love with you here."

She gave him a tremulous smile. "I want to feel good things again instead of fear when a man touches me."

He furrowed his forehead. "No other man better touch you or I'll give *him* reason to fear."

She smiled.

He took her lips in a passionate kiss, running his hands lightly down her back then up her ribcage, using great control to stop under her breasts. "How is it so far?"

A smile of pleasure bloomed on her full lips. "Good enough to record for all prosperity. Maybe I should start a new diary."

He thought about all the things he wanted to do with her. "You better get one with a key."

* * *

The sky turned dark outside by the time the colonel came back, his expression just as grim as when he'd left. Gabe's stomach sank.

"The congressman is denying knowledge of the half dozen crates we found on board of his yacht. He claims they must have been smuggled on board when he wasn't looking. And that's not our only problem. We can't take the gold to the U.S.

"That would be out and out theft from the people of Afghanistan. Not to mention, we can't have a U.S. congressman implicated in something like this when half the Middle East believes we're only warring over there to steal everything that's theirs."

He seemed to have aged five years since he'd left the room earlier. "We can't give the gold back to the warlord, either, or he'd use it to buy arms against us. And we can't give it to the Afghan government without confessing everything."

He took off his hat and sat, his eyes tired as he looked up at Gabe. "Any ideas what in hell I'm supposed to do with eleven million dollars' worth of gold coins?"

Gabe swallowed hard. "Eleven?"

"Could be more," the man said in a tone of disgust. "They're still counting."

"There's this garment factory I heard of in Afghanistan. In North Village," Jasmine spoke up. "It's a non-profit gig to give work to widows and support orphans."

The colonel shot a questioning look to Gabe, then nodded. "There's one more thing," he said after a moment. "I had a quick teleconference with the FBI about this. They'll be investigating. They want a small team, preferably people who are already on the ground and already know the case."

Gabe thought those words over long and hard. As long as Congressman Wharton was flying free, people who knew the truth about him would never be safe. They needed to figure out what Brent had been blackmailing the man with and bring him down.

"The pay won't be what private security promised you, but it'll be decent," the colonel said. "Do you know anyone who might be interested in the job?"

Gabe looked at Jasmine. The expression on her face said she'd been thinking the same thing as he had. They needed to tie up all loose ends to have any chance at a normal life together.

"I waited ten years already. I can wait another couple of months," she told him.

One in a million. He smiled at her. *One in a million.* And she was his.

The colonel cleared his throat. Gabe caught himself and stopped staring at her, wiped the goofy grin off his face.

He refocused on the topic at hand, considering Jake Tekla and Troy, two men who already knew all about Wharton, men he trusted. They both had what it took to take on an op that would be more dangerous than the mess they'd just survived.

He took Jasmine's hand and looked at the colonel. "I think I can put a small team together, sir."

The End

GUARDIAN AGENT, **AVENGING AGENT** (Jake Tekla's story), and **WARRIOR AGENT** (Troy's story), are now available in a 3-in-1 discounted collection: AGENTS UNDER FIRE.

www.danamarton.com
First Edition: June 2011

ABOUT THE AUTHOR

New York Times and *USA Today* bestselling author Dana Marton has thrilled and entertained millions of readers around the globe with her fast-paced stories about strong women and honorable men who fight side by side for justice and survival.

Kirkus Reviews calls her writing "compelling and honest." *RT Book Review Magazine* said, "Marton knows what makes a hero . . . her characters are sure to become reader favorites." Her writing has been acclaimed by critics, called, "gripping," "intense and chilling," "full of action," "a thrilling adventure," and wholeheartedly recommended to readers. Dana is the winner of the Daphne du Maurier Award for Excellence in Mystery/Suspense, the Readers' Choice Award, and Best Intrigue, among other awards. Her book *Tall, Dark and Lethal* was nominated for the prestigious RITA Award. *Deathscape* reached the no. 1 spot on Amazon's Romantic Suspense Bestseller list.

Dana has a master's degree in Writing Popular Fiction, and is continuously studying the art and craft of writing, attending several workshops, seminars, and conferences each year. Her number one goal is to bring the best books she possibly can to her readers.

Keeping in touch with readers is Dana's favorite part of being an author. Please connect with her via www.danamarton.com or her Facebook page (www.facebook.com/danamarton).

Having lived around the world, Dana currently creates her compelling stories in a small and lovely little town in Pennsylvania. The fictional town in her bestselling Broslin Creek series is based on her real-life home, where she fights her addictions to reading, garage sales, coffee, and chocolate. If you know a good twelve-step program to help her with any of that, she'd be interested in hearing about it!

Made in the USA
Columbia, SC
12 December 2023